THE DOCTOR'S DILEMMA

PRAISE FOR DALY WALKER

Emily Dickinson's famous lines warning the surgeon to be careful about disclosing the "culprit life" have never been more aptly or gracefully applied than in Daly Walker's *The Doctor's Dilemma*. Walker may be retired as a surgeon, but he has not lost a step in his ability to carefully open a subject and make it live anew. These rich stories, written in taut, clean prose, give us the culprit life in every dimension. There is tenderness here, as well as skill, both undergirded by the feeling, known to every able doctor, that life remains more wondrous and mysterious than any science that addresses it. I love this book.

— ROGER ROSENBLATT, AUTHOR OF
COLD MOON AND *RULES OF AGING*

The Doctor's Dilemma is a beautiful and deeply perceptive collection of stories. Daly Walker's writing is artful and profound.

— ELIZABETH MCKENZIE, AUTHOR OF
THE PORTABLE VEBLEN

These stories are tender, wise and loving. A doctor as well as a writer, Daly Walker offers new ways of looking at the frailties of the human heart, and the intricate and powerful ways in which it works. Bravo to Walker for this beautiful collection.

— ROXANA ROBINSON, NOVELIST AND
BIOGRAPHER OF GEORGIA O'KEEFE

In this wonderful collection of stories, Dr. Walker writes about the intimate secrets in the hearts and minds of his characters who happen to be physicians. His beautifully crafted prose portrays their struggles with gut-wrenching decisions, their feelings of pride and pleasure, of doubt and uncertainty, of guilt and sadness, of longing and love, and so much more. In short, he demonstrates and celebrates their humanity.

— ROBERT B. SANTULLI, MD,
DARTMOUTH COLLEGE

Subtle, pure, and stunning, the collection will entertain, challenge, and move readers.

— THE PRAIRIES BOOK REVIEW

The Doctor's Dilemma chronicles life in the hospital frontline, but even more importantly, it faithfully encapsulates the lives of the men and women underneath the scrubs and the people behind the mask, allowing readers to see beyond the stethoscope they carry, and making it relatable at a deeply personal level for anyone who has ever suffered pain and loss.

— THE BOOK REVIEW READER

THE
DOCTOR'S
DILEMMA

SHORT STORIES BY

DALY WALKER

TEMPE, ARIZONA

Grand Canyon Press
Tempe, AZ 85282
www.grandcanyonpress.com

Cover Image: Luke Fieldes, *The Doctor's Dilemma*, used with permission of the Tate Museum, London. Cover design by Jonathan Weinert.

Names: Walker, Daly, author.

Title: The doctor's dilemma : short stories / by Daly Walker.

Description: Tempe, Arizona : Grand Canyon Press, [2021]

Identifiers: ISBN: 978-1-951479-64-0 (hardback) | 978-1-951479-56-5 (paperback) | 978-1-951479-54-1 (ePIB) | 978-1-951479-55-8 (epub) | 978-1-951479-57-2 (ibook) | 978-1-951479-40-4 (Kindle) | 978-1-951479-60-2 (audio, individual) | 978-1-951479-61-9 (audio, library)

Subjects: LCSH: Physicians--Fiction. | Surgeons--Fiction. | Mortality--Fiction. | Medicine, Military-- Fiction. | Medical ethics--Fiction. | Healing--Fiction. | Physicians--Psychology--Fiction. | Surgeons--Psychology--Fiction. | Medical fiction, American. | Short stories, American. | LCGFT: Medical fiction. | Short stories.

Classification: LCC: PS3623.A35895 D63 2021 | DDC: 813/.6--dc23

Stories in this collection have previously appeared in the following magazines: *TSR: The Southampton Review* published "Nui Ba Den," "Blood," and "Two Corks in the Ocean;" *Catamaran Literary Reader* published "Bobolinks" and "At the Door;" "At the Door" also appeared in *The Saturday Evening Post*; *The Louisville Review* published "One Day In the Life of Ivan Jones;" *Not Like the Rest of Us—An Anthology of Contemporary Indiana Writers* included"Pulsus Paradoxus" in its anthology; *MD Magazine* published "Palliation;" "The Crystal Apple" first appeared in *The Sewanee Review* as "Shadows;" *Lifelines: Dartmouth Medical School's Literary Journal* published "Boots on the Ground;" *Hospital Drive: The Literary Magazine of the UVA School of Medicine* published "Old Dogs;" *Hektoen International: A Journal of Medical Humanities* originally published "Pascal's Law" as "Auscultation;" Columbia University's *Intima: A Journal of Narrative Medicine* published "Resuscitation."

FOREWORD

Daly Walker is a storyteller and a doctor, or maybe he is a doctor who is a storyteller, in the long tradition of writer/poet/physicians who write. It's no surprise that as a surgeon Daly is able to give us scenes where death may be the outcome, whether futile intervention in a hospital, or a life-and-death choice made at home, or violence at some desolate outpost in Vietnam. However, Daly's are mostly stories about life, a far more confusing, stressful, and eternally interesting subject.

His characters are us, we who think of ourselves as good-hearted, decent Americans struggling with life's twists and turns, wishing to do the right thing. Daly's are engrossing stories, all the more for his quiet unfolding: an old man feeling purposeless until the appearance of a young stranger; a boy meeting a murderer on death row; another returning to his childhood home to discover a secret he had been blind to.

In sum, Daly is a writer with a firm grasp on the anguish and beauty of the human condition.

Jane Fletcher Geniesse
Author of *American Priestess*
Boca Grande, Florida
April 2021

ALSO BY DALY WALKER

Surgeon Stories

Little Creek

Golden Graduates

Lichen and Haiku

In memory of my mother
Betty Daly Walker
(1917-2004)

In every single one of those ten cases, I have had to consider, not only whether the man [person] could be saved, but whether he was worth saving.

—GEORGE BERNARD SHAW, from his play *The Doctor's Dilemma*

Healing is a matter of time, but also opportunity.

—HIPPOCRATES

CONTENTS

PART I

MORTALITY

I learned to take death as an old debt that sooner or later should be paid.

— ALBERT EINSTEIN

AT THE DOOR

AN ANGRY FIST beat against the door of Harold's log cabin. The noise awakened him from a recurring dream. In the dream, his deceased wife, Marge, was still alive but for some unknown reason she had disappeared. Desperately calling her name, Harold went from room to room in a big empty house. But there was no answer. Now, in the real world the fist banged harder. The window glass rattled.

Since Marge's death, the ninety-three-year-old retired doctor lived alone deep in a hardwood forest on a narrow gravel lane four miles from his nearest neighbor. He slept naked. His once wavy dark hair had thinned and whitened. He had let it grow long, and he tied it back in a ponytail. His body was lank, tough, and lean as a strip of jerky. But his ancient skin hung on his frame, much like the pleats of an oversized garment.

Harold had been a busy and beloved family physician, someone who saved lives and brought comfort to his patients no matter their station in life. Now, he believed his greatest accomplishment was survival. He threw back the cover. Groggy, Harold thought it must be Marge at the door. She's come back, he thought. His heart leapt.

"Wait a minute, dear," he said. "I'll let you in."

The haze of sleep lifted, and Harold rolled onto his side. The old doctor squinted at the luminous numbers of the clock beside the urine bottle on the bedside stand. It was 1:30. He lay still and listened. The pounding grew louder.

"Stop it, for Chrissakes," Harold muttered. "Be quiet and leave me alone."

Normally, Harold wasn't afraid of threats from the external world. What he feared were the inner ravages of old age: losing his memory or becoming blind with macular degeneration so that he could no longer see the dogwood and redbud blossoms in the spring. Or, maybe the problem wouldn't be his sight at all. Otosclerosis could steal his ability to hear the barred owl whose call to him at night asked, "Who cooks for you?"

But now a suffocating dread coiled around Harold's chest. Cold sweat beaded his brow. He sat up and listened. Although he didn't believe in a god who meddled in the lives of individuals, he said a prayer for whomever was at the door to just leave. The knock crescendoed. Harold thought of calling 911, but a thunderstorm a month ago had knocked down his phone line. For a moment, he wished he still had his double barreled Winchester 21, but with old age, he had changed his thinking about guns and killing living creatures. Once an avid hunter, he no longer could shoot a bird, let alone a human being, even at the risk of his own life. Marge's death had solidified his belief in not only the impermanence of everything, but also the interconnections between all that existed. Harold was convinced that the entire universe was bound together.

The pounding stopped. Harold closed his eyes. He waited. For a moment, he thought his hypocritical prayer had been answered. But the angry fist against the door shattered the silence.

Last week, a few miles away on Plum Creek Road, the body of a young college girl had been discovered. She had been bludgeoned to death with a big sandstone rock. A mailman had found her lying in a ditch with dark blood pooled under her head. Police and National Guard troops were searching the vast forests of the county for her killer. Earlier in the day, Harold had heard the bark of their dogs echoing through the valley of his land. Was it her murderer at the door? His heart beat furiously. He reached over and touched the pillow where Marge's head had once rested. In his fingertips, he could feel the texture of her skin. He believed that in whatever form she existed she could still hear him when he spoke.

"Don't worry, dear," he whispered. "It's nothing to worry about. Just some poor soul who doesn't know where he is. I'll go talk to him. Get him headed in the right direction."

Harold swung his feet over the edge of the bed. He put on his thick, wire-rimmed glasses and looked out the window. The sky was moonless and black. Darkness had swallowed the world and everything in it. A feeling of inevitability, of finality, descended on Harold. Darkness is where we begin, he thought. And where we end.

The pounding grew louder. If whoever it was kept that up, the panes would break. He pictured a tall, black-clad figure carrying a scythe. He considered climbing out the window and hiding on the roof over the laundry shed or locking himself in the bathroom. Sadly, he knew it would merely prolong the inevitable. He rose from the bed. His joints were stiff and painful. From a rocking chair, he picked up a pair of gray work pants. He pulled them on awkwardly and struggled to keep his balance. He looped the suspenders over his shoulders. Harold put on a faded denim work shirt that Marge had given him because it matched the pale-blue color of his eyes. He groped through the dark to a fan-shaped window that overlooked the entry to the cabin. His pulse raced. A tingling prickled the back of his arms. Harold looked out the bedroom's window. A big pickup truck's headlights were aimed at the cabin. Harold remembered that the newspaper said the man suspected of murdering the college girl may have driven a RamCharger.

"What in God's name does he want with me?" Harold asked as if Marge were there. "I'm just an old man with nothing of value."

"Open up," a husky voice yelled.

Harold pried open the window. A gust of night air assaulted his face. The dark form of a big man stood at the door. The figure was tall and thick, but a little stoop-shouldered.

"Who are you," Harold yelled. His high-pitched voice cracked in mid sentence. "What do you want?"

"I'm a deputy sheriff," the man called.

Harold didn't believe him.

"Step into the light so I can see you," he commanded.

The man moved back so that he was illuminated by the truck's headlights. He wore a campaign hat with a wide brim, the same hat as state troopers wore. Trying to see him better, Harold squinted. He couldn't make out the man's face or tell if he had a gun. The man held up his hand and waved.

"Here's my badge," he said.

Harold couldn't see that either, but he said, "Okay, I'll come down and let you in."

Clutching the rail, he descended the steps to the

cabin's one-room first floor. He went to the door and turned on the porch light. He took a deep breath and opened it. In a pool of yellow light, the tall man stood with feet set apart and hands on hips. He wore a khaki shirt with epaulets and a zippered front. His wide belt holstered a big revolver. He pushed a silver star toward Harold.

"I'm Deputy Armstrong from the sheriff's department," he said.

Harold studied his face. Up close and in the light, he was clean-shaven with wide-set inquiring eyes and a big jaw. Harold thought he looked respectable, but he still wasn't convinced he was who he said he was.

"I'm Harold," he said, shaking the deputy's broad hand. He no longer introduced himself as doctor because it had been so many years since he was in practice, that he believed he didn't deserve the privilege anymore.

"I'm sorry to bother you, sir. But we got a 911 call from your number."

"How could that be?" Harold said. "My phone hasn't worked since that storm a month ago."

"Sometimes, a broken line will short out and trigger a call."

"I wish the damn phone company would come fix it," Harold said.

The man lowered his head. He looked past Harold, and his eyes roamed the cabin.

"You sure you're all right?" he said.

"I'd be fine," Harold said, "if I could just get a good night's sleep." He stepped back from the door. "Since you're here, you might as well come in and have a drink."

"I'm on duty," Armstrong said, "but I would be glad for some water."

The deputy returned to his truck and doused the headlights. When he came back to the cabin, Harold led him to the pedestal oak table in the corner of the room. He turned on the Waterford crystal chandelier he had bought for Marge in Dublin on their twenty-fifth anniversary. Dusty light from its flame-shaped bulbs played on cobwebbed crystal prisms and shone on the deputy's face.

"Sit," Harold said. "Be my guest."

The officer found a ladder-back chair. He took off his hat and placed it on the table. Harold went to a sink stacked with dirty dishes. He filled a Ball jar from the tap. With a trembling hand, he set it in front of the officer. Then he poured himself a glass of red jug wine and sat across from the deputy.

"I thought you were the man who killed the girl over on Plum Creek," Harold said.

"We caught that guy today," Armstrong said. "You don't have to worry about him anymore."

The deputy studied the cabin's family heirlooms and folk art that Marge had furnished tastefully. On a worn Navajo rug that covered the cherry wood floor were fragments of acorn shells that chipmunks had left. A walnut bookshelf held Marge's favorite books with their yellowed pages—*For Whom the Bell Tolls, The Sheltering Sky*, all of Flannery O'Connor's stories, and Carson McCullers's *The Heart Is a Lonely Hunter*. Harold had read them to her in the latter stages of her illness. On the mantel of a stone fireplace stood two duck decoys and a metal cricket. Even though the nights had grown cool, he had yet to refill the brass bucket for kindling on the hearth. In the chandelier's harsh light, everything looked faded and old and covered with dust.

"This is quite a place," Armstrong said.

"You should have seen it in Marge's day," Harold said. "I don't keep it up like she did."

Armstrong took a drink of water. "Marge was your wife?"

"Yes. The dear sweet lady's been gone for a while." He made a sweeping gesture with his hand. "Everything you see in here is her."

"How long have you been here?"

"About thirty years. We lived in an Airstream trailer down by the pond while the cabin was being built. Billy Wheeler, who owned a sawmill up the road, helped me lay these poplar logs. But I did a lot of the work myself —the chinking, the roofing." Harold paused for a drink of wine.

"Boy, you sure live in the boonies," Armstrong said, "I had trouble finding this place."

"Yeah, a few years back Marge and I decided it was best to live off the grid for a while. Sometimes solitude is just what a person needs. Harold paused a moment, remembering.

"I had just come through a rough patch. A kind of nervous breakdown you'd call it. I couldn't sleep. I couldn't think, couldn't focus on anything. I was a doctor then. My patients became like windows I was looking through. I was pretty much a mess. Marge said I needed to be where it was quiet so my mind could heal. That's when we bought the property."

Remembering the evenings he and Marge had spent in a swing on the cabin's porch. Discussing their days—what Marge had painted or harvested from her garden, the bridges and stone walls Harold had built, what they were reading. Sometimes they just sat without talking, swinging gently, holding hands, and sipping white wine. Looking back on it, their life together in the near wilderness seemed timeless—as if it were the only life he had ever led or wanted to lead.

"Marge was right," Harold said. "Working with my hands. Living close to the land. Stone. Wood. Water. There was something elemental about it. Something tactile and authentic. It made me feel my life was worth something again. I actually began to look forward to the next day and the day after that." Then Harold added. "I loved my work here the way I once loved medicine. I just wish I still had the strength to do all the upkeep. But that's how it goes."

Something about the way the officer listened made Harold wonder if he already knew the story. A silence followed. Harold was afraid the man was going to excuse himself and leave.

"I'll bet you're hungry," Harold said. "I have some cookies. Let me get you a cookie."

"Thanks," Armstrong said. "But I need to get moving."

He finished his water, put the jar on the table, and stood. He tamped down his hat. "I won't take up any more of your time."

"No! No! Sit!" Harold said, leaping up.

The deputy smiled. "Okay. One cookie, then I have to hit the road."

Harold went to a Hoosier cabinet where he found the bag of sugar cookies he had purchased in town. He put them on a saucer. His hand trembled when he set the cookies on the table.

"My life has sure had its ups and downs," he said. "And plenty of regrets. But for the most part it's been a good life."

Armstrong took a cookie from the plate.

"Exactly how old are you?" he asked.

"As old as the hills," Harold said. "Ninety-three to be exact."

"Wow. That's quite an accomplishment."

Harold shook his head.

"Old age isn't an accomplishment," he said. "It's an ordeal. It's like flying an airplane through a thunderstorm. Once you're in the tempest and being tossed around, you can't bail out. You just keep flying and try to be smart about it." He traced the rim of his glass with a finger. "You're lucky, son. You're young and strong and with a lot of good years ahead if you mind your p's and q's."

"Hope you're right," the deputy said. "Did your wife used to show her work in the gallery in town?"

"She did."

"My wife always wanted one of her paintings, but we couldn't afford it." He glanced at his watch. "Mind telling me what happened to her?"

"Cancer," Harold said. "It was what they call a small-cell carcinoma. It started in her lungs and spread from there. Chemo and radiation didn't work."

"I'm sorry to hear that. I'll tell my wife. She will want to know."

"I took care of her here at the cabin until the end," Harold said. "It's where she wanted to be."

Harold remembered the night she died, and sadness welled up in him. Delirious with pain, she'd fallen when trying to get out of bed. With her nightgown up around her waist, disheveled and exposed, she'd lain on the floor. He'd muscled her bulky body back onto the bed and slipped a down pillow behind her head. He apologized for hurting her, and then gave her morphine with a medicine dropper until she let out a little sigh and quit breathing.

The memory caused Harold's chin to tremble. He swallowed the lump in his throat.

"She was cremated," he said. "I hired a crop duster to spread her ashes over the land. She loved it here as much I do. She knew where all rare wildflowers grew and where the morels were."

"You took good care of her," Armstrong said. "That's the best a person can do. She was lucky to have you."

Harold pointed to a series of botanical watercolors that hung on the log wall behind the deputy. There was a Siberian iris. A fiddlehead fern. A red maple leaf with a curled edge.

"That's Marge's work," he said reverently.

"I recognize it from the gallery."

Armstrong rose from the table. While he studied the paintings, Harold pictured Marge in her studio above the barn. She was standing at her easel, her long white hair in a blue bandanna. An opera played on the radio. She wore a white, paint-smudged lab coat that Harold had worn when he saw his patients. Harold's rheumy eyes teared. He wiped them with the back of his hand.

"Look at the veins in those leaves," the deputy said, hands clasped behind his back. "They look real."

"She was a fine artist," Harold said. "And she was a fine woman. I loved almost everything about her."

"I'm sure you miss her." The deputy sat back down. "Did you have children?"

"No," Harold said. "We weren't lucky that way. It was a medical situation."

"So, you're alone way out here in the middle of nowhere."

"I've got the flora and fauna to keep me company," Harold said. "I have lunch every day with two finches. They always let me pick up the tab." Harold took a drink of wine. He closed his eyes, savoring the memories of Marge. "You probably think I'm demented. But I'm just different than most folks. This is the kind of life I like. It's what keeps me sane."

"How long do you intend to stay out here?"

"As long as I can. I don't make plans. I guess you'd say my forward-looking days are behind me."

"Don't you get lonely?"

"Sure. At times. But then, sometimes, it's loneliest when there are people around." Harold paused for a moment. He looked out the window at a dark sky. He could hear the barred owl, its plaintive call mocking the night. "It's not that I don't like people. I do, but not swarms of them and all their buzz. What I like more than anything out here is the silence of the land."

The deputy nodded as if he understood. Then he looked at his wristwatch again.

"I need to report in," he said. He raised the Ball jar. "Here's to you, Harold. A man of independence, longevity, and grit."

"Longevity for sure. What's the old joke? If I had known I was going to live this long, I would have taken better care of myself."

The deputy chuckled. He drained his glass and set it on the table. Harold was feeling warm from his wine. He wanted Armstrong to stay and talk some more.

"Sure you don't want something else to drink? A little glass of wine would go well with another cookie."

"Thanks, but I'm still on duty." The deputy rose and put on his hat. He creased its brim with his fingers. "I'll see to it your phone gets fixed, pronto," he said.

"I'd appreciate that."

"I'll come by and check on you once in a while. If you don't mind."

"That would be fine, too," Harold said. "Just don't show up in the middle of the night."

The officer smiled. He turned and headed to the door.

Harold followed him. "You a fisherman?"

"Yeah," the deputy said. "I guess you could call me a fisherman."

"Fly- or spin-casting?"

"I prefer fly-fishing."

"Good man," Harold said. "Maybe you'd like to

come out and try your luck. The ponds are well stocked with bass and bluegill."

"I'd like that," Armstrong said. "I've got a boy who likes to fish. Maybe I'll bring him along. You can teach him to fly-cast."

Harold thought back to eighty years ago when his father first brought him to these rugged hills in a Model A Ford. He had taught Harold how to bow hunt for deer. Up the road, they'd gone bass fishing in Yellow Wood Lake. How wonderful that had been—how it had changed his life and the way he considered the Earth.

"Bring him out," Harold said. "I've got rods you can use. I make the rods myself. They're bamboo. I split the cane with a special knife," he said, although he hadn't made a fly rod since Marge's death. "I'll get one and show you. They're in the barn."

"I'll bet they're dandies," the deputy said. "I'd like to see them, but I've got to hit the road." He touched his hat. "Good night, Harold. You take care."

"Good night. Thanks for stopping by."

The man shook Harold's hand and walked to his truck. Harold slid the deadbolt into its receptacle with a reluctant, metallic click. He turned off the chandelier. Slowly, he climbed the stairs. He paused a second to rest halfway up. He couldn't believe how weak his legs were. Harold's ninety-three years had taught him it was better not to count too much on things, but something told him he would soon see the man again. Harold entered the bedroom. He felt very tired. Without bothering to take off his clothes, he climbed into his side of the bed. He lay in the dark, his breathing slow and even. He heard the truck pull away. The drone of its engine. The crunch of tires on gravel. The sounds stopped briefly, then resumed and soon faded away. The silence that remained was deep and complete. No breeze in the leaves. No insects pinging the window. No owl calling out. The logs of the cabin seemed to let out a sigh. Harold rolled toward Marge's side of the bed.

"See, dear," he said. "I told you. Nothing to worry about. He seemed like a nice guy. He's going to come fishing someday. His wife liked your watercolors. Maybe I'll give him one."

Harold looked beyond the bed out the arched window. Two stars had appeared in the black sky. A nimbus of creamy light surrounded them. Like a magician's scarf, a cloud drifted by and made them disappear. When they reappeared they seemed brighter and more clearly defined. Harold believed Marge was one of the stars and he was the other. There was a chill in the air. Winter was coming soon and he wasn't prepared. He closed his eyes and thought of the day ahead and what he had to do. He hoped for the strength to cut and split a rick of firewood.

INDIA'S PASSAGE

EARLY IN THE morning of India Blue's surgery, Conner visited the young college student in the preoperative holding area where she lay on a gurney. The surgeon wore blue scrubs, a paper hat, and white clogs that he considered lucky. The operation he was about to perform on India was a laparoscopic cholecystectomy, a routine procedure to remove her gallbladder; the stone inside it had been giving her pain. India's light brown hair peeked from beneath a paper hat. A sheet covering her was pulled up to her chin, exposing her feet. Her toenails, painted with purple polish, reminded him of grape jellybeans. It amused him but made him aware of her youth and vulnerability. Beside India, her single mother, Jean, stood stroking her daughter's hair. Jean wore paper shoe covers and a paper gown. Conner thought her dimpled cheeks and her hollyhock eyes, more oval than round, were striking. He marveled at how much mother and daughter looked alike.

"Have you done a lot of these?" India said, groggy from preoperative sedation.

"Over 1,000 without a major complication," Conner said with a confident smile.

A dark-skinned orderly with a gold cross around his neck came to take India to the operating room. India, her blue gown hanging loosely on her narrow shoulders, struggled to a sitting position on the gurney. She embraced her mother who gave her a kiss on the cheek.

Jean turned to Conner.

"Take good care of her, Doctor," she said. "She's my treasure."

"Of course, I will."

Before the orderly wheeled India away, the girl said, "I'm afraid."

Conner rested his hand on her shoulder and felt her shiver.

"Don't worry," he said. "This will be a piece of cake."

IN THE OPERATING ROOM, Conner approached the table. For a second, he peered over his mask at India's face. Her eyes were patched to protect her corneas from trauma. The bird-like chirp of the heart monitor and her warm breath frosting the endotracheal tube reminded him that a life was at stake. No mistakes, he told himself. Do no harm.

Conner returned his gaze to India's abdomen and held out his hand. Monique, the scrub nurse, smacked the scalpel into his palm, and Conner put everything else out of his mind but the procedure he was about perform. Quickly he went about inflating the abdominal cavity with carbon dioxide and inserting a camera. Like a spelunker's headlamp in a cave, the tiny camera's light illuminated the dark recesses of India's belly. Watching the video screen, Conner scanned her organs. Her liver crouched, shiny and cinnamon brown, beneath the dome of the diaphragm. The coils of her small intestine writhed, pink and snake-like. To Conner her organs were strangely beautiful, but the gray-green gallbladder embedded in the liver appeared shrunken and thick-walled from inflammation and gave him pause. It was not the piece of cake he had promised.

He took a deep breath and began dissecting blood vessels and bile ducts. At the *porta hepatis*, the doorway to the liver, the tissues he encountered were edematous and swollen. He knew a mistake here could be fatal, and his pulse speeded. Go slow he reminded himself. Beads of perspiration broke out on his forehead. A drop of green bile appeared on the camera's screen. Then another. Then a trickle of blood. He knew he had made a mistake. A queasy dread came over him, and his stomach tightened.

"Cautery," he commanded.

Monique handed him a stick-like instrument with a wire on the end that produced an electric current that both cut through tissue and coagulated bleeding vessels.

Cautiously, he moved the tip of the cautery to where the blood was leaking. He pressed the button to activate the current. Like a miniature lightning strike, a blue spark leapt from the instrument's tip. A shower of red hit the camera's lens.

"Oh God. No," he said.

Instantly the gallbladder was swimming in blood.

With shaking hands, Conner tried irrigating and suctioning, hoping to find a pumping artery that he could control. But clots kept stopping up the sucker.

"Her pressure's dropping," Riley, the anesthesiologist said. He opened an IV's valve to allow saline solution to stream into India's vein.

In her abdomen, the sea of red beneath the liver kept rising.

"Transfuse her," Conner said. "Come on. Let's go. I'm going to open her up."

Monique slapped a scalpel into his hand. With a single deep stroke of the knife, he opened India's belly. Desperately, blindly, he used a big vascular clamp to stop the bleeding.

"What's her pressure?" Conner's heart was tripping.

"Sixty and dropping."

"Jesus," Conner said. "Start a transfusion. Come on! Where's the damn blood?"

"Oh God," Riley said. "No pressure. She arrested. We're going to lose her."

Riley threw back the sterile drapes. With his gloved hands on her sternum, he compressed her chest with desperate thrusts of his arms.

"One, two, three," he grunted. "One. Two. Three."

Conner reached deep in her belly and felt her aorta. There was no pulse.

"Pump that blood," Riley said to the nurse who was starting the transfusion. "Let's go. Pump it."

It's over, Conner thought. She's gone. But in a few seconds, his fingers felt a faint aortic pulse. He looked up at the cardiac monitor. A green line of blips appeared on the screen.

"She's coming back." Conner could feel the pulse in the aorta strengthen. "She's coming back."

"Praise the Lord," Monique said.

Riley stopped his chest compressions and watched the monitor's wavy green lines.

"She's got a pressure," he said.

Conner began a search for the source of the bleeding and found a tear in the main artery to the liver. The vessel's edges were charred, and he knew the electric current had caused the damage. He asked Monique for his vascular instruments and started the repair of the artery. It was delicate work, and Conner's hands were shaking.

"You're doing good, Mon," Monique whispered in her island accent. "You're doing good."

Her soft manner soothed him, but Conner's hands still shook. It took him an hour to suture the torn vessel. All the while, a deathly silence settled over the room.

"Should we send out word to her mother?" Riley asked.

Conner pictured Jean Blue, her head in her hands, sitting in the waiting room for much longer than he'd promised. He knew there was nothing truthful he could say that would soothe her.

"No," he said. "I'll speak to her as soon as we're done."

When the artery was repaired, and he was satisfied the bleeding had stopped, Conner stepped back from the table and took a deep breath. His stomach was queasy, his legs weak. He quickly closed the abdominal incision, turned from the table, and stripped off his gown and gloves to look around the room. He saw the rows of blood-soaked sponges on a blue sheet, empty transfusion bags on the floor, a snarl of instruments in a metal basin. A blood bath, he thought. His gaze settled on India. Her eyes were still covered with gauze pads. Her face was gray, swollen. Her naked chest rose and fell in the steady rhythm of the ventilator. Her skin was pale as paper and mottled with blue blotches. Conner shook his head and left the operating room. He couldn't believe what he had done to her.

AT THE ARCHED entryway of the surgery waiting area, he looked into the room with its stained dark carpet and table cluttered with Styrofoam cups and old magazines. India's mother in stocking feet sat under a muted, flickering television set on the wall. She held her head in her hands, a veil of tangled hair covering her face. Conner's heart was tripping, his brow beaded with sweat. Taking a deep breath, he stepped into the room. India's mother leapt to her feet.

"How is she?" she asked. There was fear in her eyes. "What took so long? Is my girl all right?"

"She's not good," Conner said.

"Not good? What's that mean?"

"We need to talk," Conner said. "Please. Sit down so we can talk."

"I want to see my daughter," Jean said. "Where is she?"

"Please," Conner said. "Have a seat. I'll explain the situation."

Jean returned to her chair, and Conner sat near her. In a low, hesitant voice, he described the operation.

"There were anomalies."

"Anomalies?" Jean cocked her head and frowned. "What are you talking about?"

"Her anatomy wasn't like it should be." Conner's hands were shaking, his mouth dry. "There was a lot of inflammation that distorted things." He searched for lay terms, words that wouldn't incriminate him. "The cautery unit severed a blood vessel. There was bleeding. We were able to control the hemorrhage and repair the vessel. But when she went into shock, her heart stopped."

"Oh God, no," Jean cried. "Her heart stopped. You mean she's dead?"

"No, no." Conner shook his head. "We were able to resuscitate her. But her condition isn't good. She's critical."

"Is she awake?" Jean asked as if she hadn't been listening. "I want to see her."

"She's in the recovery room. You can see her when the nurses get her settled. No, she's not awake."

"Not awake. Is she in a coma? Are you saying she's in a coma?"

"She's still under the effect of the anesthetic," Conner said.

"I don't understand. How could this happen?"

Conner felt Jean's eyes on him. When he looked up, her eyes met his. Her pupils were dilated and shining.

"There are risks to everything in medicine," Conner

said. "Serious complications are very rare with gall-bladder surgery, but they happen in a certain percentage of cases. I'm very sorry about this."

"Is she going to make it?" Jean said. "Tell me she's going be all right."

"She's critical," Conner repeated. "But she's young and strong. She has that going for her."

"How can I help her? What can I do?"

"Everything possible is being done," Conner said. "It's a matter of waiting now." He rose from his chair. "I need to get back to her. The nurse will come get you in a little while."

He started toward the doorway, but Jean stopped him by taking his arm.

"You told me the operation was nothing to worry about. 'A piece of cake' you called it."

"I'm very sorry," Conner said. "God, how I'm sorry."

"You should be."

Wishing he had never become a surgeon, Conner hurried from the room.

A WEEK PASSED. Trapped in a web of wires and tubing, India lay totally unresponsive in ICU, an electric beep counting out the rhythm of her heart. Her chest rose and fell with the click of a respirator—otherwise, she was perfectly still. In the last few days there had been a miraculous transformation in her appearance. Transfusions had restored pink to her cheeks. Most of the edema had left her face, and the curves and hollows of her features—those that made her pretty—had returned. The nurses had braided her hair. To Conner, she looked like a napping child. One of the cruelties of brain death, he thought, is that the person looks alive.

Next to him at the bedside stood Dr. Helen Anderson, a stern, studious neurologist with no lipstick and prematurely gray hair parted down the middle. In the pocket of her long white lab coat were a tuning fork, a rubber reflex hammer, a penlight to shine on the patient's pupils, and a big safety pin to test for pain.

Across the bed, Jean Blue stood, wearing a hospital gown over her clothes. With dark circles under her eyes, she looked as if she had been assaulted.

While Dr. Anderson performed a neurological exam, tapping tendons, pressing her knuckles into India's sternum, scraping the soles of her feet with a tongue blade, Conner looked at photographs of India on the bedside table. Baby India in a crib. India in a strapless prom formal with a boyfriend wearing a white dinner jacket. India in Dr. Denton pajamas sitting on her mother's lap, hand in a bowl of popcorn. India in a witch's hat on Halloween. India wearing the gauze-and-wire wings of an angel. Conner fought off the urge to weep.

"Do you think she's in pain?" Jean asked. Her voice had no strength. "I can't stand to think of her in pain."

"No," Dr. Anderson said. She reached out and rested her hand on India's shoulder. "She's not in pain. She doesn't feel anything. She's in a very deep sleep. When I test her, she doesn't respond."

"I can't stand to see her like this." Jean picked up India's hand to stroke it. "I wonder what's going through her mind."

Nothing, Conner thought. No memories. No hopes. No desire. Nothing. Nada.

"You're sure she can't feel anything?" Jean asked.

"I'm sure." Dr. Anderson's voice was low, consoling. "Her electroencephalogram shows minimal electrical activity. Her reflexes are gone, and she doesn't respond to painful stimuli. I think it is safe to say she isn't suffering."

"She's really just existing then," Jean said. With tears in her eyes, she stared down at her daughter. "Isn't that it? She's just existing."

"Yes," Dr. Anderson said. "You could say that."

"Oh God." Jean sighed. Then she began to weep. "It seems like yesterday that I brought her into this world. I can't believe God would bless me with a child like her, then allow this to happen." She dabbed at her eyes with a tissue. "What about her breathing? How would she breathe if she was taken off the machine?"

Dr. Anderson looked to Conner for the answer.

"She still requires high levels of oxygen to keep her

lungs functioning," he said. "It's unlikely she could tolerate being off the ventilator."

"Sometimes, we try patients off the machine to see how they do," Dr. Anderson said.

"What if she couldn't make it?" Jean asked. "What if she couldn't breathe on her own? What then?"

"You would have to decide about letting nature take its course," Conner said.

"That's a decision that should be made before she's taken off," Dr. Anderson said. "You need to consider what the quality of her life is going to be, and then do what's best for her under the circumstances."

Jean kept staring at her daughter, seeming not to hear.

"They talk about a vegetative state," she said. "Is that what she's in, a vegetative state?"

Yes, Conner thought, I have made her a vegetable. Hating himself, Conner listened to the ventilator's click and sigh.

"Yes," Dr. Anderson said. "In all honesty, you could say that."

"I don't want her to spend the rest of her life in a nursing home," Jean said. "I'll take her home with me. I'd rather she die than end up in a nursing home." Jean choked. "If I could only take her place. I've had a chance at life. She's not going to get her chance."

"Don't feel pressured to make your decision," Conner said. "If you have any other questions, Dr.

Anderson and I are available anytime night or day to answer them. If anything changes, you'll be the first to know."

He heard himself talking. The words sounded hollow. He thought he should be the one to take India's place.

Jean raised her eyes from her daughter and glared at Conner.

"You're the one who did this to her," she wailed. "I want you off the case. I don't want to see you again." Her voice rose. "You're going to pay for this." She opened her purse and rifled through it as if there was something in it she could use to harm him. But then she snapped it closed and began to sob.

FOR TWO WEEKS India remained in a deep coma on the ventilator. Brain dead. Neural nothingness. "Do Not Resuscitate" was plastered in bold letters to the front of her chart. In the afternoon, Helen Anderson called Conner to tell him India's mother had decided to call off life support. Although he knew it had been inevitable, the reality—the finality of the decision—was more than Conner could bear. Shaken, he asked Helen to meet with him before she turned off the ventilator.

In the doctor's on-call room, Conner stood at the window, looking out at the courtyard below where

India's friends were holding a vigil with candlelight and guitar music. He pictured India being rolled away to surgery. He pictured her anesthetized on the operating table. He pictured the blood in her belly. He pictured her in a coma on the ventilator. He couldn't stop seeing her. He knew he was going to be sued, and he welcomed it, believed he deserved it. The door opened, and Helen Anderson entered the room like a white-coated grim reaper.

"Everything is set," she said. "The girl's mother is meeting me in ICU."

"What a nightmare." Conner shook his head.

Helen sat down on the chair by the window. "I have to keep telling myself this is an act of mercy."

The door to the room was open, and a strange man in a hooded sweatshirt stopped and look in at them. Conner closed the door and took a seat on the cot where the on call doctors slept. For a moment, he thought of the future's unpredictability, the miracles of the past, and the medical misjudgments he'd made. Could the EEG be wrong? What if India's brain wasn't dead? What if a cure for brain death was right around the corner? Who could say what the value of the life of someone in a coma really is? That he was responsible for her death magnified his agony.

"You're sure it's not too early to make this decision?" he asked. "Should she be given more time to see what happens?"

"That will just prolong everyone's suffering, including yours, Conner. There's a time to live and a time to die. Sad as it is, it's her time to die."

"She's way too young to die." Conner sighed. "My God, the incompleteness of her life."

"Yes, it's a great tragedy." Helen paused a moment, thinking. She was backlit by gray moonlight shining in through the window. "Try to look at it as a form of palliation, like sedating someone in pain."

"Except it's forever," Conner said.

"Who knows what forever is?" Helen asked. "Who is to say when a life is complete?"

"How is Mrs. Blue taking this?"

"She's totally despondent. She says India is all she has in her life."

"What does she say about me?"

"You don't want to know."

Conner looked at Helen. Her face was shadowed, and he wasn't able to read her expression. "What did she say?"

"She thinks you have destroyed two lives. India's and hers."

"And mine makes three," Conner closed his eyes and shook his head. "God, I can't stand this."

Helen looked at her watch.

"It's time. I need to go." She wrapped her arms around Conner and patted his back. "I'm sorry. You're a good doctor. Just remember that."

"Thanks for all you're doing." Tears blurred Conner's eyes.

"It's my job."

After Helen left, Conner stood, looking down into the hospital's lawn. India's friends were still there. The flames of the votive candles quivered, about to go out. His stomach was a tightly wound ball. Afraid that he was going to throw up, he flung himself on a cot and turned to face the wall. He was in a dark cave, staring into a futureless abyss. He pictured what was happening to India. The click of the switch when the ventilator was turned off. The waiting while life seeped out of her. The flat green line. Helen's fingers on the girl's carotid artery. Helen's stethoscope listening to the silence of India's heart. India's mother wailing at the bedside. He felt a pain deep in his bone marrow.

After a while, Conner picked up the phone and called ICU. The nurse, Jan, answered.

"Is it over?" Conner said.

"Yes, it's over." Jan's voice was soaked with sorrow. "Dr. Anderson turned her morphine drip wide open so she wouldn't experience air hunger. Then she stopped the ventilator. India died peacefully."

Conner swallowed the knot in his throat. "Is her mother still there?"

"She left."

"Please keep India there. I want to see her."

"Yes, Doctor."

In a daze, he moved heavily through hushed empty corridors redolent with the odor of illness. In dimly lit rooms, families gathered around beds, talking in hushed voices. Somewhere in the distance a siren whined. An elderly woman cried out for a nurse.

In the ICU, his heart thudding, Conner stepped into India's glassed-in cubicle. Moonlight poured through the window, bathing India in blue light. The respirator, the monitors, the IV poles—had all been removed. The room was eerily quiet. Conner moved to the bedside and stared down at the girl's lifeless pastel face. She looked as if she were sculpted from pale stone. Her lips were curved in a slight smile of someone seeing something glorious.

"India," he said in a low voice. "How could I have failed you so miserably? I am so sorry."

Conner had a strange urge to crawl up on the bed, to lie down beside her, hug her. But instead, he turned, and with glistening eyes, walked from the room and down a back stairway. Opening a heavy door, he stepped out into the night. The world was silent and empty. He looked up at a black sky with its sprinkling of stars. The entire universe surrounded him. High above, he saw the red and green lights of an airplane moving slowly across the sky. He watched the lights blink until they disappeared, leaving him alone and filled with regret.

～

IN THE YEAR THAT FOLLOWED, the memory of India's death was always with Conner, like a spike in his brain. He continued his medical practice but restricted the surgery he performed to minor procedures done under local anesthesia in his office. Even though they were technically simple and of minimal risk to the patient, in doing them he felt unsure of himself. For Conner, surgery had been his calling, the operating room his sanctuary, but there was no longer joy in the work that he had once loved.

When Jean Blue's malpractice suit against him was settled for three million dollars, Conner believed she deserved the money, but the publicity of the settlement left him humiliated and guilt-ridden. He no longer attended county medical society dinners, hospital staff meetings, or social functions at the country club. Then one day, to Conner's amazement, he received a call form Helen Anderson telling him that Jean Blue was asking to see him at her home.

"Why would she want to see me?" Conner asked. "I killed her daughter. The lawsuit's been settled. What good would it do?"

"If that's what she wants, you owe it to her," Helen said. "I'm going to tell her you agreed to come. It's the decent thing to do."

The following week, Conner found himself on the stoop of Jean Blue's gray stucco cottage. The street in front of the house was quiet and empty of cars. Dead geraniums gave window boxes the appearance of something lost. A harsh wind blew withered leaves across the yard's brown grass. When Conner dressed, he had chosen somber colors. A gray sweater and navy corduroys. Despite the cold, he was perspiring. What could he say except that he was sorry? And what good would that do? Taking a deep breath, he rang the doorbell. A dog barked, but no one came to the door. He was about to turn and flee, but the sound of footsteps held him in place. The door swung open, and Jean was there holding a black-and-white mutt by the collar. She wore a cotton peasant blouse and jeans with faded seams. Her lips were pale, nearly white. Conner noticed faint circles under her eyes and thought how haggard she looked. The dog, straining to break free, let out a yelp.

"Good afternoon, Doctor," Jean said without a smile. "Please come in."

"Thank you for inviting me."

He bent over and offered the back of his hand to the dog. The pooch licked it with a long pink tongue.

"Gandhi's friendly," Jean said. "He just gets excited when there's company."

Aha, Conner thought. India, Gandhi. Now, he knew who'd given the dog its name.

With the dog trotting behind her, Jean led Conner into the living room with its baby grand piano, pinewood floors, and hooked rug. The air was pungent with the scent of nutmeg and ginger, an aroma that reminded Conner of autumn. Jean directed him to an overstuffed chair next to a coffee table made of distressed wood. He lowered himself into the cushions.

"Would you like a cup of tea?" Jean asked.

"Tea would be fine," he said, although he rarely drank it.

With Gandhi at her heels, Jean left the living room through a glass-beaded curtain. Conner studied the room and its furnishings. The overstuffed chairs. The love seat upholstered in faded red velvet. A hutch with a smiling Buddha on the shelf. Leopard-skin pillows. The shabbiness seemed calculated and appealed to his taste.

He rose from his chair and moved to a bookcase behind the piano. Fiction, philosophy, religion, and poetry were randomly arranged without regard to subject matter. He read some titles: *Interpreter of Maladies, The Essential Writing of Thich Nhat Hanh, The Raft Is Not the Shore, Peace in Every Step, The Seven Story Mountain.* From a shelf, he pulled E. M. Forster's *A Passage to India.* He opened it and read a line at random. "I'm a doctor. Snakes don't bite me." He shook his head at the irony. He returned the book to its place, thinking his own story's title, should be "The Passage of India."

From the kitchen came the whistle of a teakettle, and Conner went back to his chair. Soon Jean, carrying two white china mugs, came through the beaded curtain. She handed a mug to Conner then settled onto the couch with Gandhi beside her.

"I'm sorry, Doctor," she said, no life in her voice. "I forgot to ask. Do you take sweetener? I have honey."

"No sweetener, thank you."

For a while, they sipped tea in awkward silence. The brew was strong with a hint of orange flavor. As Jean drank, Conner noticed her fingers holding her cup. They were long and thin, without rings. The hands of a pianist, he thought. He was aware of his own hands, the hands that had made the fatal mistake. He despised them. He motioned with his head toward the piano.

"Do you play?" he asked.

"Yes," she nodded. "I teach piano."

"What kind of music do you play?"

"Classical, popular, show tunes. A little bit of everything. I prefer jazz."

"I'm a big jazz fan," Conner said. "I'd like to hear you play. Do you perform?"

"Some lounge gigs. Nothing big." She put her mug on the table, and her face darkened. "You can't imagine how I've hated you," she said.

Her abrupt change startled Conner. He stirred in his chair to brace himself.

"India was everything to me. You stole what I treasured most in life. The money I got means nothing to me." Jean clasped her hands. "I have wished you dead. I have never felt like that about anyone before."

Conner's face flushed.

"All I can say is I am terribly sorry," he said. "I'd do anything to make it right. To bring her back."

Jean continued as if she hadn't heard him. "All that anger." She strained to get the words out. "It eats me up. My soul aches. Sometimes I want to die. I've become a prisoner to my bitterness."

When Conner saw her eyes glisten with tears, a lump came to his throat. He swallowed it down with a sip of tea. He wished he'd never come, wished he could disappear. Conner stared into his tea. After a very long time, Jean wiped her eyes with a napkin and began speaking again.

"There's a well-known Buddhist story," she said. "It's about two monks who encounter each other years after being released from prison, where they'd been tortured. One of them asks the other if he had forgiven their captors. When he responds that he will never forgive them, his fellow prisoner says, 'Well, I guess they still have you in prison, don't they?'" She looked directly at Conner with cold eyes. "So you see, Doctor, like that monk I've been in a prison that you put me in." She paused for a sip of tea. "But then one night, India came to me and said, 'Mom, you need to leave that prison you're in and be free again to lead your life.'"

The idea that India had spoken to her mother caused Conner's heart to seize.

"I'd give anything to free you from that prison," he said. "I didn't want to put you in it."

"It's not in your power to free me," Jean said. "I am the only who can." After a few seconds she continued. "I heard you took time off from your practice. Are you back to being a surgeon?"

"Not really," Conner said. "I do some minor procedures in the office, but I haven't been able to face the operating room."

"That's a shame," Jean said. "Dr. Anderson told me you were a good surgeon. You have the gift to save lives. You should use it."

Conner was baffled.

Then Jean looked at him quizzically. "I think you're in a prison too, Doctor, and like me you're the only one who can set you free. India wants you to be free, same as she wants me to be free."

Conner nodded, thinking of his own anger and guilt, the way he hated himself for who he was and had become and what he did to India.

"What happened is in the past," Jean said. "Think of it this way. You'll never be the same person you were before."

"I know that's true." He kept thinking she was the one who deserved to be comforted, not him.

"Every person is a river that flows. Keeps changing. Keeps moving on." Jean put her hands to her knees. "Oh gosh. I forgot something."

She hurried to the kitchen and returned with two plates. On them were two forks and two slices of bread, the color of dark molasses.

"Pumpkin bread," she said, returning to the couch. "I make it with coconut milk and toasted walnuts."

"I love pumpkin bread." Suddenly Conner was hungry. "My mother made it when I was a kid. I haven't had it for a long time."

He looked at the slice of cake on his plate and remembered telling India before her surgery that her operation would be "a piece of cake." He shook his head. The arrogance, the flippant foolishness of his statement made him ashamed.

They both began to eat. The bread tasted tangy with spices Conner couldn't identify. He watched Jean chew each bite methodically. Dark crumbs stuck to her white lips. He detected an air of sad tranquility about her. Or was it simply resignation?

"Delicious," Conner said.

"Thank you." Jean put down her fork and dabbed at her mouth with a napkin. "You said you wanted to hear me play the piano. Would you like for me to play something?"

"That would be terrific."

She went to the baby grand and sat on the bench. Jean laced her long fingers together and stretched them. Then she closed her eyes and began to play. Conner listened to the soft riffs and runs of "Misty." How beautifully Jean played, blending "Misty" in with bars of Debussy's "Arabesque." The melody, full of melancholy and yearning, came to Conner, hovered around him, and clutched his heart. He took another bite of pumpkin bread and held the morsel in his mouth. It turned sweet on his tongue.

DRUMLINS

FLYNN WAS knowledgeable about the pathology and prognosis of malignant melanomas. The retired surgeon knew the thinner the melanoma, the better the survival rate and that younger and female patients tended to have a more favorable outlook. That he was a male and the melanoma that had appeared on his face was thick caused great dread to bloom in his chest. The thick, darkly pigmented lesion had a scalloped border.

It was the morning after a Mohs surgeon had excised the melanoma from Flynn's cheek. Flynn had arisen early to prepare for his day at the clinic for the indigent in Muncie, Indiana, where he volunteered every other Friday. The haze of sleep was still with him. His incision ached, and the side of his face felt swollen and tight. Flynn showered carefully to avoid getting the wound wet. It was late autumn, and Flynn's furnace wasn't working properly. When he dried off, a rash of goose bumps covered his chest and back. With a towel tucked around his thickening waist, he stood in front of the mirror in his bathroom. He studied the bluish discoloration beneath his left eye—his face looked like bruised fruit. He was afraid of what he would find beneath the strip of white gauze that angled across his features. Slowly, grimacing, he peeled off the tape the surgeon had applied. The length of the incision startled Flynn. He counted fifteen nylon stitches. He forced a smile and saw that the cut didn't quite conform to the natural lines of his face. His smile melted into a frown.

Flynn had been a rather handsome man. In spite of thinning hair, an unfortunate iguana neck, pouches under his eyes, and sun-damaged skin, he was someone whose looks had not totally succumbed to the ravages of old age. For the most part, his appearance had pleased him. But now he didn't care if the inevitable scar would mar his face. With his guarded prognosis, what difference would it make? He applied Bacitracin ointment to the incision and taped a strip of Telfa dressing over the wound. He was glad not to have to look at it. Before he buttoned the collar of his shirt, he felt his neck for metastatic lymph nodes. Flynn's fingers found none. He tried not to think of next year or the year after that, but he couldn't avoid weighing the odds. "Fifty-fifty," he muttered, referring to his chances of survival. "The flip of a coin." He exhaled a great sigh of regret.

BEFORE HIS DEATH, Annette's father had been a tenant hog farmer in Winchester, Indiana, a small county seat just over the Ohio border. A cheerleader for the Winchester Community High School's Yellow Jackets, in high school Annette had been a good student. Planning to become a nurse, she'd enrolled at Ball State, but she had to drop out to support her widowed mother and baby brother. For the twenty years that followed, Annette had worked as a housekeeper.

At first, she'd been resentful that her father's death had deprived her of an education, but after a while, she began to enjoy her work as a domestic. In an unschooled way, she understood the chemistry and microbiology of bathrooms and kitchens and how to disinfect sinks, toilets, and tubs with household ammonia, sodium hypochlorite, and isopropyl alcohol. It was as if she were practicing preventive medicine. To clean and care for people, to protect them from disorder and disease, was the essence of who she was. Then, a mammogram had revealed a suspicious shadow in her breast, and suddenly it was her own welfare that concerned her.

Ten days earlier, Dr. Price, a surgeon at the hospital

in Muncie, had removed Annette's left breast. Because she had no medical insurance, the diagnosis had been made at Volunteers in Medicine, the clinic for the indigent, where she received free health care. After the results of the biopsy were known, the clinic nurse referred her to the mannerly but arrogant surgeon who performed the operation pro bono with the understanding that follow up would be provided by the clinic. At her preoperative visit, Price had told her the good news: her tumor was a ductal carcinoma in situ, which was the earliest form of breast cancer and nearly a hundred percent curable. The bad news was that her breast had to be totally removed to assure a cure. He tipped his head back when he talked as if she were a medical journal he was reading through bifocals. When Dr. Price called the operation "a simple mastectomy," Annette had nearly laughed out loud. Her breast was more than just a body part to her. It was the essence of her womanhood. Losing it wasn't simple at all.

The day she was to go the clinic and have the skin clips in her incision removed, Annette rose early. It was a misty fall morning, and the wind was blowing. Outside her window, the leaves of oaks and maples were in their final fall blaze. The surgery had depleted her, left her tired and glum with a sore chest and stiff shoulder that made it difficult to comb her hair. Annette stepped from the tub and stood in front of the full-length mirror on her bathroom door. As she toweled off, she looked at the angry incision that traversed her left chest. Tentatively she touched the reddish and slightly swollen skin where her breast had been. The operative site was numb and bruised. The row of staples the surgeon had used to close the wound looked like a track for a miniature train.

Annette had been raised in the Nazarene Church. Although she no longer attended worship services, she still believed in a loving God who had a hand in everything that happened to her. But when she studied her chest in the mirror, she thought that if this was God's work, she didn't want anything to do with Him. She moved her eyes to her remaining breast. Pert and with a small, dark nipple. It seemed lonely, like an identical twin whose sibling had been lost. She felt unbalanced as if she were listing to one side and might soon topple over. Her eyes glistened.

Annette had loved her well-formed boobs, loved to sit in the bathtub and look down at them. She wondered what it would be like to date again, to undress in front of man? The thought of nakedness brought a pain to her chest. She felt as if something had been stolen from her. She taped a strip of gauze over the wound and was glad to have it out of sight.

BEFORE HE LEFT for the clinic, Flynn stood on the veranda of his beautifully restored Federalist farmhouse, its pillars as tall as the hardwood trees that lined the drive. The furniture in his home was mostly Midwestern antiques—a solid oak Hoosier cabinet, an Amish farm table, and a parson's bench. He wore a Harris tweed jacket, a blue Oxford cloth shirt and corduroys. At his collar was a necktie decorated with reclining Labrador retrievers. During his forty years in practice, he wouldn't have considered seeing a patient without a necktie and coat. The casual attire young doctors wore to work distressed him. It showed a lack of respect for the profession that had become part of Flynn's being, part of everything he did. Although he believed access to good medical care was the right of everyone and not a privilege, he dreaded the day ahead at the clinic. The patients' noncompliance with his medical advice, their obesity, their smoking and other unhealthy habits, and their utter poverty depressed him. His efforts to effect any meaningful change in their lives were in vain, and he wished he didn't feel obligated to donate his time to their care. Furthermore, he didn't want to be seen with his face bruised and bandaged and have the nurses question what was wrong with him.

Cautiously, he touched the dressing on his cheek. He thought of the scar that would form there. Since his divorce two years ago, he had been seeing Adrianne, an accountant for Ball Corporation in Muncie. She was young—in her early fifties and with a long life and fine career ahead of her. Would she still find him attractive? With his prognosis, he didn't feel it was right to burden her with the desolate days that likely lay ahead. The right thing to do would be to break off their relationship.

Halsted, a chocolate lab named for the father of American surgery, leaned against Flynn's leg. The dog had white whiskers and a bad hip. Flynn heard him wheeze, and he envied his pet's indifference to his own infirmities.

"You know, old boy," Flynn said, looking down at the dog. "I've had this face for seventy years. I don't like the idea of it changing."

Halsted stared at him with dark, noncommittal eyes.

"I know," Flynn said. "Get over it, man. Who gives a rat's ass what us old dogs look like?"

Flynn gazed out over his rolling, green acreage. His ancestors, who were among the first settlers in eastern Indiana, had emigrated from Ireland in the late 1700s, and the fertile farmland had been in his family for close to two hundred years. The low, elongated hills reminded him of the drumlins, the oval mounds smooth-sculpted by Cork County's glaciers. His malignancy had sprouted on his cheek like a mushroom. Again, he felt his neck for metastatic lymph nodes. Cancers, particularly melanomas, were devious and often occult. Even now, malignant cells could be coursing through his bloodstream. A surge of dread circulated through him.

Flynn looked at his watch. It was a gold OMEGA Seamaster given to him by his physician father when Flynn graduated from I. U. Medical School. Flynn saw that he was already five minutes late to work at the clinic. He didn't like to keep anyone waiting. He patted Halstead's broad head. "Time to get this show on the road, old boy," he said.

Flynn reached in his pocket and found a quarter and a Milk Bone treat that he gave to the dog. "Heads you survive," he said. "Tails you don't."

He flipped the coin and caught it. Tails. He shook his head. "Luck of the Irish," he muttered, giving Halsted another pat. "You know, old buddy, one day you're here. The next you're not. But the world goes on."

Flynn looked out at the rolling hills of the land he so loved. When the time came, it was here he would like his ashes scattered.

ANNETTE LIVED next door to a dairy farm at the edge of town. With a thermal mug of coffee in her hands, she sat on the steps of the two-bedroom rental. The white clapboard house needed a coat of paint and a new roof.

What Annette liked best about the house was that it had purple shutters, and she could leave her bicycle outside without fear of it getting stolen. Across the road, a fine mist layered over a pasture where a small herd of black-and-white belted Galloway cattle grazed. The panda-like cows chewing their cuds seemed to be part of a simpler life and reminded of her childhood on the hog farm.

Annette was dressed in high-heeled sandals. Her flowered summer dress was out of season and clung to her legs. She wore no bra, minimal make up, and the blue cardigan a lawyer's wife she'd worked for had handed down. Around her neck hung a string of imitation pearls her ex had given her before he left her for a blackjack dealer at Belterra Casino down on the Ohio River. She didn't mind that he was gone. She knew he wouldn't have had the inner strength to deal with her mastectomy. She'd managed to drag herself out to the porch. Later that morning, she'd be lying on the clinic's hard, cold examining table. It would hurt when the clips came out. She dreaded the pain and resented having to receive her health care at the free clinic. She didn't like being on the dole. The doctors and nurses treated her well enough, but, often preoccupied, they acted as if they were doing her a favor.

Annette turned her eyes to the pasture. A sparrow hawk circled above the Galloways. She watched the bird, with its brown-and-red feathers, dive into the clover. In an instant the little raptor rose with a field mouse in its talons. The violence of nature brought a hollow feeling to her damaged chest. She decided she wasn't up to riding her bike. So, with her coffee mug, she headed to the truck she'd parked in the side yard. She didn't want to be late and have them think she was some irresponsible airhead.

IN THE CLINIC, Edith, a veteran nurse with a silver pixie cut who years ago had worked with Flynn in the operating room, helped him into a starched and pressed white lab coat. His name and MD was embroidered on the left pocket. That the monogram confirmed he was still a physician pleased him.

Edith pointed at the dressing on his face. "Basal cell?"

"Melanoma," Flynn said.

He saw her expression darken.

"Don't worry," he said. "I'll be around for a while."

"I'm sure," the nurse said. "You're too ornery to die."

"Flattery will get you everywhere," Flynn said.

He glanced at a mural on the wall above the copy machine. It was an amateurish painting of a golden sunrise over a village of small houses. Red lettering printed on the sun said:

WE WELCOME THOSE WHO NEED CARE TO
COME WITHOUT FEAR. AND WE INVITE THOSE
WHO SERVE TO COME WITHOUT PRIDE.

For a moment, Flynn considered why he volunteered. Maybe because his presence at the clinic made
him believe that he was involved with something larger
than himself.

Edith handed him a chart.

"Go get 'em, Doc," she said.

Flynn took a deep breath and trudged off to see his
first patient.

A GOOSENECK LAMP. A metal chair. A sink. A dirty
window that overlooked a dumpster. The examining
room where Annette waited for the doctor was bleak
and cold. There was a noise in her head, a kind of
cacophony of fear and uncertainty. She noticed three
dead flies on the sill. The place needed a good scrub-
bing and a plant or a picture—anything with a little
color. Annette lowered the window blind and slipped
down the top of her dress. She looked at her incision
with its grillwork of metal staples. Once she had loved
to get naked, to show what she had. She shook her
head. She put on the flimsy paper gown the little nurse
had given her. She thought of the mural she had seen

on the wall of the nurses' station. It welcomed the patients to come to the clinic without fear. Fine for them, she thought. But she was afraid. Scared to death of dying. Plus, no man would ever touch her again. And, if she had cancer, what were the chances her daughter would one day get it, too? A chill passed through her. She draped her sweater around her shoulders. She decided to leave on her necklace.

SOON THE DOOR OPENED, and Dr. Flynn stepped into the room. Annette rose from her chair. She looked at the doctor's silk tie with the dogs and at his tasseled loafers and well-pressed corduroys. Rich man's clothes. She didn't mind that he was wealthy—all the doctors were—as long as he would listen to her and at least pretend to care. Even with a bandage and bruised face, he wasn't bad looking for someone his age. Her nervousness had dried her mouth. She licked her lips. With the back of her hand, she brushed strands of hair from her forehead.

"Good morning, Doctor," she said.

Flynn liked being addressed as "Doctor", a show of respect.

"Good morning, Annette," he said. "Please. Have a seat."

Annette like being called by name, but she detected

a tone of weariness in the doctor's voice. She dropped back into her chair and gathered her sweater around her. She started to thank him for seeing her. Then she thought, No it's his job, just as I don't need to be thanked for showing up to clean a house. If he treats me well, then I will thank him. He was holding his hand in front his face, and she wondered what he was trying hide, wondered what had happened to him. Had he fallen? Doctors didn't get into fights. She thought his wound somehow made him more human.

FLYNN STRADDLED a stool in front of his patient. He could feel her eyes on his incision. He turned himself to present his good side to her. He opened the chart and read the face sheet. She had listed her occupation as housekeeper; her only child was a daughter. Annette's age was thirty-nine. Her diagnosis was "post mastectomy for in situ carcinoma of the left breast." Flynn raised his eye from the record, and for a moment he studied her. She wore no rings. Her face and arms were freckled. Her reddish hair tied back in a long ponytail suggested an innocence and lack of sophistication. He was captivated by her ice-blue eyes. What were the circumstances that brought this attractive young woman to her place in life? Flynn wanted to put her at ease and to not seem hurried. He asked her where she lived and where her daughter was.

"She's going to beauty school," she said. "Hoping to become a hairdresser." Then she asked Flynn if he knew where the dairy farm with belted Galloway cattle was. Flynn said he did, and Annette said she lived across the road from it.

"Those are the loveliest of animals," Flynn said. "It must be nice to see them every day."

"It's nice if the wind is the right direction," Annette said.

Flynn smiled, pleased that she maintained a sense of humor in spite of her illness. He thumbed through the chart until he found the pathology report from her breast biopsy.

"So, Annette," he said, "I see you've had breast surgery."

The way he talked made him sound as if he already knew the answer to everything. Were his real concerns somewhere else? He seemed sad. She wondered why.

"I had cancer," she said. "I'm here to get my clips out."

"Yes," Flynn said. "I know. Your diagnosis was carcinoma in situ. Do you understand what that means?"

"Sort of," she said. "The surgeon said it was an early stage, and I was probably cured."

"Yes," Flynn said. "Your outlook is excellent." Flynn

patted the examining table. "Hop up here and lie back. We'll check your incision."

Slick cold paper covered the table. After lying down, Annette arranged her ponytail on the pillow. Flynn loomed over her. The scent of his shaving cream and shampoo wafted down. In anticipation of pain, her pulse quickened.

Flynn parted her gown. He smelled the coffee on her breath. He turned on the gooseneck lamp and examined her chest wall. He noted the red ring of inflammation around each staple and the violet and yellow bruising below the incision. Although he had performed hundreds of mastectomies in his career, the absence of a breast on a woman's chest always gave him pause. It made modern-day surgery seem as barbaric as bloodletting back in the days of leeches. The incision on his own face now suddenly seemed trivial. He gently palpated her incision and found no evidence of infection. He slid his hand into her left armpit and felt nervous sweat. He was relieved not to encounter enlarged lymph nodes.

"Is everything okay?" Annette asked. She was staring at a water spot on the ceiling.

"Your wound looks good," Flynn said. "Well healed. The surgeon did a nice job. He kept the incision low, which will allow for a better reconstruction."

"I wish I had my own breast back," Annette said.

"I'm sure you do," Flynn said. "You do know you

can have reconstruction done, don't you? There are various techniques using silicone implants or even your own tissue."

"I could never afford anything like that," she said. "I'll just get me a . . . What do they call it? A 'prostheta'?"

"Prosthesis," Flynn said. "They make some very nice ones now."

He knew she was right about the unaffordable costs of breast reconstruction. The artificial breast she would undoubtedly wear and the cheap necklace around her neck made her seem like a woman who had been denied life's bounty. The utter poverty of the world, all of its inequities, troubled him. At times, he felt as if he were a participant in a great scam. He wanted to figure out a way to help her.

"It's not something you have to decide now." He unwrapped the staple remover and wiped its jaws with an alcohol swab.

Annette clasped her hands together on her abdomen."

Is it going to hurt?" she said.

Flynn saw the tension in the muscles of her shoulders and arms.

"Relax, dear," he said. "This won't be bad."

He pried out the staples one at a time and dropped then in a plastic basin. In the past couple of years, he had developed a tremor that worsened when fine movements of his fingers were required. He steadied his right hand with his left. His diminished skills had forced him to retire, and he missed the operating room. But with the poor prognosis of his melanoma, it didn't matter that his days as a surgeon were over. In fact, nothing mattered now.

When he dropped the last clip in the basin, Flynn said, "That's it. We're done."

"That's all? I didn't feel a thing."

"Good," Flynn said. "Things are seldom as bad as we think they're going to be."

After wiping the incision with saline-soaked gauze squares, he patted it dry. "You don't need a dressing now."

Flynn could feel that the adhesive on his bandage was coming unstuck. He pressed the tape down with his fingertips.

"I have a question," Annette said.

"Go ahead and ask," Flynn said. "That's why I'm here."

"Why did the surgeon have to take my whole breast?" Annette said. "My aunt had breast cancer, and they did a lumpectomy on her."

Flynn thought for a moment.

"Because your type of tumor is often multi-centric," he said. "To get it all required removing the entire breast."

"Multi-centric?"

"Occurring in several locations within the breast."

"Okay," Annette said. "I get it."

"A total mastectomy was the surest means of cure," he said. "Now you don't have to worry about it coming back."

"What about my other breast?" she said. "Will I get cancer there?"

"We'll need to keep a close watch," Flynn said.

"Will my daughter get it?"

For a moment Flynn considered how he should phrase the answer.

"She has a greater chance than someone who doesn't have it in her family history. When she's a little older, she should begin getting regular mammograms and checkups."

"I was afraid of that," Annette said. "It doesn't seem fair."

"You're right," he said. "It isn't fair." He gave her a comforting pat on the shoulder. "You can get dressed now."

Annette rose from the table. She turned her back to Flynn, pulled up the top of her dress, and retied the ribbon that held her ponytail. When she turned around, she saw Flynn sitting at a desk fixed to the wall. While he wrote in the chart, the adhesive on the tape that held his dressing let go. The bandage fell down, exposing his incision with its reddish discoloration and bruising, the whisker-like sutures. Flynn peeled off the bandage. He looked at Annette with an embarrassed smile.

"What happened to you?" she asked.

"I had a little surgery," he said. "A dose of my own medicine."

"Was it cancer?"

"A type of cancer."

"Did they get it all?"

Should he be talking to a patient about his prognosis? Flynn started to say that with any malignancy you never knew, but he changed his mind. "Hopefully I'm cured. Just like you."

"I hope so," Annette said. "Don't be sad. You're still a good-looking guy for your age."

Flynn chuckled, amused at her bold remark.

"You didn't have to say 'for your age'," he said. "But thanks. And don't you be sad either. You're still a beautiful woman."

Flynn watched Annette blush and lower her eyes. He liked her: her humility, her spunk, and lack of pretension. He wished there was something more he could do for her. He finished his note and closed her chart. Flynn had an urge to gather her in his arms and reassure her everything was going to be right. Instead, he gave Annette his warmest smile.

Annette saw his smile and thought to herself that he was a good doctor and a decent man. She believed that in his heart he didn't consider himself any better than her. She wanted to give him a hug, but she didn't want to make him uncomfortable. So, she just returned his smile and thanked him for seeing her.

Flynn held the door open. Annette stepped through it into the room with the awkwardly painted golden sunrise on the wall. She thought one of the houses in the sunlit village represented her home. The noise that had been inside her head when she came to the clinic was gone.

With her chart in hand, Flynn followed Annette out of the room. The mural's golden rays seemed to be shining on him. Knowing he had helped the young woman, he felt lighter, as fulfilled as he once had felt after a successful operation.

ONE MORNING THE FOLLOWING SPRING, a warm breeze blew out of the west. Across the road from Annette's house, a black-and-white belted calf suckled its mother. Overhead in a cloudless blue sky, a sparrow hawk, seeking its prey, circled on thermals. Annette rose early to prepare for her six-month follow-up at the clinic with Dr. Flynn.

After her bath, Annette examined herself in the mirror over the sink. The incision on her chest was well into the remodeling phase. The once angry red scar had flattened, retracted, and whitened. What remained was only a pale remnant of the ordeal. Her missing breast was like a dream that she'd once had and longed to have again. She raised her eyes to the reflection of her face. She felt the thump of her heart beneath the ribs of her thin and damaged chest wall. It told her she was alive, and for that she was grateful.

ON THE OTHER side of town, early sun burned away a silver mist that layered over the fields of Flynn's farm. The sky shone with unusual brightness. Halsted's asthmatic bark awakened Flynn. He climbed from his bed. He was looking forward to his morning at the clinic. He had seen his schedule and knew he would be seeing Annette in follow-up. Flynn had talked to a plastic surgery friend and convinced him to reconstruct her breast in exchange for a case of single malt Scotch.

Before he shaved, he focused on the reflection of his face in a mirror above the bathroom sink. From the time of his surgical residency many years ago, he had been an expert in the science of wounds. He knew about macrophages, neutrophils, and fibroblasts—the body's cells that mediated the healing process. He could tell that the scar on his cheek was well into the maturation phase of healing. Flynn marveled at the work of the fibroblasts; they had remodeled his wound into a barely visible scar, a thin whitish line that linked the present to the past.

On the way to the car, Flynn stopped and looked down at the rolling landscape of his property. The beauty of the green and undulating drumlins gave him a little chill. As he often did, he felt his neck for metastatic lymph nodes. He found none, and a smile of gratitude spread across his face. For a moment, he thought of his fifty-fifty chance of survival. He reached into the pocket of his corduroys and took out a quarter.

"Heads you live," he said. "Tails you die."

He flipped the quarter with his thumb. The silver coin spun high in the air and glinted in the sunlight. Flynn caught it. For a moment, he held it in his hand. Then without looking at it, he returned the coin to his pocket and headed to the clinic to see Annette.

BOOTS ON THE GROUND

LT. COLONEL STONE'S pulse pounded from the adrenalin rush of the resuscitation. The career Army medical officer was in the trauma bay of a surgical hospital he commanded in Afghanistan. A Navy SEAL had been shot in the chest and femoral artery. Stone had stemmed the bleeding in the man's mutilated leg. He had inserted a chest tube in his left pleural cavity to expand a collapsed lung. In the SEAL's left subclavian vein, Stone had placed a large bore line and rapidly infused a crystalloid solution that brought the soldier out of shock. The patient was now in the operating room having his leg amputated. The floor was dappled with blood: red paint flung from a brush. Stone exhaled a long, deep breath and slumped into a chair. The strain of war lined his narrow face. He was pleased with the way he and his team had performed. A leg lost but a life saved. He had developed a way of thinking that made the maimed seem not quite so maimed.

Stone's tour of duty ended tomorrow. Then he would fly home from this bleak and savage land. The idea of going from war to peace seemed somehow daunting to Stone. It was as if he had lost touch with all the beauty and wonders of life. The telephone on the nurse's desk rang. An African-American master sergeant in scrubs answered it. He looked up at Stone and offered the receiver.

"It's for you, Sir," he said. "The morgue."

He reached for the receiver. "Colonel Stone here."

"Sorry to bother you, Sir," an accented voice said. "Sergeant Martinez here. We need you for a death certification."

Stone could have assigned the task of filling out death certificates to a lower ranking medical officer, but he chose to do the job himself. It kept him in touch with the darkness of war and cognizant of the human sacrifices battle required.

"I'll be right there."

Stone stepped out into the Afghan afternoon. A blast of scorched air greeted him. The sun beat down and made him squint. He put on a pair of silver aviator shades that blanked his eyes. On a sandy path, he headed toward the morgue, a ramshackle, tin-roofed building near the airstrip. Stone's blue shadow passed scraggly trees and piles of rock. From somewhere in the distance came the thud of artillery fire. Stone felt weary, weary of a war he believed nobody knew how to win. He wasn't even certain what winning would mean.

Stone opened the metal door to the morgue and stepped inside. He was relieved to be out of heat and wind. The pungent odor of embalming fluid stung his nostrils. Martinez, a muscular sergeant on the mortuary affairs' staff, saluted him. A member of an Army Reserve unit from San Juan, the noncom wore a rubber apron over an olive-drab T-shirt and fatigue pants. His cheeks were acne-scarred, and his black hair and mustache were turning gray. There was something sorrowful in the way he moved and in his downcast eyes.

"Good morning, Sir," he said in a hushed voice.

"*Buenos días*, Martinez," Stone said. "How's it going?"

"Like always, Sir."

Martinez lead him to a stainless steel embalming table. On it lay a body encased in a heavy-duty black vinyl bag. Stone worked his hands into a pair of latex gloves. There was a chemical taste in his mouth that he tried to swallow away. He reached down and slowly, almost reluctantly, unzipped the body bag so he could examine the remains. In his deployments to Iraq and Afghanistan, Stone had seen the most mutilating wounds possible—decapitations and quadruple amputations from IEDs, children with half of their faces blown away by bombs. Sometimes, there were just body parts. In spite of all his years as a war surgeon, he always dreaded what he might find inside a body bag.

Stone looked down at a mangled soldier. His face was scorched. His hair and eyebrows had been burned away. Stone picked up the soldier's left arm. It was stiff with rigor mortis. The fingers of his hand were gone. White bones and tendons were exposed. The heat of the explosion had melted the Kevlar strike plate of the man's body armor and welded it to his chest. Stone thought he had seen everything that weaponry could do, but this was something new. He shook his head. Who was this young man in the real world? Somebody's son, he thought. Somebody's brother. Maybe he was married. Maybe he had kids. Stone picked up the dog tag that was on a chain around the man's neck. He looked up at Martinez.

"What do you know about Private Nelson?" he asked.

"He was a door gunner, Sir," the sergeant said. "His Black Hawk was shot down yesterday. An RPG hit the fuel tank. His body was retrieved early today."

"Where'd it happen?"

"Zhari district, up by Kandahar," the sergeant said. "If you want to watch his chopper crash, you can see it on an Islamic web site. It shows towel-heads dragging him by his ankles through the street."

The desecration of Private Nelson's body caused

Stone to shudder. He tried to find some meaning in the soldier's death. But he found none. He had come to believe that only in living was there significance. Stone stripped off the rubber gloves and dropped them in a wastebasket.

"You know," he said. "Dying should be an old man's game."

"Yes, Sir," Martinez said. "But it won't be. Long as there's wars."

"Sad, but true," Stone said.

He turned and walked slowly to a desk in the corner of the morgue. From a file he pulled out a blank death certificate. Medical school had taught to be a keeper of life, but now he was a certifier of death. The thought depressed him. Stone sat on a stool and stared at the wall. He couldn't stop brooding about the dead door gunner. Why had Nelson joined the army? Was it starry-eyed patriotism? A broken heart? Maybe he couldn't find a job. Maybe he just wanted to fight. Stone started filling out the form, but he kept thinking about the young soldier. Why had this had happened to him? Why did it happen the way it did? Everything about war seemed cruelly accidental and random and made no sense. When he finished with the form, Stone took out a leather-bound journal from the pocket of his fatigues. Recorded in its pages were the names of all the men whose death certificates he had signed. Keeping score that way made their deaths more real. As he entered

Nelson's name in the journal, a heaviness bore down on him that pushed him deep inside himself. Stone wanted to cry but didn't. He had come to doubt that there was a loving God, but he bowed his head and silently asked the Lord to bless Nelson's soul and end the war.

The phone rang. Martinez answered it. He covered the receiver with his hand and called to Stone, "Trauma bay, Sir. They need you. They've got a wounded Taliban."

"Oh, good," Stone said. "He stable?"

"I don't know. They said, 'stat.' It might be the guy who killed Nelson. I wouldn't be in any hurry."

"Do no fucking harm," Stone told himself.

He looked at Martinez.

"Unfortunately, that's not the way it works, Sergeant," Stone said. "Tell 'em I'm on the way."

Stone rose from his chair. He hurried out the door into a hot wind. He could feel ground heat rising through the cleated soles of his rapid-deployment combat boots.

THE FOLLOWING DAY, Stone walked toward the helicopter that was to take him on the first leg of his trip out of Afghanistan. The air was hot and dry, the sky the color of smoke. A fierce wind blew the stench of burning garbage to him. From the entry to the morgue,

Martinez appeared in his rubber apron. He came to attention and saluted. The colonel returned the salute and gave him a thumb's up. Beside the sergeant was Pvt. Nelson's metal casket, draped in an American flag. The coffin was waiting for an honor guard to load it onto a C-130 that would transport the dead soldier to the States. For a moment, Stone pictured the horror Nelson had been through—his chopper bursting into flames, the Kevlar body armor fusing to his chest. The name politicians in Washington gave soldiers like Nelson came to Stone and echoed in his mind: "Boots on the ground." Stone took a deep breath. He turned and headed toward the helicopter. From the mountains to the north came the thump of artillery fire. Stone's footsteps left powdery tracks in the dust.

PULSUS PARADOXUS

THE SNOW BEGAN in the morning and continued into the afternoon. It was Saturday and I was the surgeon on trauma call. As was my habit when I was tethered to the telephone, I decided to listen to opera. I wanted nothing but a little time to myself so I could lie on the couch and let the music drain me of loneliness and allow me to escape the sadness of my life—my estrangement from my troubled daughter, Polly, and the recent and unexpected death of my wife. The opera I chose was a favorite of mine: Mozart's *Magic Flute*. The overture began, its heavy chords sounding like knocks on a door. Through the window, I watched the snow fall and let the orchestra's glistening shimmer of sounds flow through me. The music did as I wanted it to. It transported me into a state of reverie where I became the heroic Prince Tamino rescuing my love Pamina from the forces of evil. But then the phone rang.

"Damn it," I said.

Medicine is a fickle and inconsiderate mistress who holds no regard for her lover's other life, and I knew it would be the emergency room and that the music was over. I muted the sound system and picked up the receiver. The ER nurse's voice was high-pitched with excitement. I was needed stat to attend to a young man who had been shot in the chest. She said he was in shock when he came in, but his blood pressure rose with a rapid infusion of intravenous fluids. I told her to call the OR and have six units of type-specific blood available. I was on my way. I hung up the phone and took a deep breath, dreading what lay ahead.

I pulled on a pair of snow boots and a parka and hurried through the house to the garage. I passed the open door of Polly's room and saw her empty bed. A feeling of abandonment and failure chilled me. I pictured Polly asleep, her hair loose on the pillow. What if it was my daughter on that gurney in the emergency room? The young man, however good or bad he was, was someone's child—someone's Polly. Age was beginning to take its toll on my surgical skills. My fingers weren't as nimble as they once had been, and operations were harder. Did I still have the power to save him? I wished for a magic flute.

I backed my Land Rover out into the falling snow.

The radio was playing bad, repetitious rock, the kind of music that Polly would like. I turned it off and tried not to let myself think of her in the grimy motel apartment where she'd lived with Andy Mitchell. I tried not to let myself think of the checks she forged or her mother's jewelry, sold to buy their drugs. I wanted to remember her the way she was in the days before Andy Mitchell, the years when her mother was alive and Polly was a high-spirited and utterly happy child who filled my heart with gladness. I wanted to remember her as a willowy high school girl with wonderful pale blue eyes and a sense of humor that hit me just right. I wanted to remember the dance of her long brown ponytail as she loped over grassy hills with her cross-country team. I wanted to hear the sound of her voice reciting French vocabulary. I wanted to laugh with her and feel together and blameless. It stopped my heart to think how Andy Mitchell ruined her life, and mine, too. The thought of him nearly drove me mad.

On the slick street to the hospital, the urgency in the nurse's voice over the phone came back to me, and my thoughts returned to the man who had been shot. I blew my horn and skated the Land Rover through a red light. The fishtailing of my rear wheels heightened my excitement. Big flakes splattered on the windshield. A swirling cloud of white surrounded me with a sense of duty and uncertainty.

Ahead, under the ER's canopy, a cone of red light

from an ambulance circled in the white gloom. My heart pounded harder. As I had first done thirty years ago as an intern working the Saturday night "knife-and-gun club" in the Cook County ER and later as a battalion surgeon with the infantry in the Mekong Delta, I recited to myself the ABCs of trauma resuscitation. A for airway. B for breathing. Would I have to trach the guy? C for circulation. I told myself to watch for cardiac tamponade or a tension pneumothorax. Bullets ricochet off bones and pinball, boring unpredictable paths through the body. I cautioned myself not to get trapped into assuming that the obvious chest wound was his only significant injury.

I turned on to the plowed obsidian surface of the parking lot, thinking of all the nights I'd spent at the hospital. The stabbings. The shootings. I tried not to harden my heart against everything I'd seen. In Nam, it was punji sticks, AK 47s, and Claymores. Here it was Glocks, switchblades, shotguns, and even assault rifles. You thought you lived in a civilized country, but sometimes, it felt like you'd spent your life working in a war zone. I knew ballistics, had seen what guns do to people. I detested them and the wounds their bullets created—the lives they destroyed.

I parked next to a police car. Through the windows of the emergency room, I could see a woman pushing an X-ray machine. Nurses flitted about like a covey of white birds in flight. Everyone was moving in fast forward. I had the feeling that comes from watching disaster from a distance. It was the same way I'd felt in Nam hovering above a fire fight in a helicopter. I climbed out of the Land Rover and hurried through a dense white snowfall. My breath condensed in little puffs like smoke. From somewhere in the distance came the howl of an anguished dog. Metal doors sprang open, and I burst into the ER. Angie, a tall, gangly nurse with ash-blond hair and wearing blue scrubs, raised her hand in greeting.

"Look what the cat drug in," she said feigning cheerfulness.

"What you see is what you get," I said stomping snow from my boots and casting my parka aside. "Okay. Where's this fine denizen of our fine city?"

She thrust an X-ray at me and pointed down the corridor. "Trauma two. He's rocky. Can't keep his pressure up."

For a second, I held the chest film with its smoky images up to the ceiling light. I saw the boot-like shape of his heart and the bullet, a white button superimposed on a gray sternal shadow. My adrenal surged, heating me up.

"What can you tell me about him?" I asked as I hustled behind Angie toward trauma two.

"He's nineteen. Otherwise healthy. Shot with a twenty-two revolver. An accident, of course."

"Bet his best friend did it. Just slipped cleaning his gun."

"Doctor! So cynical." She shook her head and sighed. "Actually, it's a shame. He's a nice-looking kid."

"A real choir boy, I'll bet."

I grabbed a stethoscope and stepped into the trauma cubicle. A burr-headed policeman with a pistol on his belt bent over the stretcher and tried to restrain a thrashing, moaning young man. As I approached them, I glanced up at a cardiac monitor that was beeping in a rapid staccato. The kid's QRS complex looked good, and he was in a sinus tachycardia, but I didn't like the digital printout that said his blood pressure was only seventy over forty.

I stepped up to the gurney across from the policeman to begin my examination. I lowered my eyes to the patient's ashen face. Long lashes. An aquiline nose. A little blond mustache. His features were delicate, almost pretty. In disbelief, I recognized Andy Mitchell, and my heart constricted. I felt as if the blood puddled on the floor was mine, that it had suddenly drained from me. I gathered myself and made a quick assessment of his wound. His shirt had been ripped open, and over his left nipple there was a tattoo of little blue-and-red devil wearing a cape. On the right, I saw a small blood-encrusted hole in the skin below the clavicle. I tried to put his identity out of my mind, but it was impossible to do. I wondered what I had done wrong to cause my daughter to be with someone like him.

Andy jerked his arm away from the policeman and swung it wildly. I grabbed his wrist. "Lie still, Andy," I said.

"You know him, Doc?" the policeman asked.

"Yeah. Unfortunately, I do."

Andy flung his head from side to side. He raised up from the gurney and screamed, "Help me! Help me!"

His plea blew through the room like a cold wind. I started to grab him by the hair and jerk his head down, but before I could, the policeman reached up with his big hand and pinned Andy's head to the stretcher.

"Easy, son," he said. "Let Doc do his job."

"Let me up." Andy flailed his arms like a drowning man. "Let go. I can't breathe."

"Lie still, goddamn it," I said. "Don't talk."

I wondered who'd shot him and if Polly had been there. I wondered where she was now and if she was safe.

Suddenly, Andy quit struggling. His body went limp. I knew if I didn't act quickly, he would die.

I'D LAST SEEN Polly at the Candlelight Motel. The rundown motor inn's blue-neon sign advertised apartments, efficiencies, or rooms—by the day, the week, or the month. Inside Unit 10, Polly, sipping a can of Mountain Dew and smoking a cigarette, sat at a Formica-topped table. Her cornflower blue eyes looked haggard. Her skin was pale as paste. In the corner, the coils of a space heater glowed orange, but the room felt cold. The air smelled like singed paper.

For a moment, I scanned the linoleum-floored efficiency. There was a sofa, a television set with rabbit ears, a kitchenette with a sink, a hot plate and a small fridge. In the corner was Andy's electric bass guitar. Through a door, I could see the metal bed where he and Polly slept. The starkness of the place, the poverty of her life, made me want to cry.

"You look thin, honey," I said. "I wish you didn't smoke. Have you been sick?"

I reached across the table and touched her forehead to feel for fever. She pushed my hand away.

"Where's Andy?" I asked.

She eyed me suspiciously.

"At work," she said. "He works at a music store. Why do you want to know?"

"Just wondered."

"Why are you here?"

"I want you to come home."

I said it gently. My voice sounded thin. I inhaled deeply. I could barely breathe. I rose from my chair, moved around the table, and laid my hands on her shoulders.

"Don't touch me."

I stepped away and looked down through her tangled hair at her slim back. Her shoulders were as narrow as a little girl's.

"Come home, Polly," I said. "We can make a new start. You can get off drugs and go to college."

"I'm off drugs," she said. "I'm with Andy." She looked at me with icy blue eyes. "You don't like Andy because he's different from you. Well, I love it that he's different. He's not like you think. He's off drugs. He has a job. He's playing in a band and writing music. He wants me to go back to school."

"Polly," I said, "please come home."

"Why should I? When I was home, you were hardly ever around, and when you were, nothing I did suited you. My grades were never good enough. I wasn't dressed right. My friends weren't good enough." She stuffed her cigarette into the Mountain Dew can. It sizzled, and smoke spun out of the hole in the top. "Nothing I do will ever be good enough for you. Why should I come home?"

Suddenly, I was aware of my age and my history of cardiac disease—I might not have long to live. I dreaded nothing more than dying alone, estranged from Polly. A feeling of desperation came over me. Time was running out.

"I'm sorry," I said, fighting back tears, swallowing to get the words out. "It'll be different now. I've made mistakes. We can learn from our mistakes. We can start over. It's not too late to turn things around."

"I'm not coming home." She lit another cigarette.

"Polly, you can't stay here. This isn't the way to live. You need to come home and get your life together."

"I said I'm not coming home. Now leave me alone."

She turned from me and walked into the bedroom. I looked through the door at her sitting on the metal bed, backlit by the neon candlelight of the motel sign winking through a window. We remained lost to each other.

I PLUGGED the stethoscope into my ears and put the bell against Andy Mitchell's chest. The lub dub of his heart was muffled, a distant and sinister sound as if played softly on a kettledrum. I glanced up at the monitor. My left hand rested on his chest while I felt his pulse with my right. When his ribs rose under my touch, my fingers on his wrist could feel his blood pressure dampening. It was an ominous sign, pulsus paradoxus, a rare physiological phenomena that I had learned about in medical school. I had seen it in Vietnam with frag wounds to the chest and once when a cardiologist perforated a heart during cardiac catheterization. The paradox of his pulse told me there was blood in the pericardial sack. The blood was tamponading his heart and restricting its beat. He needed to have a needle stuck into the pericardium and the blood aspirated. He needed it now or he would die. I looked at his eyes. His pupils were big black tunnels to the brain. They seemed to be staring at me, and I stared back.

"Doctor," Angie said. "His pressure's dropping."

His pulse faded under my fingers. Each beat became weaker. The intervals between the green blips of his heart-tracing were a lengthening green line. As if paralyzed, I felt the rise and fall of his chest. His respiration was slowing. Each breath was a labored gasp. Then his chest stopped moving.

When I was a resident, I was part of a surgical team that severed Siamese twins who were joined at the chest. We knew that we were killing one twin to save the other. As I watched Andy with his heart drowning in its own blood, I told myself that if I let him die, I would be sacrificing him to save my daughter. The power of the idea twisted around me like a rope.

A spasm passed through Andy. His body jerked like that of a condemned man in an electric chair. Through the window over the sink, I could see that it was snowing harder. I sensed that my wife, wherever she was, was watching me through the murky light.

"Oh God," Angie gasped. "We're going to lose him. He's about to arrest."

"Crash cart," I barked.

Frantically, she rattled a red metal cart on rollers to the bedside. From it, I grabbed a long eighteen-gauge spinal needle attached to a 50cc syringe. I plunged the needle into Andy's chest just below his sternum and directed its tip toward his left shoulder. I advanced the needle slowly at a forty-five-degree angle toward the heart while applying suction on the syringe. I kept my eye on a flurry of agonal blips on the heart monitor. My own heart was pounding. Tiny beads of sweat clung to my forehead. Suddenly, I felt the suction pressure give way. I looked down at the syringe. Dark blood flowed into the glass cylinder. As the syringe filled and the pericardial sack emptied of blood, the ECG waveform returned to normal, and Andy's blood pressure rose to 80 mm of mercury. It was magical. Sleight of hand. A white dove appearing out of a silk handkerchief. The work of a magic flute. Or maybe it was Biblical. Lazarus rising from the dead. I stabilized the needle against Andy's chest with my hand. Like clay, his skin felt sticky and moist. With her hands trembling, Angie held out a metal basin. I detached the syringe from the needle and emptied the blood. Then, I repeated the aspiration three times. On the fourth attempt no blood filled the syringe. I felt Andy's heart tapping the tip of the needle. The ECG waveform changed to an injury pattern, telling me I was touching the heart. I quickly withdrew the needle from Andy's chest. I watched the tracing return to normal. I let out a great sigh. Was it one of relief? Or was it only resignation?

"Praise the Lord," Angie said.

With the syringe still in my hand, I stepped back from the gurney and waited to see if his vital signs would hold. When I saw his pulse and blood pressure were stable, I laid the glass syringe on the crash cart. I turned to Angie and told her to notify surgery that we were on the way with the gunshot wound.

Then I turned to the policeman. "Do you know who shot him?"

"Some guy was trying to rob the music store where he works," he said. "They've got the guy downtown." He cocked his head and looked at me. "How'd you know him?"

I hesitated a moment, and then I answered, "When you've been around as long as I have, you get to know a lot of people."

THE SURGERY WAS ANTICLIMACTIC. With a little supervision a second-year surgery resident could have performed the operation. The bullet had only creased the left ventricle of Andy's heart, sparing his coronary arteries and the electrical conducting system. I quickly repaired the lacerated cardiac muscle with three simple sutures tied over felt plegettes. In my hand, his heart was heavy and rubbery. It rhythmically clenched and unclenched like a determined fist. Its beat felt like forgiveness. Before I closed the chest incision, I cut a small window in the pericardium to prevent tamponade if bleeding reoccurred.

After I changed from my scrubs into street clothes, I stopped by the recovery room and looked at Andy, still asleep on the gurney. He was breathing on his own. His slight body looked white as the snow falling outside the window. His eyes were closed, and his mouth was set in almost a smile as if he possessed some secret knowledge. Bathed in fluorescent light, he seemed to glow with a kind of innocence. I pictured my daughter held tight in Andy's thin arms. In the dizziness of the moment, I suddenly felt tired, but somehow enlightened.

For a long while, I stood there with my fingers on his pulse. The green blips of his heart monitor marched across the screen above his bed. The dots seemed to be spelling out a coded message. What had brought Andy and me together was more destiny than coincidence. Something told me things would be different from now on.

When I left the hospital, I stepped out into the silence of a snowy night. It was as if I had entered a large, cold white room. A freezing wind made my eyes water. Big flakes were falling. Illuminated by a streetlight they crisscrossed in the wind like yellow ashes.

Everything was blanketed in snow: the winter trees, the roofs of houses where families were eating supper, the police cars in the parking lot, the deserted street. I pictured the snow falling on my wife's lonely and windswept grave. I envisioned it falling, too, on the Candle Light's blue neon sign with its flickering flame. I turned up the fur collar of my parka against the cold and headed to the motel to tell Polly that Andy was alive and all was well.

PART II

MORALITY

Compassion is the basis of morality.

— ARTHUR SCHOPENHAUER

NUI BA DEN

I HADN'T SEEN Jen for many years, not since I'd met her in Hong Kong in 1967 when I was a young battalion surgeon on R & R from the Vietnam War. For a long time, memories of Jen haunted me. But, finally, I was able to put her in the past—in recent years, I seldom thought of her. On the rare occasions that I did, my recollections were hazy and fragmented, as if I were looking back through cataract-clouded lenses. Then one night she appeared in a dream. In this dream, Jen and I, naked and drunk on margaritas, were making vigorous love on the shag carpet of an empty house. A Lincoln Town Car pulled up in the driveway. A real estate agent and his clients came to the door, and I awakened in a sweat, thinking I'd actually been caught in a sordid act.

Beside me, bound in twisted sheets, her long gray hair splayed on the pillow, was Julie, my wife of thirty-five years and the mother of our two grown daughters. A slim, aging author of children's stories that she wrote in both French and English, Julie no longer cared if she was the best-looking woman at a party, even though she often was. Easygoing, witty, she was also shrewd and independent. Our marriage had survived two affairs, one of mine with an OR nurse, and one of Julie's with the illustrator of her books. But now we had moved beyond foolishness and settled into a comfortable life together that, for the most part, we both liked.

"Are you all right, sweetheart?" she asked, her voice groggy.

"A leg cramp," I said.

"Want me to massage it?" Julie asked.

"I'm okay now. Just need to walk it off. Sorry to wake you up."

Shaken by the dream appearance of my long-ago lover, I arose from the warmth of the bed. Feigning a limp, I made my way through the dark downstairs to my walnut-paneled office. The panes of windows were black, the house silent. I turned on my laptop, and the screen's ghostly glow illuminated the room. I sat at my desk and keyed the letters of Jen's name into the Google search box. The computer seemed to hesitate for a moment, as if its chips and connections were reluctant to open this Pandora's Box. But to my surprise an image of Jen's face appeared on the screen among the faces of prominent women with the same name as hers. In her photograph Jen's head was slightly tilted to the left. Her hair, once brown, was now blond but in the same pixie cut she had worn when I last saw her those many years ago. Long, gold, feathered earrings hung from her earlobes. A small mole still dotted her upper lip. Her smile, revealing perfect white teeth, was still luminous and seductive.

As if I were adjusting the lens of a camera, my blurry remembrance of our rendezvous in Hong Kong slowly came into sharp focus. The venerable Peninsula Hotel with Chinese lions painted on its glass doors to guard against evil spirits was more than I could afford. But I splurged, using up all my combat pay so that Jen and I could stay there in luxury for the week. We spent most mornings in the room, keeping the drapes drawn, taking warm baths together, washing down chocolate croissants with champagne, getting to know one another again. Suntanned, playful, her figure was toned from modern dance and waterskiing. As always, her appetite for intimacy was voracious. But something about her seemed different from the days when I had been a surgical resident and she a physical therapist at University Hospital and we were living together in a studio apartment. It was as if a shadow person had come between us. Or was it me who was different, changed by war?

In the mild sunlight of afternoons, we strolled the streets of Hong Kong, carefully avoiding conversations about Vietnam—the danger I was exposed to, the atrocities I was seeing, the gruesome wounds I treated. And Jen mentioned nothing of the war protests going on in the States because, I assumed, she believed hearing about them would anger me. We could tell each other the truth when I returned home.

In the markets of Kowloon, plucked fowl and great sides of pork swung from meat hooks. The blood of eels and fish-fillets stained beds of crushed ice. A temple's fiery dragons lured worshippers bearing gifts to please the gods. The scent of incense spiced the heavy, humid air. It was an exotic, occidental world far away from the battlefields where my comrades were being maimed and dying in droves. It seemed as if I had momentarily escaped from hell to a life of pleasure so remote from war that I couldn't possibly be living it. At a booth in a Mong Kok flower market, I watched Jen select a lavender orchid for our hotel room. What if she becomes pregnant? I wondered. What would I do? The thought both frightened and excited me.

Early in the week, I took Jen to the garment district of Hong Kong where I bought her a Shanghai-style sheath with a Mandarin collar and myself a powder blue Nehru jacket. I can still see her slipping out of the dress. She arranged her hair in the bathroom mirror, then posed naked and fell laughing into bed.

The evening before she was to return home, we sailed on a Chinese junk in Victoria Harbor and drank

Beefeater gin and tonics. I remember the moon being full and unusually white, the silhouette of Hong Kong's skyline dark purple, and the salty sea breeze. With their girlfriends and wives, American soldiers on R & R strolled the ship's deck. The men would soon be back in the paddies and jungles of Nam. One out of ten of us would be wounded or killed. Who would survive and who wouldn't? Would I come home to Jen?

Our dinner that night was a dim sum banquet at a floating restaurant in Aberdeen. Delectables were spread around us as if they were a Thanksgiving feast. I felt we made a stunning couple: me in my Nehru jacket, Jen in the Shanghai sheath with a strand of cultured pearls around her neck, a small white flower in her hair, her lips shining. The way someone who is happy wishes for immortality, I wished the week that was soon to end would last forever. I reached across the table to cover her hand with mine.

"I love you," I said. "I want to marry you when I get back from Nam."

Jen was quiet. She stared down at plates of shrimp dumplings and sticky rice as if there were something troubling about the food. Then she looked up at me with her pale, brooding eyes.

"If you want to marry me," she said, "marry me now. Tomorrow before I leave."

I released her hand and took a long drink of wine while I pondered the temptation.

"There just isn't time," I said.

"I know other couples have married on R & R," she said. "I'm sure the concierge at the hotel could help us find a way."

"I have to get Vietnam behind me. I'm not fit for marriage."

"Tim," she said, "marry me now."

"When I get home, we'll have a proper wedding with music and flowers, our families and friends. We can come back here on our honeymoon if you want."

"Your answer's no?" she said in an even tone.

"Can't we wait?" I asked.

Jen didn't answer. The downward curve of her mouth expressed resignation. Or was it sad relief? After that, she ate very little. Her conversation turned hollow —about popular music and movies I hadn't seen and about people she'd met since I left the States, people I didn't care to know. That night we made love. Moonlight filled the hotel room. When I looked up at Jen, pale as a ghost, I saw a shiver pass through her. I noticed a tear trickling down her cheek.

The next afternoon we rode to the airport in one of the Peninsula Hotel's Rolls Royce Phantoms. Hong Kong's teeming streets were choked with bicycles and exhaust fumes, the odors dank. We sat in silence like two strangers. Jen stared out the window. I tried not to dwell on what it was going to be like without her in Nam. Why hadn't I agreed to marry her? Should I change my mind, go AWOL, and marry her this minute? Was her proposal an ultimatum? Why didn't she say she would wait until I returned from the war? It was a question I was afraid to ask.

At the departure gate, she held me awkwardly and gave me a dry-lipped kiss. "Good luck, Tim," she said. "Be safe."

Through the terminal's dirty plate-glass window, I watched her mount the boarding steps of the winged silver jet that would take her home to America. Her short white skirt clung to her hips. Her dancer's calves tensed with each step. I kept waiting for her to turn and wave, but she disappeared through the door without looking back. For a long time, I stood, staring at her plane. Finally, it taxied away and lifted off the runway. I watched the gleaming jet make a long sweeping turn and become lost in the clouds.

I returned to my Tay Ninh base camp, to its concertina-wire perimeter and stench of burning shit. The letters I sent to Jen went unanswered. Not even a "Dear John" appeared in my mail. In desperation, I hitched a chopper ride to Tan Son Nhut airbase in Saigon where I tried to call her on the MARs radio system. But the ham radio operator who was the intermediary for my call said her number had been disconnected. I was certain she was with another man, some draft dodger, while I was risking my life for a cause. The thought of Jen in bed with someone else drove me mad.

At night, alone in my sandbagged hooch, I listened to the Rolling Stones on a tape recorder and drank vodka. I volunteered for dangerous MedCap expeditions to remote villages to treat the Vietnamese and flew on medevac missions to hot LZs to rescue the wounded. I hoped to be wounded myself and that she would learn of it. Who could reject a hero with a Purple Heart?

Finally, a letter came. It was in one of those tissue-thin overseas envelopes bordered in red, white, and blue. It was from my sister, Liz, whom I had asked to try and locate Jen. I was standing in the scorching sun waiting for a dust-off chopper to take me to an aid station on the top of a mountain honeycombed with Viet Cong tunnels and caves. I was dressed in a flak jacket and steel pot, a .45 caliber single action revolver on my belt. My destination was named Nui Ba Den, "Black Virgin Mountain." Dreading the message, I opened the envelope and began to read Liz's left-handed scrawl.

Dear Tim,

I've finally located Jen. She has married a man named Tom Martin. They live in Kansas City where he practices law. That's all I've found out. I do know, however, that you are heartbroken, but somehow, I think you will be better for this. Although she is quite beautiful, there was always something about her that didn't seem right for you, a narcissism, something I didn't trust. I guess I always believed you deserved more.

Keep your head down but your chin up.

Love,

Sis

I returned the sheet of onionskin paper to its envelope and boarded the Huey. The chopper lifted me to the top of the dark and dangerous mountain. That night the Tet Offensive began with a mortar attack that blew me off my cot, a fragment of its shrapnel embedding itself in the flesh of my forearm. It was a wound that would take months to heal. Soon after the mortar attack, a VC suicide sapper penetrated our perimeter and killed two of my corpsmen. It seemed like the end of everything that mattered.

BELOW JEN'S picture on the computer screen was a posting of a newspaper article about her. She was the director of "Puppets for Pediatrics," a charitable organization that entertained sick children in a Tampa, Florida pediatric hospital. I shook my head. How could someone so seemingly benevolent have been so cruel and caused me so much pain? I reread the article about her twice. My curiosity swelled. Was she still married to

Tom Martin? I returned to bed and lay awake beside Julie, wondering. Did Jen have children? What would life with Jen have been like? What children would we have had? Would the marriage have lasted? Was she as beautiful and seductive as she once was? Did she ever think of me?

The next morning after Julie had gone to Pilates, I Googled "Puppets for Pediatrics" in Tampa and found the organization's phone number. When I dialed it, a friendly secretary with a Southern accent answered. I convinced her that I was a physician who wanted to contact Jen Martin about a puppet show for some of my patients. She gladly gave me Jen's home phone number and wished me and my patients well. I hung up the receiver and pulled up Jen's picture on the computer screen. Her face was beautiful for sure, one that men would still fall in love with. From the photograph, her seductive smile beckoned me as it had many years ago. I picked up the receiver and punched in her number. Her phone rang like an alarm sounding, which made my heart speed.

"Good morning," a voice answered. "Jen here."

Her sweet Midwestern twang hadn't changed in all those years. A liquid warmth washed through me.

"This is a voice from the past," I said. "Do you recognize it?"

"Oh my gosh," she said. "Tim Russell. After all these years. How in the world are you?"

"I'm great," I said. "And how are you?"

"I'm okay. Not great, but okay."

For a while Jen talked about her life and family. She had retired from physical therapy and spent her time doing volunteer work for the puppet shows and a hospice. She said that she and Tom were still married. He was twelve years older and, after a radical prostatectomy for cancer, in poor health. Their son was married. He lived on the West Coast and worked in insurance. She seldom saw her twin granddaughters. There was something empty about her voice, a longing.

Finally, Jen asked about my family. I told her about my daughter Ann, a radiologist in Indianapolis, and her sister Sally, who taught first grade in a charter school. I said I had retired to Naples, Florida, after practicing general surgery for thirty-five years, and now spent my time playing tennis, sailing, and doing primary care at Volunteers in Medicine, a clinic for the indigent. I wanted her to know I'd had a good life without her. I didn't mention Julie, and Jen didn't ask about a wife.

"Why, you're just down the road from me," Jen said. "I'd love to see you."

"Really?" I was surprised. Then I remembered her husband was most likely impotent. Was that a factor in her wanting to see me?

"Really," she insisted.

I pictured her as she once was, her luminous smile, her jaunty walk.

"It would be nice to see you again," I said.

There was a long moment of silence. Had her husband entered the room and caused her to hang up? Then, to my relief, she said, "I have an idea. There's an old inn in Boca Grande. It's halfway between us. Do you know it?"

"I do. The Gasparilla."

"Let's meet there," she said.

I paused a minute, thinking. For years I had guarded myself against reviving the distant and painful past. Jen would be an old lady now. And me? An old man with an uncomplicated life and a marriage to a woman I loved. What was to be gained from reconnecting with Jen? Would she break my heart again? Would this change my marriage? How far would I go?

"Are you sure this is what you want?" I asked.

"Very sure."

As a surgeon, my decision about whether to operate or not was always guided by a risk/reward assessment. For a moment, I weighed the pros and cons of meeting Jen.

"Okay then," I said. "Let's get together."

We made plans to meet at the Gasparilla Inn on the following Monday afternoon. I hung up the phone in a state of mild excitement, but trepidation, too. Had fate blessed me or condemned me?

∼

I CHOSE my attire carefully for the rendezvous with Jen—pressed khakis and a navy-blue blazer, a pale-yellow shirt open at the collar, and a silk pocket-square to match. When I came down the stairs to leave for Boca Grande, Julie—in jeans, a loose-fitting T-shirt, and flip-flops—was waiting for me.

"My, my," she said. "Don't we look spiffy?" She cocked her head. "Now who is it you're going to see?"

"A college fraternity brother," I said. "Old Spider Mills."

"You got all dressed up for a fraternity brother?"

"Spider belongs to a fancy club."

Julie smoothed the shoulders of my jacket. "Well, you be careful," she said. "Stay out of Spider's web. But have a good time."

THE GASPARILLA INN'S tall white columns and Jamaican bellmen bespoke of privilege and tradition. Guilt grappled with anticipation as I entered the lobby with its potted palms and sailors' Valentines on the wall. I settled into a white wicker chair upholstered in green and yellow chintz. A young mother and her two blond daughters, dressed alike in flowered Bermuda shorts, peered at a shell collection under glass. The trio reminded me of Julie and my daughters when they were that age. How inquisitive my girls were; how Julie loved being their mother. Everything her daughters did seemed to fascinate her and often became material for the stories she wrote. I steered Julie from my mind and turned my thoughts to Jen, remembering the pleasure and pain she once inflicted on me. It made me wonder what my real reason was for being here. I had recently broken my right incisor, and the dental extraction had left a gap in my gum. I reminded myself to not smile too widely.

Soon Jen appeared, descending the staircase at the end the room. She looked stunning in white linen slacks and a stylish aqua Mandarin jacket piped in white. Its high collar harkened back to the Shanghai sheath I had bought her in Hong Kong. Was her choice of apparel intentional, a reference to our Asian rendezvous? She came to me with her broad, white-toothed smile. I rose, and we embraced, the citrus aroma of her shampoo washing over me. For a moment, I felt her breath on my cheek. My pulse quickened.

"Good to see you, Tim," she said in my ear.

"Good to see you, too," I said, surprised by how much I meant it.

I drew back slightly and examined Jen's face. The picture of her on the Internet had been taken when she was much younger. Now, there were crow's-feet at the corners of her pale green eyes and pleats of puckered skin above her upper lip. But despite aging, Jen still had a look about her, a sultriness that would draw men in.

"Isn't this a lovely place?" she said, looking around.

"Old Florida," I said. "Very classy."

"But not as classy as the Peninsula."

"Ah, the Peninsula," I said. "So you remember?"

"Who could forget?"

"That was some hotel," I said. "Nearly bankrupted me."

"It looks as if your finances have recovered quite nicely." She touched my silk pocket-square.

"I have enough to buy you a drink," I said. "Shall we have one?"

"Show me the way."

I placed my hand on her lower back and steered her toward the Silver King Lounge just off the lobby. In the pecky-cypress-paneled room, a gigantic, open-mouthed tarpon was mounted above the bar. We settled into rattan chairs at a table overlooking a golf course, a manicured Eden of sugar-white sand traps and rolling greens where ex-presidents and ambassadors played. A paddle fan stirring the air made me think of Bergman and Bogart in Casablanca. My gaze moved up and down Jen.

"You look terrific," I said. I wondered what it would be like to make love with her again.

"As do you," she answered warmly.

Suddenly I was aware of my little paunch, of my iguana neck wattle, my thin white hair, and missing tooth.

"A little worse for wear," I said.

"No, you look great, Tim. Time has been good to you."

"Kind of you to say."

The waitress wore a pink button-down shirt with a green and pink striped tie. She dealt out two cocktail napkins. "Welcome to the Silver King. What can I get you?"

"A silver queen," I said foolishly, trying to be light.

Jen managed a polite smile, then thought for a moment.

"Gin and tonic." She looked at me. "For old times' sake."

"I'll have one, too," I told the waitress. "Beefeaters, of course. And bring something salty to munch on."

While we waited for our drinks, I wasn't quite sure of what to say. My stomach was churning. Through the window, I watched a foursome of young golfers appear on the green. One of the men was an amputee with a pipe-like metal prosthesis protruding from the leg of his shorts. Iraq or maybe Afghanistan?

"No doubt a wounded warrior," I said, pointing at him.

"You weren't wounded, were you?" Jen asked.

"Not critically." I pulled up the sleeves of my blazer and shirt and showed her the purple ridge of scar on my forearm. "I took a piece of shrapnel in a mortar attack. It was during the Tet Offensive on top of a mountain named Nui Ba Den. It happened soon after you left me in Hong Kong."

Jen reached across the table and touched my scar, lightly, tenderly with her long fingers.

"I can't imagine what you went through," she said.

Or what you put me through, I wanted to say but didn't.

On the golf green, the man with the artificial limb sank a long putt and did a fist pump. When he knelt, struggling to retrieve his ball from the cup, I felt sorry for him and what had been taken from him. The waitress returned with a bowl of salted almonds and our gin and tonics in sweaty glasses.

I raised my drink to Jen. "Here's to old friends."

Jen touched her glass to mine.

"More than friends," she said. "Much more."

"Yes," I said. "Once upon a time."

The gin seemed to relax us both. For a long while, we reminisced with ease and amiability about our time together—our friends at the med center; the crazy, wild parties we gave; the drinking; the marijuana-laced brownies; and the skinny-dipping. Jen still had that charming way of tilting her head and listening expectantly when I spoke.

"Those were the days," she said. "Do you remember when we got caught in that house that was for sale?"

I felt a slight skip in my heart. "I've had dreams about it," I said, remembering our nakedness, our lust.

"I can still see you scrambling around trying to put your pants on," Jen said. "The look on you face was pure terror."

"No," I said. "Disappointment."

She smiled at me and then grew quiet again. The waitress brought us another round of drinks. Jen nibbled on an almond and washed it down with gin.

"So," she finally said, "After all these years, what prompted you to track me down?"

"I don't know. I've wondered that myself." I swirled my glass, watching ice cubes collide with the lime wedge. "Curiosity I suppose, but there was probably more to it than that. Why did you decide to meet me?"

"Curiosity, too. Or maybe it was because I felt I owed you something."

"Owed me something? Why do you think you owe me anything?"

"I know I hurt you. I could tell by the letters you sent me after Hong Kong."

So, she had read them. Suddenly, resentment awakened in my chest and cooled the feeling of warmth that had just been there.

"Why didn't you answer me?" I said.

"I had decided to marry Tom. I didn't want to prolong the agony. Both yours and mine."

"You were in love with him when we met in Hong Kong," I said, somewhat curtly. "Weren't you."

"I thought so," she said. "He had asked me to marry him."

"So why did you ask me to marry you?" I asked.

"I knew you wouldn't agree. Maybe I wanted the blame for breaking up to fall on you."

"What if I had agreed?"

"You always had trouble committing," she said. "Tom was so sure. I felt confident with him." Jen was quiet for a moment. Then she reached across the table and took my hand.

"I have a room here," she said.

"You're staying the night?"

"I am. Join me."

"That honeymoon we never had?"

"I'm lonely," Jen said. "I want to be with you."

I took a long swallow of gin and tonic. There was a knot in my stomach.

"But you're married," I said. "And so am I."

"I'm worn out by marriage, Tim."

For a few moments, I thought of the sadness that had to be part of her weariness.

I contrasted it to my own happiness. I was lucky to have been denied what I once had wanted so desperately.

"I'm sorry to hear that," I finally said. "I really am sorry."

Again, a silence followed. I thought of Julie at home waiting for me and the lie I had told her about meeting

Spider Mills. I felt like an imposter, a cheat. I picked up my glass, turned it in the air, and downed what remained of the drink. I looked at my watch.

"It's getting late," I said and rose from my chair.

"You're not leaving, are you?"

"I have to go."

"At least stay for dinner."

"I promised to be home for dinner."

"Please don't go. Just say something came up."

I bent down and kissed Jen's cheek, my kiss as dry as the one she had given me at the Hong Kong airport.

"Are you sure this is what you really want?" Jen asked.

I hesitated a moment and then nodded. "Take care of yourself," I said.

I moved quickly to the bar and paid the tab. Then I walked out of the cypress-paneled room without looking back. At the entry to the inn, a bellman held the door for me and wished me a good evening. I was feeling unsettled, and his soft-spoken dignity soothed me. I stood on the hotel veranda and looked to the west where the sun was setting over the Gulf of Mexico. The last rays of the day tinted the clouds with shades of lavender and orange. The landscape lay half in light, half in shadows. A sea breeze brought the fresh salty scent of the ocean to me. I turned to go back to Jen. But something told me no, and I continued down the steps toward the car that would take me home.

PASCAL'S LAW

ON HIS WAY to the hospital to accompany his father on rounds, Fred slumped down in the Chevy wagon's passenger seat. The teenage boy was dressed a tweed sports coat and white shirt with a necktie that his father, a specialist in internal medicine, had insisted he wear. The March sky over Lake Michigan to the north was brown and strange from the smoke that spewed from steel mills in Gary. The morning traffic streamed along—farmers in pickup trucks, businessmen in dark suits commuting to Chicago, steel workers with lunch-boxes on their way to the blast furnaces. Fred's father drove carefully, seemingly lost in thought. Then he reached over and patted Fred on the leg.

"We're going to see something a little different today," he said. "Unlike what you've seen before on rounds."

"What's that?"

"We're going to see Charlie Woodhouse. I believe you know who he is."

When Fred heard the name, a shiver of revulsion passed through him. He pictured Woodhouse as he had seen him on the evening news a year ago in handcuffs and an orange jumpsuit being led away from the courthouse after his trial. Fred remembered his crime. Amy Yoder, a young teacher at the Mennonite Christian School in nearby Goshen, had gone shopping for her seven-year-old twins. In the parking lot of a Walmart, Charlie Woodhouse had forced her into his truck. He bound her wrists and ankles with duct tape and drove her to a remote cabin in the woods; he raped her then bludgeoned her to death with a log-splitter wedge. An eyewitness of the abduction led the state police to Woodhouse who confessed to the murder. Fred remembered reading that when the judge pronounced the death sentence, Woodhouse's reaction was a smirk.

"Why are we going to see that animal?" Fred asked.

"He's a patient of mine," his father said. "I believe there is something you can learn from him."

"What is there to learn from a murderer on death row?"

"We'll see."

Just beyond Michigan City's limits, the car passed the brick walls of the Indiana State Prison. Except for the guard towers and concertina wire, the brick buildings looked like the campus of a small college. Fred pictured Charlie Woodhouse with his head shaved, guards strapping him into "Old Sparky," the big wooden electric chair. Fred wondered what Charlie would want for his last meal and who would be there to see him die. He wondered what had gone wrong to make the man so evil.

"So," he said. What's the matter with Woodhouse?"

"He has pneumonia."

"Is that bad? I thought people got over pneumonia."

"They usually do, but he has Staphylococcal pneumonia. It's a particularly virulent form. He's also in congestive heart failure. He's very sick."

Good, Fred thought, although something told him it would be sacrilegious to say the word out loud.

Just ahead, the hospital's tall smokestack fumed lazily above the trees. On the sidewalk a crowd of protesters milled about. People in raincoats and slickers were waving signs that read REMEMBER AMY YODER and LET THE KILLER DIE! Hoping not to be seen, Fred slid down in his seat. In the parking lot, his father wheeled into a space beside a trash dumpster. He turned off the engine, swung around in the seat, and looked at Fred.

"Remember what I've told you about patient confidentiality," he said.

"Yeah. I remember."

"Good, then. Anything you hear about Charlie Woodhouse, you'll keep in confidence. Won't you?"

"Okay," Fred said. "If you say so."

His father opened the driver's-side door and climbed out of the car. Fred followed him across wet asphalt toward the hospital's back entryway. The wind was blowing hard, whipping his necktie. The cold air stung Fred's eyes. He couldn't understand why a murderer deserved confidentiality. Why should he have any rights at all? As they entered the building, he asked his father what Woodhouse was like.

"He's mean," his father said. "He smells. He's ugly. His body is covered with obscene tattoos. He's a total jerk."

"How can you take care of someone like that?"

"When I graduated from medical school, I took the Hippocratic oath," his father said. "It's an oath that all doctors take. It states that 'Into whatever houses I enter, I will go into them for the benefit of the sick.'" He swept his hand around. "Charlie's sick. This is his house."

In the intensive care unit, his father led Fred to the nurses' station. Behind the desk was a woman with yellow curly hair and bright red lipstick. Her uniform was white and starched.

"Irene, this is my son Fred," his father said. "He's making rounds with me."

Over her fancy half-glasses, the nurse looked at Fred. "You planning to be a doctor like your daddy?"

"I'm just in high school," Fred said. "I don't know what I'm going to do."

"You could do worse."

For a few minutes, his father and Irene huddled at the desk over a chart. They spoke in low whispers. Fred looked over at a burly, uniformed guard with a revolver belted to his waist. He was sitting on a metal chair reading *Argosy*. Behind him was a glass cubicle with a flickering fluorescent light. Fred moved a step closer and tried to get a better view of the prisoner. The officer glanced up from his magazine and eyed Fred suspiciously. Fred turned away. At the desk, his father, seated on a stool, scribbled something in the chart. He folded it closed and then stood and turned to Fred.

"Let's go see the patient."

"Am I allowed to?"

"If I say so."

His father moved toward the entry to Charlie Woodhouse's cubicle. Knees trembling, Fred followed. From a metal cart by the door, his father picked up two yellow cloth gowns. He shook one out and tossed it to Fred.

"Put it on," he said. "And wash your hands."

Fred wrestled into the garment, and his father tied it. Fred scrubbed his hands at a sink with cold water and strong pink soap. He could feel the eyes of the guard on him. Fred slid by him into a small glass-walled room.

On a narrow bed, Charlie Woodhouse lay blue-lipped, gulping for breath. He was towheaded and chinless, much smaller than Fred had imagined. His eyes were the pale yellow of a cat's. The plastic prongs in his nostrils connected to a long tube. Adhesive tape held an IV line to the bend of his elbow. Shackles locked his ankle to a metal bedrail. When his father stepped up to the bedside, Woodhouse turned his face toward the wall. His father reached down and picked up his wrist and felt the pulse. Fred saw the tattoos on the prisoner's fingers. The right hand said LOVE, the left HATE. On his forearm was a faded-ink portrait of a naked woman with large, pointed breasts and red pubic hair.

"How do you feel?" his father asked.

Fred could hear neither approval nor disapproval in his voice.

"Can't breathe," Woodhouse gasped.

His father pulled down the sheet that was covering the prisoner. A sour odor filled the air. Fred felt a little faint. He looked at the nearly naked little man. His body was almost delicate, like a child's. Fred didn't think he seemed dangerous at all. Instead, he appeared sick and afraid. Then Fred remembered how Woodhouse killed Amy Yoder, and he wished him dead.

His father picked up stethoscope and plugged it into his ears.

"Deep breaths," he said. "In and out through your mouth."

As he pressed the black bell to Woodhouse's chest, his father closed his eyes and turned his head as if he were listening to distant music.

"Can't breathe," Woodhouse panted through blue lips. "Help me."

His father reached over and turned up the oxygen valve. Then he placed his hand on Woodhouse's shoulder.

"I'm going down to X-ray to look at your chest film," he said. "Then I'll come back to talk to you."

Fred and his father stepped out of the cubicle and shed their gowns. Fred's father turned to the guard.

"In his condition, Woodhouse isn't going anywhere," he said. "Could we get rid of the shackles?"

"It's the rules, Doc. This guy's a murderer on death row."

His father nodded and walked away. As they passed the nurses' station, Irene and all of the staff swung their eyes toward Fred's father as if he were a judge ready to hand down a sentence. His father ignored them and continued on into the tiled corridor outside of intensive care.

"He's going to die, isn't he?" Fred asked.

"If nothing's done. He's a sick, sick man."

"He seems afraid. I don't think he wants to die."

"I think you're right."

"Why would he want to go on living?"

"It's human instinct." On the stairs to the X-ray department, his father turned to Fred. "Maybe Woodhouse wants to live so he can make amends for what he did before he goes."

Fred wondered what Woodhouse could possibly do to make up for killing Amy Yoder.

They entered a small room with a wall of lighted view boxes. A man with dyed reddish hair sat sipping a mug of coffee and reading a magazine called *The American Spectator*. His father put his arm around Fred's shoulder.

"Harry," he said. "Meet my son Fred. Fred, this is Dr. Stevens."

Fred shook the radiologist's hand firmly, as his father had taught him.

"What grade you in, son?" Harry said.

"A junior."

"Fred's first in his class," his father said.

"Good for you."

"Can I see the Woodhouse film?"

Standing, Harry walked over to an X-ray film up on one of the view boxes. "Sir Charles Woodhouse, that fine, upstanding denizen of the world. A splendid piece of humanity."

"This is his heart," his father said to Fred, pointing with his pen at a boot-like shape in the middle of the chest. "It's enlarged. That's what happens to the heart when it fails." He moved his pen. "These are his lungs. What you see is pneumonia. Four-plus, bilateral pneumonia and pulmonary edema."

"A white out," Harry said. He smiled a broad, ominous smile. "This guy's in deep doo-doo." He swiveled in his chair and looked up at Fred's father. "So what you going to do with him?"

"I don't know. He needs to be on the ventilator and have his heart failure treated."

"A ventilator," Harry said. "How about a little skillful neglect? Let nature takes its course. You could save us taxpayers some dough."

"Maybe death would be too easy for him," his father said.

It hadn't occurred to Fred that keeping Woodhouse alive could be punishment. He was becoming confused about what should be done.

"Jesus Christ, he's a killer waiting to die," Harry said. "Give the world a break. Let the bastard go."

"We'll see," Fred's father said. "Thanks for the advice."

In the tiled corridor outside of the X-ray department, Fred saw beads of sweat on his father's furrowed brow. Fred could tell it wasn't easy to hold someone's life in your hands, even a killer's.

"Did you notice Woodhouse's face?" his father said.

"It was kind of flat," Fred said. "He didn't look too smart. Why?"

"You're right. His face is flat. That little upturned nose. The thinness of his upper lip. The funny folds around his eyes. We call those dysmorphic features. They're typical of fetal alcohol syndrome."

"What's that?"

"His mother was a drunk. Her drinking damaged him when he was inside her womb. I'm sure he was abused, too."

"Is that why he's so bad?" Fred asked.

"It might help explain it," his father said, "but it doesn't excuse what he's done."

"Do you feel sorry for him?"

"No. I can't stand him."

"So what are you going to do?"

His father hesitated a moment. Then he said, "I'm not sure. I need to talk to him."

Back in the ICU, his father stepped up to Woodhouse's bedside. Fred retreated to a place by the window. Through the glass panes, he saw smoky clouds drift by and mute the sun. The picketers were gone, but a LET THE KILLER DIE! sign remained propped up against a leafless tree. Fred was aware of the electric hum of the fluorescent lights, the cricket-chirp of a heart monitor, and the hungry rattle of Woodhouse's breathing. He looked at Woodhouse. That the little man seemed so alone caused a strange emptiness inside Fred. His father fitted the stethoscope into his ears and listened to Woodhouse's lungs. When he finished, he motioned Fred to the bedside. He handed the instrument to Fred.

"Here," he said. "Take a listen."

"Who me?" Fred asked, amazed.

"Yeah, you. Put the bell here and listen carefully."

His father pointed above the left nipple on Woodhouse's hairless chest where the word SOUR was tattooed. With shaking hands Fred placed the listening bell where his father had indicated. The prisoner's skin felt cool and as sticky as clay. Fred could hear the two-note thud of Woodhouse's heart and the labored gurgle of his breath. Woodhouse stared up at him. Fred saw the glaze of fear in his eyes. He thought of the fear that must have been in Amy Yoder's eyes when Woodhouse was raping her. Fred closed his own eyes and listened.

When he finished, his father said, "What did you hear?"

"A bubbling kind of wet sound."

"That's good. We call it 'rales'. You get it with pneumonia and heart failure. Did you hear his heart going 'lub dub, lub dub'?"

"Yeah, I think so," Fred said.

"That's the sound of the valves in the heart closing. His heart has an extra sound because it's failing. We call it a gallop rhythm." His father took the stethoscope from Fred. "So, what do you think it's like to be a doctor?"

"I don't know. It's okay I guess."

Suddenly, a fit of coughing seized Woodhouse. His odd, flat face contorted and turned purple. His eyes rolled up. Fred gasped, thinking the man was going to die. But Woodhouse stopped coughing and lay gulping for air. His father offered Woodhouse a glass of water with a straw. The prisoner sucked in a drink. He choked, and a trickle of water ran out the corner of his mouth. For an instant, Woodhouse and his father looked at each other. It seemed to Fred that some kind of an understanding had just passed between them.

For a few seconds, his father stood, stroking his mustache as if waiting for the right answer to rise up and announce itself. Woodhouse was sucking air through pursed lips, tensing his neck muscles with every breath. Fred could see that breathing was taking all of the prisoner's strength. His desperation made Fred anxious. He didn't see how the man could keep it up much longer. He didn't want to be there if the man died.

Finally, his father said, "Charles, your heart and lungs aren't able to do their job. I need to put a tube in your throat so a machine can breathe for you." He paused a second. "Is that what you want?"

The room was quiet except for the ragged rasp of Woodhouse's breath. Slowly he turned his face toward Fred's father. The prisoner's lips quivered as he fought for the strength to speak.

"The machine," he gasped. "Get it."

Fred's father closed his eyes, and his shoulders sagged.

"Okay, then," he said. "We'll get it."

He rapped on the window of the cubicle and motioned to Irene. The nurse nodded and began to roll a ventilator with corrugated tubing and a glass canister of bellows into the room. While Irene injected a syringe of medicine into Woodhouse's IV line, Fred's father popped on a pair of rubber gloves. The prisoner's eyelids fluttered closed, and his limbs went limp. Quickly, Fred's father pried open the patient's mouth with a lighted, silver blade. Fred watched, wondering again what made a convicted killer want to go on living. Was it only the fear of death? He didn't think it had anything to do with making amends as his father had speculated.

His father slid a plastic breathing tube through the vocal cords and into Woodhouse's trachea. Woodhouse coughed and his whole body heaved. His father connected the tube to the respirator and switched the machine on. He pointed to the bellows, squeezing air into the killer's lungs.

"Hydraulics," he said. "Do you know Pascal's Law?"

"Yeah. We studied it in physics."

"So what is Pascal's Law?"

Fred thought for a moment, then he said, "A change in pressure on a confined fluid causes a change in pressure equally throughout the fluid."

"You got it right," his father said. He reached up and adjusted a dial on the respirator. "You know, Pascal was a philosopher as well as a scientist," he said. "He wrote that life is a prison in which we are executed. He said we are all living under a death sentence."

Fred watched the rise and fall of the sick man's chest synchronized with the puff of the bellows. The color of Woodhouse's skin slowly turned from dusky blue to pink. He lay quietly with his eyes closed. Fred wondered if the sick man was reliving the darkness of his past or dreaming of whatever awaited him.

His father bent over and placed his stethoscope on Woodhouse's chest. The movements of his hand with the bell were slow and deliberate, priestly. Fred stood, listening to the sigh and wheeze of the ventilator. He was aware of the changes in the pressure of his own lungs, the naked beat of his heart.

THE CRYSTAL APPLE

BEN WILSON'S mother died suddenly last winter, and already his father has sold their old family home. Ben loved the roomy but comfortable house. He keeps asking himself why Ben Sr. is getting rid of it. To Ben, the house was a part of his mother, and in selling it, his father has disposed of all that remains of her. Ben doubts that he will ever forgive him.

Today, Ben is returning to the small Indiana farming community where he grew up. His task is to clean out his room and get it ready for the nameless new owner. As he drives slowly down Main Street through the flitting sun and shadows of maple trees, he tries to think of all the things of his past, tries to remember life as it was when his mother was alive. Just ahead, he sees his father mowing the lawn. Ben Sr. is a big rangy man who once pushed the mower with a long easy stride, but now hunches over the handle of the Lawn Boy, barely lifting his scuffed wingtips from the turf. Ben thinks he looks haunted, forlorn. A denizen of nowhere. The yardman.

Ben's father always wanted his lawn manicured, perfectly weedless, and clipped like the fairway of his country club. When Ben was a boy, the lawn was one of the battlegrounds where he and his father fought their Oedipal war. Cutting other people's lawns, Ben was a diligent worker and eager to please those who employed him. But when his father ordered him to mow the yard at home, Ben became such a sullen, shiftless brat that his father would grab the mower and attack the lawn himself to try to make Ben feel guilty. Now, as Ben watches him, a tottering old man struggling to push the Lawn-Boy through the grass, he supposes his father still wants him to feel guilty.

Ben eases his Buick Riviera to the curb and climbs out of the silver car into the sharp light of late spring. The air smells sweet and green. Ben kills the Lawn-Boy's motor, and under maple leaves that are green and filled with sunshine, they greet each other with their usual formal handshake. Ben's father's hand is as broad and rough as a fence rail, his grip too firm. Even with the curvature of his spine that old age has caused, he still towers over Ben.

Ben studies the frayed pockets of his dad's gray gabardine slacks, the food stain on his yellow Banlon shirt, the bulge of chewing tobacco in his cheek. If his mother had seen him so unkempt, she would have had a fit. She'd picked out his clothes at L. Strauss & Co.'s men's store in Indianapolis and kept him looking sharp. Ben dreads thinking what his father's life without her will be like.

"It's good to see you," Ben Sr. says. Absent is his usual smile, the smile he once used to disarm farmers and car dealers who wanted to borrow from the savings and loan bank where he was the President.

"Good to see you, too. The yard looks great. I wish mine looked as good. Some lucky bastard is getting one hell of a nice lawn."

"There's nothing magic about growing grass," his father says. "All it takes is fertilizer and water."

Ben bends over and plucks a blade of Kentucky bluegrass.

"I have a sprinkler system," he says, "and Lawn Doctor sprays it with fertilizer four times a year, but it doesn't look like this."

"You still bag your clippings?"

"Well, yeah. Sure."

Ben Sr. shakes his head.

"You ought to let them lay. They make a good natural fertilizer. I thought I told you that once." He mops nervously at his brow with a big workman's handkerchief and lifts his eyes, gray and spent, to the house, the place that both confined and defined them for years.

With this sale, the two of them are being redefined, Ben thinks. The uncertainty of their futures gives him a chill.

"Aren't you going to miss the lawn?" he asks.

"Naw."

His father spits tobacco juice in the gutter, a habit Ben dislikes intensely, and one his mother wouldn't tolerate.

"You've lived here over fifty years," Ben says. "It must kill you to leave."

Ben Sr. doesn't respond. He stands staring down the quiet street. He seems preoccupied by a dog sleeping in the gutter. Then he turns and spits again.

"This house is too much for one old man," he says. "Besides, it was your mother's more that it was mine."

"Oh, come on," Ben says. "It was ours. It belonged to all of us. I'd think it'd be damned hard to give it up after all these years."

"Time to move on," his father says.

Ben's gaze moves to the east side of the street and Dr. Nick Nicoletti's two-story colonial brick with its white shutters and American flag fluttering from a pole in the front yard. Nick's immigrant father had made a small fortune in scrap metal during the war, and he sent his bright son to Yale, then to New York City for medical school at Columbia and an internship at

Bellevue Hospital. Nick was the Wilson's family doctor. He and his wife Ann were friends of Ben's parents, although Ben's father was critical of the amount of money Nick made from other people's misfortunes. He often belittled Nick's Ivy League airs, his lack of military service, and his Catholicism. Six months earlier, Nick suffered a massive stroke. Now he is bedridden with live-in caretakers.

"How's Nick doing?" Ben asks.

"For shit," Ben Sr. says. "He's a vegetable."

"What a shame."

"It is a shame," Ben Sr. says.

He doesn't look at Ben. He bends over to adjust the choke on the Lawn-Boy and grips the starter cord. He jerks it hard. The engine coughs but doesn't start.

Ben reaches for the mower. "Want me to push that thing for a while?"

"Naw, I've got it." His answer is tinged with self-pity.

"Just for old times' sake? A couple laps around the yard."

His father waves him away.

"Have it your way," Ben says. "I'm going inside and pack up a few things. Maybe later we can run by the cemetery."

"Sure. Whatever."

Ben starts for the front door, but his father's voice stops him. "Ben, there's something . . ."

His hesitation concerns Ben. "What is it?"

"Never mind."

"Something's bothering you. What is it?"

"Nothing important. I'll talk to you later."

Ben shrugs, thinking, "Yeah, sure you will." He believes his father has spent his life putting him off, pulling back, promising something for later. But later never happened.

Ben leaves him yanking the starter cord on the mower. Finally, the motor chatters to life, and Ben Sr. heads to the backyard. Ben climbs the brick steps between stone-cast pinecone pedestals. He pauses for a moment on the stoop and listens to the soft music of his mother's wind chime, hanging from a limb of a magnolia tree. The notes have a Far Eastern, mystical sound like one might hear in a Tibetan monastery. Ben wonders again what's on his father's mind. He was always such a self-contained man. Ben could never put his finger on the why of him. What did he want from me? Ben thinks. From my mother? From himself? What does he want now?

Ben continues up the steps and shifts his focus to the house. He remembers when it was a two-story box, painted green and white and with an ugly concrete verandah. It was not nearly as appealing as the venerable Victorian homes on Main Street. But his mother, with her flair for decorating, transformed it into one of the most attractive homes in town. The concrete porch and pillars came down and were replaced by a brick stoop with copper carriage lanterns. She had the roof shingled with cedar shakes, and the siding painted the color of Swiss chocolate. Ben likens the way she approached the house to the way she raised him, with a fierce determination to make something better for her son than her life had been. Ben sees himself there on the porch as a small boy during World War II when his father was off on a submarine in the Pacific. Ben, the boy, is rocking back and forth in a squeaky glider while counting the cars that roll by on Main Street and wondering if his father will ever come home.

Now, Ben opens a white wooden door with a brass knocker and enters the house. He knows it will be painful, but he wants to peer deeply into the place he came from and remember who he was. He wants to honor his origins and say goodbye to the past. The metal of the latch clicks behind him.

The foyer is high-ceilinged with two long windows. On its south wall, a stairway rises to the second story. The walls are papered with a silk-textured grasscloth that is the color of key lime pie. Only two pieces of furniture remain in the hall, a walnut chest of drawers and an antique Stickley chair upholstered in flame stitching. With a lump in his throat, Ben remembers what his mother stored in the chest—his knit caps and mittens, her own pillbox hats and soft kid gloves, and her alligator purse. In the dimness and silence, the house seems even more empty than it is.

Ben looks up to the large portrait of his mother that dominates the entryway. It is an oil, done in pastel shades. When it was painted, she was a pretty woman in her forties, with bright brown eyes and dark hair streaked with gray. The painting is rather amateurish, Ben thinks, but he likes the way the artist has captured her expression, a confident cheerfulness that says she is proud of her home and her little family. But for the first time, he sees something else, a mysterious cast to her eyes as if there is something beyond her gaze´that she longs for. He wonders what was on her mind. What did she want that she didn't have? What did she have that she didn't want?

He sits in the Stickley chair, trying to remember what his mother was like when he was growing up. He thinks of her as a kind of premodern mother giving birth and nourishment and shelter. Her identity seemed to be linked to him, her only child. When he succeeded, she acknowledged it with a tight-lipped smile as if she'd expected as much, but when he failed, it was as if her own worth was diminished, and she didn't try to hide her disappointment. As if she were standing in front of him, Ben can hear her voice saying, "How could you do this to me, Ben?"

Now, beneath her gaze, he pictures the entryway with a tall Christmas tree, a flood of gifts wrapped in green-and-gold foil spilling from beneath the branches. Although age and cynicism have limited Ben's access to ecstasy, he tingles with the same excitement he felt on cold Christmas mornings when he and his mother tiptoed down the stairs at dawn. With Ben Sr. still asleep, she would unwrap the piece of Steuben crystal sent to her every year by her Aunt Martha in San Francisco while Ben emptied the presents from his stocking. They adored Christmas, the two of them.

Ben rises from the chair. He steps though an arched entry into the living room. Sunlight shining through a mullioned window casts a shadowed grid on the light carpet. The room has always seemed formal. It reminds him of the lobby of the Canterbury, a small, chic hotel in Indianapolis, where in the days his marriage was breaking up, he once discovered his wife, Marg, rendezvousing with an old college beau. Heartbreaking at the time, it now seems somewhat humorous, as if it were merely an act in a Noel Coward play. Against one wall, a herd of ivory and brass elephants, advertising his father's Republicanism, poses on the shelves of a walnut secretary. It would embarrass Ben to admit it to anyone, but he knows that if Nixon rose from the dead to run again, his father would campaign for him.

Ben turns from the elephants to the living room's east wall, where a bay window juts out over a bed of ivy. Beyond the ivy, he sees his father's immaculate green grass sloping to the gray slate sidewalk. Years ago, when the stones were smooth, the sidewalk was a fine place to roller skate or play hopscotch and monkey-in-the-middle. Now, the roots of curbside maples have cracked the concrete slabs. Everywhere he looks, Ben sees something that brings the sadness of lost innocence. Ben remembers how, when he was a boy, his father was always too busy chairing Chamber of Commerce meetings or spearheading Community Chest drives to teach him baseball or basketball, but Dr. Nick, who, in spite of his small stature, had lettered in both sports at Yale, would invite him to play pitch-and-catch or shoot hoops at the basket in the driveway. Unlike Ben Sr., Nick had the instincts of a parent. Ben always wondered why the Nicolettis had never had children of their own.

As vividly as if it were yesterday, Ben can picture Dr. Nick backing his big Buick Roadmaster out of the driveway onto Main Street, the tires spinning gravel as he raced off to the hospital to deliver a baby or set a bone or suture a cut. He was always on the run, a man on a mission. Ben had watched him and dreamed of someday being on that same mission. Also, his mother had dreamed of a career in medicine for Ben. Both of their dreams had come true. Ben became a surgeon with a busy practice in Indianapolis where he is chief of his department at Methodist Hospital.

When Ben was a premedical student, home on vacation from college, Nick would take him on rounds or have him observe during surgery. Ben smiles to himself, remembering the first time Dr. Nick took him into the operating room to watch an appendectomy. When Ben saw the wet red line of blood that followed Nick's scalpel across the skin of the child's belly, Ben had turned gray and his legs gave way. The circulating nurse helped him to a stool in the corner where he slumped in humiliation with a cold washcloth pressed to his forehead. After the appendix was in a jar of formaldehyde and Nick finished suturing the skin, he helped Ben into the doctors' lounge and gave him a bottle of RC Cola.

"Low blood sugar," he said kindly.

Even though Ben longed to wield a scalpel someday, he said, "This isn't for me. I can't even stand the sight of a little blood."

"Nonsense," Nick said. "I almost passed out my first day in gross anatomy lab. You'll get over your squeamishness in no time. Listen, Ben, you'll make a fine doctor."

Nick reached into his pants' pocket and pulled out a big gold watch that he handed to Ben. Its case was engraved beautifully with a cornucopia of flowers and a bird in flight.

"It was my father's," Nick said. "He gave it to me when I graduated from medical school."

"It's a beauty," Ben said, handing it back to Nick.

"No," Nick said. "I want you to have it. I was going to give it to you when you graduated, but today seems like a good time. There's a stipulation, though. You have to finish med school."

"I'll do my best," Ben said.

The watch felt heavy in his hand, like a gold hammer.

A few months after Nick gave Ben the Elgin, he was unexpectedly widowed when Alice, his pale, somber-eyed wife, drove her Olds convertible into the path of a passenger train. Ben feels like finding his old Harvey-Kuenn-model fielder's mitt and a baseball and trotting across the street to meet Nick on the sidewalk for a little pitch and catch. He reaches into his pocket and pulls out the gold watch that he stills carries on occasion. He pushes the release, and it snaps open like a gold clam. The Roman numerals on its face say three o'clock. Even though he knows seeing the man in his debilitated state will be hard to bear, Ben decides to visit Dr. Nick before he goes.

Turning from the window, Ben moves across the room to a glass cabinet on the wall next to a reproduction of Renoir's "Girl with a Blue Sash." On the shelves, his mother's collection of Steuben crystal gleams. There is a glass cat, the crystal apple, a dove, a heart, and a snail. Ben picks up a glass frog and holds it up to the light, thinking how her expensive tastes and impulses were so like his own. He wonders why his mother had such an insatiable appetite for fine things. He decides it must have been because she was a daughter of the

Depression, raised poor by her widowed mother, and that she became like someone who had once known hunger and could never get enough to eat. His father, in spite of his own ordinary tastes, didn't seem to mind financing her extravagances. Ben thinks it must have been compensation for the way he ignored her need for conversation and affection.

He recalls how, of all her pretty possessions, she treasured the Steuben crystal most. Its tasteful elegance seemed to epitomize her. Ben decides to take the collection with him. Maybe he'll give the apple to Marg, his ex-wife. She loved the crystal, and she loved his mother. He knows his father won't care if he takes all of the Steuben. He never liked it. When he finally made his appearance on Christmas morning, as though he thought he was being slightly witty, he would pick up a figurine and say, "Great. Another piece of good old Steuben crystal. Old Aunt Martha must have robbed Wells Fargo to afford this stuff."

In the laundry room, Ben finds a cardboard box. He carefully wraps each figurine in newspaper and places each one in a box that he leaves by the front door. He resumes his farewell tour. Entering the dining room, a great fatigue and anxiety settles over him. His emotions turn to thoughts about medicine. The only doctors who have practiced in town since Nick retired are ill-trained hacks or alcoholic malpractitioners. For an instant Ben thinks of making the new owner of the house an offer he couldn't refuse. He could come back home and open a practice in Nick's old office downtown by the post office. It would be as if he were a missionary to his past. But he knows being a small-town doctor is not what he wants in life. Sunlight prisms through a beveled-glass window above the sideboard where his mother served dinner. The house is silent. Ben feels as if he is in an Egyptian tomb where all of a person's treasures are buried with her.

He recalls Thanksgiving and Christmas when the family gathered around a linen-covered table and with Rambling Rose sterling silver, attacked a ceremonial turkey. The tastes of his mother's favorite recipes awaken on Ben's palette: the sage of her oyster dressing, the cheddar of her cheese grits, the sweetness of her cranberry chutney.

Ben's memory turns to the worst of times here. It was the summer of 1951 when he was nine years old and the shortstop on a Pee Wee League baseball team. On a hot July afternoon, Ben wasn't feeling well when he took the field for a game. His head ached, and he felt dizzy, weak all over. By the time the opposing catcher popped up for the third out, Ben had become disoriented; his arms and legs were shaking. He collapsed on the infield's dusty base path. The coach carried him to his car and rushed him to the county hospital where Dr. Nicoletti performed a spinal tap. The diagnosis was polio. Ben spent the rest of that summer in the hospital.

The muscles of his arms and legs were spared, but the muscles of his palate and throat were paralyzed. He wasted away, unable to swallow.

When Ben finally recovered enough to come home, his parents moved his bed into the dining room. Ben looked like a refugee child. Everything about him was bone—ribs, vertebra, scapula. He barely made a dent in the mattress. He still couldn't swallow, so his mother fed him through a red rubber gavage tube that she slipped through his mouth into his stomach. Then she pumped in a gruel of food that she had liquefied in a blender. After she removed the tube, she would give Ben a Nehi grape soda to rinse out his mouth or a Baby Ruth or a Clark Bar to chew up and spit out so he could enjoy the textures and tastes of things he couldn't swallow.

Every morning that summer, Dr. Nick charged into the dining room with his big black bag. He would thump on Ben's knees and elbows with a rubber hammer and listen to his heart and lungs. Some days after he finished his exam, he would pull a chair to the bedside and read Ben a story while Ben's mother went to the grocery store or to the beauty parlor to get her hair done. If his mother didn't have errands to run, Nick would join her in the kitchen, where they smoked Dunhill cigarettes from Nick's gold case, drank coffee, and talked in low voices.

Escaping the darkness of that summer, Ben moves

on to the sunporch where the brightness of spring fills the room. With its walls of sliding glass and high-beamed ceiling, it is his favorite place in the house. His mother's touch is everywhere. The furniture is wicker, painted a light lemon yellow, the cushions patterned with calico flowers. Hanging plants, a ceramic white elephant, and a ceiling fan slowly stirring the air create a Casablanca atmosphere. His mother spent a lifetime creating a beautiful, homey environment. How can his father throw it away so easily?

Ben's memory spins, then stops in the heat of a humid August afternoon when he was supposed to be cutting the lawn. The old reel push-mower waited for him in ankle-high grass while he lolled under an elm tree caught up in a dream of a large-breasted girl who lifeguarded at the swimming pool. On the porch, his father was having a Johnny Walker and soda and putting together a business deal with the savings-and-loan's lawyer. The voices of the two men sifted through the screen, and Ben overheard them discussing the stock market and the Masters golf tournament, two topics he considered as boring as opera and Methodist Youth Fellowship. But then he heard his father brag to the attorney that Ben was first in his class and captain of the basketball team. Ben was stunned. He jumped up from beneath the elm and attacked the grass with the mower. He even trimmed around the trees and swept the walk. When his father saw the lawn that evening, he smiled and patted him on the shoulder. But he still didn't appear in the bleachers at Ben's games or look at his report cards.

From the sunporch, Ben passes back through the dining room into the kitchen with its strawberry-print wallpaper. He takes a glass from the cupboard and fills it from the tap. The water tastes of iron. This was the last drink of water he'd ever have in this kitchen. He tells himself to savor it.

Ben spins the lazy Susan in the middle of the round oak table. He remembers meals eaten and plans made here. So many lessons taught. He recalls listening to the table conversation of his parents. The tone of their voices and the looks they gave one another made him aware that there were great, unspoken forces at work in their marriage that he was being sheltered from.

In the foyer, Ben picks up the box of Steuben glass. Before he was born, his mother taught high school English. She particularly loved the plays and short stories of Tennessee Williams. Ben remembers her saying, on more than one occasion, that the crystal collection was her glass menagerie, a reference he imagines to her own translucent beauty and fragility. Outside, the sky appears mysterious, with a lone gray cloud peering over the trees. Ben carries the box to his car and slides it onto the front seat. His father shuts off the lawn mower. Mopping his forehead with his handkerchief, he approaches Ben.

"What's in the box?" he asks.

"Mother's crystal. Hope you don't mind."

"Of course not. If you didn't want it, I was going to sell it or give it away." He reaches into the box and pulls out the glass apple. "The old Steuben crystal."

For a few moments, as if deep in thought, he weighs the apple his hand. Then he looks across the street toward the flag flying in the Nicolettis' front yard. Ben Sr. takes in a deep breath.

"Listen," he says. "Take anything in the house you want. It's yours."

With a little underhanded flip, he tosses Ben the apple. Ben catches it.

"Jesus, Dad, be careful." He returns the figurine to the box on the car seat. "What about Mom's clothes?"

"Maybe I'll have one of those garage sales."

Ben pictures a covey of chintzy women pawing through the dresses that his mother picked out at L. S. Ayres on her shopping sprees to Indianapolis.

"I don't think Mother would want her clothes sold at a garage sale."

"She'll never know."

Their eyes lock for an uncomfortable moment.

"But I would."

"Okay, no garage sale, but when I'm gone, I don't give a damn what you do with my stuff. You can give it to the Salvation Army."

The tone of self-pity has reappeared in his voice. Ben doesn't find it becoming.

"The Salvation Army it is," Ben says. "I'm going back in and pack up the things in my closet. Then we can run by the cemetery."

"That's fine. Take your time. I don't have anything important to do."

"By the way," Ben says. "What did you want to tell me?"

Ben searches his father's face. It looks tight and troubled.

"It was nothing," Ben Sr. says.

Inside the house, the air smells faintly of fireplace ashes. Ben slowly climbs up the foyer's carpeted stairs. The floorboards and joists creak and moan. It is a plaintive sound as if the house were grieving, too. Ben imagines that the old wooden structure wants to be young again, to reverberate with the romp of his play, to host one of his mother's bridge parties or her Great Books Club. The banister is polished maple, supported by spindled balusters. Ben has an urge to slide down it once again. At the top of the stairs, Ben arrives at a hallway connecting three bedrooms and a communal bathroom. He is struck by how small the rooms are. As a boy he thought they lived in big rooms in a big house in a big town populated by big people. But now the rooms and house, the town and people, all seem to have shrunk. Ben feels small and insignificant himself. He pauses for a moment in the hall, wishing he could hear the buzz his father's electric razor or the drum of his mother's shower water. But the house is silent and as sad as a seaside hotel in winter.

He steps into the bathroom with its coral-tile walls. The medicine cabinet is filled with his father's home remedies and homeopathic potions: Serutan for his bowels; Ben-Gay for his osteoarthritis; Corona ointment for his wounds. Arranged on a glass dressing table are his mother's makeup and powder, her brushes and a tortoise shell comb. He unscrews the cap on a bottle of Chanel No. 5. The scent of her perfume brings her back to life for an instant.

In the mirror over the sink, Ben studies his reflection. His light brown hair is thinning on top and graying at the temples. The skin of his face is beginning to sag, pulled down by the gravity of passing years. In the mirror of his memory, he sees a naked boy with puny pecs and biceps, sparse pubic hair and pimples. A copy of *Photoplay* is in his hand. Ben devoured the pictures of Marilyn Monroe and Jane Russell in their bathing suits. Their breasts made him weak. He winks at himself in the mirror.

Ben leaves the bathroom and steps through the adjacent doorway into his own bedroom, and his heart constricts. In this small square space with its polished pine floor, two windows, and single twin bed, he slept and studied and played and dreamed. Here it is impossible for him to imagine himself not a boy.

Ben opens the closet door. He pulls the chain on the light and stands in the bulb's swaying glow. The shelves are like a museum of his youth, a shrine that smells of mothballs, dust, and bay rum. The valedictorian's trophy topped with a gilded student in cap and gown should have his mother's name engraved on it, too, and the tarnished junior golf trophy should bear his father's name, for it was the only sport that he encouraged Ben to play because the game would be something he could enjoy when was older.

Under a file filled with college notes, bluebooks, and chemistry lab manuals, Ben finds a pair of black Chuck Taylor high-top gym shoes, and a blue-and-gold basketball jersey. Although he was small, Ben was gritty and quick on his feet. The hours of practice in the driveway with Dr. Nick paid off. Ben became a deadly shooter who could handle the ball with either hand. He looks at the jersey and wishes he were back in school and could play a game again. And win.

Deeper in the cobwebbed recesses of the closet, he finds a matchbook collection, a Boy Scout mess kit, bronzed baby shoes, a fraternity paddle, a teddy bear with one eye, and an ivory Buddha from his year in Vietnam. A redwood ashtray reminds him of the summer of '53 when his father drove the family across the country in a black Ford sedan to San Francisco, where he attended the national Kiwanis convention at the Mark Hopkins Hotel. Seen in the light of day, these trinkets seem like useless prizes won on a carnival midway. But Ben can't bear to throw them out. He packs the artifacts of his boyhood in cardboard boxes. Then he turns his attention to his desk of well-fit maple, its drawers and pigeonholes crammed with the correspondence of the first thirty years of his life. Slowly, he sorts though letters and postcards, reading and remembering. An envelope with a return address of Yale University catches his eye:

Dear Ben,

I happened to talk with Dr. Nicoletti, during the Christmas vacation when we met in the Yale club in New York. He mentioned that you were interested in Yale and were considering application. He spoke very highly of you as a student and as a person. He also mentioned that you were quite a basketball player, and he subsequently sent me a couple of your press clippings, which I showed Coach Frable, our varsity basketball coach. Coach knows the reputation of Indiana high school basketball, and he said he would like nothing better than to have a guard from the Hoosier state on his team.

My respect for Dr. Nicoletti is great. For that reason, I am following his suggestion of investigating your college plans—in hopes that I might be of some help in your pursuing admission to Yale University.

Yours very truly,

    Richard Mote

    Assistant to the Director of Admissions

Ben tucks the yellowed letter back into its envelope. He remembers the fall of his senior year in high school when his mother outfitted him in a Harris tweed sports jacket and a club tie and drove him east on the Pennsylvania Turnpike to visit Princeton, Swarthmore, and Yale. On their tours of the campuses, Ben felt like a foreigner, a refugee from some undeveloped country. The students that showed him around intimidated him with their Eastern accents and sophisticated airs. Ben's nasal post-polio voice, with its Hoosier twang, embarrassed him, and he answered questions with a single word. When he attended varsity basketball practice at Yale, the players looked too big. Even the school's stone buildings seemed daunting. Ben chose to enroll at Wabash, a small Indiana men's school that was comfortably Midwestern, somewhere less risky and closer to home. His mother responded by saying, "How in the world could you do this to me? He finally redeemed himself in her eyes when he obtained his MD from Indiana's medical school.

Ben browses through the letters his mother sent to him at Pottawatomi Camp for Boys on the shore of Lake James, north of Ft. Wayne. Ben looks at her neat schoolmarm's handwriting, and his heart softens. In her perfect grammar, she coached and mothered him through the mail, urging him to do a good job on the saltshaker he was making in the craft shop, inquiring if he had been a good boy, explaining that some people were just bossy. "Learn to put up with them, Ben," she had said in her letter. "I want to see a lot of merit badges when you come home, and write every chance you get. Love Mother."

Ben moves to his bed. For a while, he sits, looking out the window. The leaves of a sycamore filter sunlight that creates a tree of shadows on the wall. Ben feels as if his blood is barely flowing through his arteries. The beat of his heart is so slow it seems that it might stop.

In almost a dream, he recalls the stifling summer heat before the house was air-conditioned. He would open the window and remove the screen. Then he would place a pillow where the roof flattened and lie half-outside in the warm breeze. Gazing at the stars, he would listen to the blues' broadcast beamed from Randy's Record Shop in Gallitin, Tennessee. The Union Pacific's railroad tracks were two blocks away, and every night at eleven o'clock, a passenger train hurtled through town on its way to Chicago. Ben recalls the clank of the engine's wheels and a low seductive whistle. The sounds seemed to be inviting him to a world beyond this house and small town. Now, the recollection of the sound lures him back into his room and the happiness of the past. But he knows that this is somewhere he can never return. It is impossible for him ever to be young and happy in that way again.

Ben rises from the bed. For what he knows will be the last time, he walks out of his room with his box of keepsakes. He closes the door behind him. He feels as if his life has slipped away almost without notice.

With glistening eyes, he looks into his parents' bedroom. It had always been a place of mystery to him, a secret world he wasn't privy to. Overcome by curiosity mixed with trepidation and feeling like an interloper, he enters his parents' private place. The window's drapes are a soft brown tapestry. The shades are pulled so that the room is buried in beige light. The bed's fluted posters remind him of phallic totems that might have been used in a tribal rite. To look at the bed where he was conceived resurrects the Oedipal feeling of his youth.

Through an open closet door, Ben sees his father's suits and sports coats hanging like the uniforms of an old soldier. He recognizes the wool Hart Schaffner & Marx suit Ben Sr. wore to his mother's funeral. Ben lifts the coat from the hanger and slips it on. The scent of his father's sweat and tobacco lingers in the fabric. The jacket sags on Ben's slim frame, and the sleeves cover most of his hands. His shoulders are not as wide as his father's, but he knows his brain is quicker. Ben thinks how different they are in almost every way.

Ben returns the coat to its hanger. He moves slowly

to his mother's big chest of drawers made of polished cherrywood. With a sense of guilt, he pulls out the top drawer. Inside, her silk underwear and nylons are interred in the fragrance of lavender sachet. Under a nightgown, he finds a sheath of yellowed correspondence and documents. Ben pages through them somehow afraid of what he might find. An envelope with Jean, his mother's name, inscribed in a back-slanted script, catches his eye. He pulls out a letter written on pale green paper.

My Darling Jean,

Merry Christmas.

Another year has passed, and here is another piece of Steuben crystal to mark it.

I dream of spending every day of the year with you. I promise that someday that dream will come true. Until then, we will have to do the best we can. When I'm in New York in February for the AMA meeting, will you join me? We can stay in that little hotel east of the park that we liked so much.

Ben is growing into such a fine young man. He reminds me so much of myself. I couldn't be prouder of him. But then I wouldn't expect otherwise with a fabulous mother like you.

All of my love,

Nick

Ben feels the blood drain from his face.

"Oh my God," he says. "No."

He feels limp and nauseated. With his hands trembling, he sits down on the bed and rereads the letter. He shakes his head in disbelief. He lies back on the chenille bedspread. He stares at the ceiling. His chest aches. He feels betrayed. It is as if his mother and Nick have shoved him off the edge of the world. Everything seems to be a deception, his very existence a lie.

After a while, he rises slowly and makes his way to the window. He peers down at Ben Sr. In the shadow of a curbside maple tree, his father stands rigidly, staring off toward Nick Nicoletti's. He has retrieved the Steuben apple from the box, and he is holding as if it were a grenade. For a moment, Ben thinks his father is going to heave the crystal sphere. But Ben Sr. gives it a low toss in the air, catches it in his other hand, and stuffs it into his pocket. He turns, blinking into the sun. Ben pulls back from the window and takes a deep breath.

With his head spinning, Ben returns the letter to the drawer. He moves heavily from the bedroom. The papered walls with pale orange flowers, the old blue wainscoting, the hallway and the rooms seem different now, even alien. Ben descends the stairs to the foyer where the Christmas tree once stood. He remembers his father accusing Aunt Martha of robbing Wells Fargo to buy the crystal apple. Did he suspect his wife was unfaithful? If so, why did he stay with Mother? Why did she stay with him? Standing in front of her portrait, Ben looks at her and sees a longing in her dark eyes. In her own words, he asks, "How could you have done this to me?"

Ben flees the gaze of her gaze and steps out the front door onto the stoop. In shrill sunlight, he squints, feeling dazed. He pictures his mother in her quilted housecoat standing here as he set off to school, waving to him but looking beyond him with longing toward Nick's house. Ben moves toward his silver Buick. His father is there leaning against the car. He searches Ben's face with his grave, gray eyes.

"So," he says. "Get everything you want?"

Ben nods. "And more."

His father takes the Steuben apple from his pocket and offers it to Ben.

"No thanks," Ben says. "I don't want it."

"Okay then," his father says and stuffs it back in the pocket of his pants.

He stands for what seems like a long time, slowly working on the tobacco in his cheek. Ben pictures his mother greeting him when he came home from the war, he in his blue uniform and white sailor's hat, she young and pretty, the illicit lover. Nick's paramour. He waits silently, fearing what his father might say. But instead of speaking, Ben Sr. spits tobacco juice into the gutter.

He wipes his mouth with a handkerchief and sighs wistfully.

"Can you believe it, Ben?" he says. "We lived here fifty damn years." He shakes his head. "You always think things will go on forever. Then you wake up one day and find out you don't live in eternity."

Ben swallows hard but doesn't answer. A man in a wood-trimmed station wagon cruises by and toots the horn. His father waves and smiles.

"You have to learn to live with things, Ben," he says, "And you have to learn to part with things, too."

Ben nods. His father points toward the once stately old Blake house next door.

Weeds sprout from the gutters, and paint is peeling from its siding. In the window, a sign says "room for rent."

"Just look at that," Ben Sr. says. "The neighborhood is going to hell in a handbasket. Your mother wouldn't want me living next door to a rooming house. It's time to move on."

Ben Sr. reaches across the open space between them and puts his big hand on Ben's shoulder. It has been years since his father touched him. The weight of his hand feels unnatural.

"In spite of everything, I miss your mother," Ben Sr. says. "I see her in every room of the house. I see you, too. It's hard for me. I need to leave. Go somewhere else."

For what seems like a long time they don't speak. Then Ben Sr. points toward Nicoletti's house.

"Old Nick's in pretty bad shape," he says. "You want to go over there and see him?"

Ben pictures Nick, pale and paralyzed in bed. Ben has a strange, dislocated feeling, as if he were standing apart from his own life. His eyes are damp and bleary.

"Not now," he says. His voice is raspy.

"He probably won't be around much longer."

"Maybe I'll come back another time."

Ben gives his father's shoulder a pat. He moves around the car to the driver's side. He climbs in behind the steering wheel. He reaches across the seat and rolls down the window. His father bends over, looking in at him with gray and watery eyes.

"When will I see you?" he asks.

"Soon," Ben says. "I'll call you."

He turns the ignition key. The motor kicks in, moaning quietly. His father steps back from the car. Ben pulls away from the curb and heads slowly down Main Street. In the rearview mirror, he sees his father silhouetted against the family home. The sunlight behind him creates a nimbus around his head. Ben speeds up, and his father and the house grow smaller and smaller.

JACOB'S WALL

DEEP IN A HARDWOOD forest in southern Indiana's
Brown County, big brown stones were piled and strewn
on a grassy hillside like the dolmens of some ancient
and unknown civilization. Swinging a mason's hammer
with crisp, rhythmic blows, an old doctor was shaping a
chunk of stone for the wall he was building. When
metal struck rock, sparks and chips flew into the air,
and an anvil-like ringing resounded through the
wooded valley below. From a pale sky, late summer
sunshine splashed through the leaves of a nearby oak
tree, dappling the ground with shadows and light. The
sun's rays were warm on his back but not too warm.
Squirrels were putting on a high-wire act gathering
acorns in the oak trees. Crows barked like dogs, and
nuthatches and tufted titmice swooped down on the
feeders that hung from the eaves of his log cabin. The

doctor-turned-mason possessed a deep and abiding awareness of nature, but now he was so engrossed in rock and wall, he was oblivious to the inspiration that flowed from his surroundings. The scent of stone was in the air. Its earthy fragrance pleased him the way the scent of his wife Martha's soap and shampoo had done, back when she was alive. While he worked, he hummed the tune of "How Great Thou Art," a hymn played on the church organ at Martha's funeral.

The doctor was Walter Roberts, a retired orthopedic surgeon who had set fractures and fused spines in Indianapolis before his retirement. Reddish rock-dust caked the white plumes of his eyebrows and overalls. Sweat had soaked his blue Colts baseball cap. To protect his eyes, he wore round tortoiseshell bifocals. He had chosen the scholarly glasses because James Joyce had done the same. The doctor admired Joyce's writing, particularly the short stories of *The Dubliners*; but even the stream of consciousness and multilingual puns in *Finnegan's Wake* spoke to him. He scored a fault line with his mason's chisel, and the rock split clean, exactly where he'd wanted the break to occur. He smiled at the perfection of his effort the way he'd once smiled at the X-ray of a perfectly aligned Collie's fracture of the wrist after he'd set the bone.

The screen door to his cabin banged shut, and a slim young woman with a dark complexion and short chestnut hair appeared at the porch railing. She wore a tank top and tight jeans that displayed what Walter considered an exceptionally fine ass. Her name was Becky. Merry Maids in Nashville had sent her to clean his cabin. The small, rustic dwelling didn't require frequent cleaning, but Walter hired her to come once a week because her presence eased the loneliness of his monastic life.

Becky leaned over the railing "Hey, Doc," she called. "You're going to knock yourself out." She spoke in a country Hoosier twang. "Don't you think you could use some help with them big stones?"

He wanted to correct her English, but thought better of it.

"Sure," he said. "Come on down."

"Not me, sweetie. I don't do rocks. Take a break. Come on up and set. I've got a glass of sweet iced tea for you."

"One more stone," he said.

He leaned down and gripped a long, meaty rock. Walter bent his knees, took a deep breath, and hoisted the stone. Straining and panting, he lugged it to the wall. The darned thing must weigh eighty pounds, and the weight bulged the veins on his forehead. He positioned the stone, butting its angled edge with the adjacent stone's edge and keeping the front edge parallel to his chalk line. He checked the wall's batter with a triangle made of wooden strips. Satisfied that the stone was properly fit, aesthetically pleasing, and strong enough to bear the weight of the earth behind it, he looked up to see if Becky was watching. He was disappointed to find she had gone back inside.

Walter pulled off his leather gloves and stuffed them in his pocket. On weary legs, he made his way up the steps to the porch. He straddled the bench of a picnic table. His arms quivered from the effort of hefting the stones. He took a deep breath. Would he live long enough to finish the wall?

"Damn old age," he thought. "Damn every friggin' thing about it."

Backing out the door, Becky carried two tall, sweaty glasses of iced tea with sprigs of mint from his herb garden. Walter rose and took off his ball cap. He was thirsty and he took a long drink.

"That mint's a nice touch," he said.

"Such a gentleman," she said. "I like a gentleman. There ain't too many of you left, at least in these parts."

She sat across the table from him and swirled her tea. Her smile revealed a gap where one of her front teeth was missing. Above the scooped neck of her top, he saw the rise and curve of her small breasts and forced himself to look away. For a moment, he fantasized about walking around the table and putting his arms around her. But she wouldn't want that from an old man. He couldn't give her what a younger man like Wes, her boyfriend, could.

"How'd a doctor learn to lay stone?" she asked.

When she spoke, she hid the gap in her teeth with her hand. How could someone so pretty allow her mouth to look that way? He'd talk to a dentist friend of his and arrange for him do a restoration. What better way was there to spend what he had plenty of and nothing that he needed or wanted.

"Summers when I was home from college, I was a hod carrier for a one-legged mason," he said, remembering the Latvian giant who quoted poetry and the Bible in an old-world accent. "Strongest man I ever knew both in physical strength and character. To him masonry was spiritual work. He believed that laying stone could teach you about things like reverence, forgiveness, and love." Walter looked down at the ice cubes in his tea. "I helped him build fieldstone fireplaces, foundations, stone houses, brick walls, and walkways. Once we built a little bridge out of hewn stone. He taught me about masonry, but more than that, about truth. Problem was I didn't always abide by what he taught."

"Well, I can see you sure love laying them old stones," Becky said.

"Beats the devil out of idleness," Walter said. "Gives me something to do." He drank what was left in his glass. "When I'm laying stone, I never think that doing something else would be more pleasant or important."

Except being with a woman like you, he thought.

"How about doctoring?" Becky asked.

Walter saw himself in the operating room—nailing a fractured hip, driving a Smith-Peterson nail through the greater trochanter into the femoral neck, wearing rubber gloves rather than leather, swinging a hammer with the same rhythm he swung a mason's hammer.

"Masonry's the equal of medicine," he said. "Neither one's just a job. They're both a calling, same as the ministry. In fact, they're both a hell of lot more noble than preaching a bunch of blarney."

Becky stood and turned toward the cabin door. Walter thought he must be boring her with his long-windedness.

"Where you going?" he said. "Sit down and talk."

"Relax. I'm getting you more tea."

The screen door banged shut. Two goldfinches perched on the wooden feeder that hung from the porch's eaves. The birds pecked nervously at thistle seed. A white-bellied nuthatch swooped down and chased them away. The finches flitted about, scolding the nuthatch and arguing among themselves. Walter thought nature was full of greed and conflict. Same as man. Why did things have to be that way?

Becky returned with a pitcher and filled Walter's glass with dark tea.

"Thanks, pretty lady," Walter said, raising his glass in a toast.

"You know, Doc," she said, "my boy Jacob could

help you lay them stones. He's strong for his size. He's on the wrestling team at school."

"When it comes to stonework, I'm sort of a loner," Walter said. "Besides, I'm too particular about how it's done, same as I was in the operating room. I'd be difficult to work for."

"I don't think you should be doing this by yourself out here in the middle of nowhere. What if you fell or had a heart attack or something?"

"If I go, I go," Walter said.

"Don't be talking like that. You ain't going nowhere soon. How about it, Doc? Jacob's not afraid to work. I'd like him to be around you and learn from you."

"You women," Walter said. "Sweet tea. Sweet talk."

But he decided he shouldn't dismiss the idea out of hand. If the boy came out to work, Becky would come, too. He could see her more often. "Okay, then. But he won't be learning from me. He'll be learning from the work itself and the stones. Can you bring him tomorrow? It's Saturday. No school."

"If my vehicle don't give out first."

"It's a deal. Ten bucks an hour. He'll need plenty of muscle and thick skin. Have him bring leather gloves and safety glasses."

"Don't be too hard on him. He's just a kid."

"We'll shape him up. Those big rocks will make a man out of him."

Becky took the empty glasses and pitcher into the

kitchen. Walter pulled on his gloves and headed down the porch steps to the work site. For a while he studied the big Brown County quarry stones in the pile. He turned and looked at the wall where the next course of stone would go, making a mental note of the size and shape that would be necessary to start the new row. He swung his eyes back to the stones. He saw one with a flat edge; the stone was thick where it needed to be. It was a beautiful rock with striations in various shades of brown and rust. He went for it eagerly.

THAT NIGHT WALTER LAY AWAKE, his mind flashing with possibilities and recurring images of the rocks, the wall, Martha, and Becky. Like an old photograph, the sky was dark brown and toned with sepia clouds. Through the window of the cabin's bedroom, Walter watched a long line of Canadian geese honk their way past a full and ghostly moon. Although the cabin and the fifty acres of land with its ponds and paths through the woods were a steadying force in Walter's life, age was making it harder and harder for him to keep up the property. He thought the barn's loft that he had made into a guest room and potter's studio for Martha. Maybe Becky and the boy could move into the loft rent free in exchange for helping take care of his place. Walter rolled onto his side. His thoughts turned to masonry and how tomorrow would be a fine September day for laying stone.

The next morning with a mug of strong black coffee in his hand, Walter went to a wooden bench he had fashioned with his chainsaw from the trunk of a fallen walnut tree. His view was of a dark-water pond ringed with native hardwoods. The sun illuminated the leaves of a sumac that had already turned red; dragonflies, blue and transparent, hovered above the cattails. When he came to this quiet place, something deep, peace-loving, and contemplative rooted him in the earth. Open on his lap was *The Essential Writings of Thomas Merton,* the Trappist monk from the Abbey of Our Lady of Gethsemane, a monastery not too far away in Kentucky. Walter was contemplating Merton's concept that the roots of violence were found within, while nonviolence required a spiritual transformation, a conversion of the heart. He wondered how that might apply to him. Was violence rooted in him? He didn't think so, but then there are things nobody knows about themselves.

Hearing the crunch of tires on gravel, he closed the book and hurried up the path to the cabin. Becky's red truck with its rusted door panels pulled into a parking area in front of the barn. When she shut the engine off, the long-suffering vehicle shimmied with what Walter likened to a senile tremor. He opened the driver's-side door with a bow, and Becky climbed out, showing a strip of bare belly above her cutoff jeans.

"Thank you, Sir Walter," she said.

Walter's heart moved when he heard her say his name. He smelled the soap from her morning bath. He reached out and put his hand on her bare shoulder. Then, knowing that touching her was a mistake, he pretended to be shooing an insect away.

Swinging a thermos by its handle, a boy in baggy denim shorts walked around the truck. He was shorter than Walter and wore his dark hair Ringo-Starr style; it covered his ears. The boy had a small, guarded face and eyes that were brown, clear, and long-lashed. His arms extended from a sleeveless blue T-shirt that said BELIEVE in bold white letters. His biceps were taut cords, his forearms sinewy. Walter offered him his hand. The boy took it with a weak grip and lowered his eyes to the ground. Walter could tell the kid had done some work by his calluses. He had his mother's coloring and good looks, but he needed a lot of shaping up: some manners, some couth.

Walter pointed at the lettering on his shirt.

"Believe what?" he asked.

The boy's cheeks turned red.

"In yourself, I guess," he said. "At least that's what Coach tells us."

"Well, do you then?" Walter asked, thinking he looked like he lacked self-confidence.

The boy thought for a moment.

"I don't know. Not always, I guess."

"Nobody does, Honey," Becky said. "Don't feel like the Lone Ranger. Isn't that right, Walter?" She reached out to pick at some raveling on the bib of Walter's overalls.

"It's something to strive for," Walter said. His skin tingled where she had touched him.

From the truck's seat, Becky retrieved a glass baking dish covered with tinfoil. "I made you a meatloaf for your supper," she said. "Brown sugar's the secret ingredient. Cook it an hour at 350 degrees, and then let it set for a while before you cut it. I'll put it in the fridge."

"You're going a spoil me," Walter said. "Say, when you come back to get the boy, why don't you and he plan on having supper with me?" Walter imagined an evening of laughter and companionship. "I've got homegrown tomatoes and roasting ears."

"Thanks, but Wes and me's going out tonight." She wiggled her hips. "Dancing."

"Suit yourself," Walter said, wounded.

He felt like Father Time, imagining his white hair and sagging face as seen through her eyes. "Guess I'll have to eat that meatloaf alone. Like my daddy used to say, 'Don't let your meat loaf.'"

Becky smiled and headed to the cabin to put her dish in the refrigerator. For a moment, Walter watched her hips move as she climbed the stairs to the porch.

He wondered how the hell she got herself into those jeans. Maybe with a shoehorn. He didn't like to think of Wes getting her out of them. Walter turned to the boy.

"Now, son, give me your name. Your mother's told me, but I can't recall."

"Jacob."

"Ah, Jacob, son of Rebecca," Walter said. "Now I get it. Do you know who Jacob was in the Bible?"

"Some guy with a ladder," Jacob said.

"He wrestled an angel," Walter said. "His mother's name was Rebecca, same as your mother's. His father was Isaac. Your Dad's named Isaac?"

"Don't know," Jacob said.

The boy's eyes turned darker, and he looked at the ground.

Walter wished he hadn't asked.

"Well, then," he said. "Time to get to work. Did you bring gloves and safety glasses?"

Jacob hung his head. "I forgot 'em."

Oh Jesus, Walter thought.

He went to the barn and retrieved an extra pair of leather work gloves and the plastic safety glasses from his chainsaw case. He gave them to the boy and led him down the hill toward the work site. The incline was steep and covered with acorns that were like ball bearings. Lamenting his lack of balance, Walter took little cautious steps so as not to fall. When they reached the rock pile, Walter showed Jacob the tools: a stone chisel, a three-pound hammer, a carpenter's level, and a long-handled shovel. Jacob asked what the purpose of the wall was. Walter said they were building it to create a terrace on the hillside that they would backfill with topsoil and plant with wildflower seed.

"The thing that's important here, son, is for us to make this wall strong. If a wall is strong, everything else falls in place."

"Where's the mortar?" Jacob asked.

"We're laying it dry," Walter said. "It's gravity that holds true masonry together. Not cement."

Carrying a laundry basket, Becky came out of the cabin and called down, "I'm taking your shirts home to iron."

"Much obliged," Walter said. "Sure you don't want to join in?"

"I told you I don't do rocks." She continued on to her truck and opened its door. "You boys behave."

"Do we have a choice?" Walter called back.

She climbed in the cab and turned the key. After two tries the truck started. She dropped it into gear and pulled away, the tires kicking up dust, black smoke billowing from the exhaust. Walter thought it must need a valve job or, better yet, a trip to the junkyard. When the truck disappeared into the tall oaks and shagbark hickories that lined the gravel lane, he turned to Jacob who was aimlessly pounding a rock with the mason's hammer. Annoyed, Walter took the tool from him.

"Your mother said you were sixteen," he said. "Do you have a driver's license?"

"Naw."

"Why not? Don't you know how to drive?"

"I know how to drive, but Mom can't find my birth certificate."

"It should be in a courthouse somewhere. Where were you born?"

Jacob hesitated a moment.

"Kokomo or Crawfordsville," he said. "Somewhere like that."

That the boy knew nothing of his father or place of origin gave Walter a pang. Life had already administered Jacob a beating.

"Well then," Walter said. "We're here to lay stone. Get me that beauty over there. The triangular shaped one. Yeah, that one." Walter, making an old man grunt in his throat, took the stone from Jacob and set it on the wall. "See how I placed one stone over the seam of two stones? It's the mason's rule of strength. 'One over two. Two over one.'"

Jacob was looking off into the distance.

"Hello," Walter said. "I'm talking to you."

"I hear you," Jacob said. "One over two. Two over one."

Walter pointed at a huge stone nearly three feet long

and six inches thick. The rock weighed nearly a hundred pounds, and he wanted to test the boy's strength.

"Fetch that big one there if you can handle it," he said. "If you can't, I'll help."

Jacob picked it up and lugged it to the wall. Walter told him to place it on the corner because he wanted something big to be the endmost stone.

"You're pretty strong," Walter said. "What weight do you wrestle?"

"One forty-seven. How'd you know I wrestled?"

"Your mother told me. You any good?"

"Good enough, I reckon," he said softly. "The heavyweight can't beat me. He knows it, and he wrestles me dirty. Tries to choke me and stuff. Next time he does it, I'll break his fingers."

Walter slid a thin chink of rock under one edge of the stone to shim it up. With the mason's hammer, he tapped the shim in tight. He liked the boy's humility, but not that business about breaking the heavyweight's fingers.

"All that's going to do is piss him off and make him wrestle dirtier," Walter said. He was thinking of what Thomas Merton wrote about violence.

"He won't be able to wrestle dirty if his fingers is broke," Jacob said with a smile.

Walter shook his head.

For a while, they worked in silence, Walter

selecting the stones, Jacob carrying them to him to position on the wall. The boy worked tirelessly and silently without complaint. As the morning wore on, Walter thought Jacob had earned the privilege of laying some stones himself. He let him select and position a few on the wall while Walter carried for him.

When Jacob placed a rock with its uneven side down, Walter said, "Not that way, son. Flat side down."

"I don't see no flat side."

"That's 'cause you're in too big a hurry. Take your time with each stone and get to know it. Even a round stone has a flat side if you look at it long enough."

After a while, Walter's back ached as if he had been bending over the operating table doing a tough spinal fusion. In spite of his gloves, his fingers were rock-sore. Walter untied the bandana around his neck and mopped his brow.

"Whew-eee," he said. "Don't ever get old, if you can help it."

He picked up a four-foot wooden level and laid it on the top course of stone. The bubble floated between the middle marks. Perfect. From a leather case, he took a brass plumb bob that the Latvian mason had given him. He held it near the wall by its string. The pendulum came to rest.

"You know where that's pointing?" he asked.

"To the ground," Jacob said.

"To the very center the earth," Walter said. "Four thousand miles deep."

"It must be cold there," Jacob said.

"Some would say it's a ball of fire," Walter said. "But I agree with you. I think it's composed of cold stone, stone that's harder than any other." He looked at his watch, surprised to see they had worked two hours. "I'm tuckered. Let's take a break." He wrapped the string around the brass weight and returned it to its case. "What I like about a plumb bob is that it never lies."

ON THE BRICK hearth was a wood stove and a brass bucket filled with kindling. The cabin's cherry-planked main room was decorated with a Navaho rug.

"Is that Indian?" Jacob said.

"Do you like it?" Walter said.

"I guess so," Jacob said. "It's kind of goes with a log cabin."

"My wife picked it out."

Jacob looked around. "Where is your wife?"

"Dead." Not looking at the boy, Walter poured sweet tea from a pitcher into two Ball jars. He handed one to Jacob and led him to the porch. Walter filled a dish with tea from his drink. At the porch rail, he offered the sugary solution to a ruby-throated hummingbird hovering at a feeder. With its needle-like beak, its wings a blur, the tiny bird flew to him and drank from the dish. Walter handed Jacob the bowl, and the bird drank for him, too.

"Cool," Jacob said.

Walter settled onto a bench at the table and swigged his tea. His body felt spent, and he was glad for the chance to recover his strength. He asked Jacob what he planned to do with the money he was earning. Jacob said he was going to save it to go to Daytona Beach on spring break with his girlfriend's family.

"You putting any aside for college?" Walter asked.

"Naw," Jacob said. "I ain't going to no college."

When it came right down to it, the boy probably wasn't college material, Walter thought. Too many kids went to college who shouldn't. The happiest men he knew were in the trades: carpenters, electricians, plumbers. That's why he'd gone into orthopedics instead of internal medicine or pediatrics, to see something concrete from his labor—a reconstructed knee, a well-pinned hip.

"Do you have kids, Doc?" Jacob asked.

"No, we didn't have any."

Walter thought how nice it would be to have a son or daughter to help him if he got sick. He looked down at the wall. Two mourning doves were perched on the stones, cooing. The love birds reminded him of Becky and her boyfriend.

"Your mother and that Wes guy pretty tight?" he asked.

"I reckon. He lives with us."

"Oh, he does? He a good guy?"

Jacob looked down at his hands and picked at the dirt under his thumbnail.

"I don't like him."

"Why not?"

"He don't bring any money in to help us out."

"He mean?"

"When he's drunk.

"Why's she stay with him?" Walter asked.

"Beats me," Jacob said.

Walter wondered if it was because she believed she wasn't worthy of anything better. It occurred to him that it was likely Wes had knocked Becky's tooth out. The thought of it tied Walter in a knot.

"Does he hurt her?" he asked.

"He'd better not. If he did, I'd make him sorry, and he knows it." Jacob's eyes were black as gun bores. "If that son-of-a-bitch lays a hand on her, I'll shoot him."

Walter shook his head. He was tired of the world's violence and hatred.

"You have a gun in your house?" he said.

"Not in my house. But my grandpa does. A double barrel twelve-gauge shotgun. He lives just up the road. I could get it if I needed it. How about you? You got a gun?"

In 1968, Walter, just out of his orthopedic residency, was drafted into the Navy and assigned to the 9th Marine Division. In a matter of months, he found himself at Khe Sanh on a surgical team. During the North Vietnamese's siege of the base camp, Walter operated through the night in a sandbagged bunker while mortar shells rained in. The body bags stacked on the landing zone still haunted him.

"I don't have any use for firearms," Walter said. "I saw enough of what they can do to people when I was in Vietnam. A gun never solved anyone's problems. All violence does is to promote more violence."

Walter pulled on gloves and downed the last of his tea. Jacob did the same and they started down the hill together.

"Do they teach you about Vietnam in school?" he said.

"Naw. I've heard of it though."

"They should teach you about it. There's a lot to learn from that sorry ass war."

LATER IN THE week at dusk, Walter stood on the cabin's covered porch. He looked down at the nearly finished wall. In the thin light of a dying sun, the stones took on the reddish-brown hue of blood. He recalled that the Mayan Indians were said to have mixed their mortar with human blood. Just as in orthopedic surgery, there was something corporeal as well as spiritual about stonework. He wondered what he would do after the wall was built. It seemed as if his life was all memory and devoid of plans.

Overhead, the clouds were ragged with dark under-bellies, threatening rain. Walter wanted to get the wall backfilled before the storm came and turned the topsoil into mud. He would be shoveling long after dark, and he wished Jacob had been here to help. Someone to talk to. Someone to lighten the load. Walter put on a beat-up Stetson hat with a hawk's feather in the band. He trudged down the hill to the pile of dirt. He picked up a long-handled shovel and began slinging topsoil over the wall. Soon, sweat beaded his brow and dripped off his nose. The fragrance of fresh damp earth filled his nostrils. Walter thought of digging a grave. His own.

The telephone in the cabin rang. He cursed and buried the blade of his shovel in the dirt pile. Walter hustled up the hill, listening to nagging jangle of the phone.

"Jesus," he said, breathlessly. "I'm coming. I'm coming."

But by the time he reached porch, the phone had gone silent.

"Damn it."

He continued on into the cabin and clicked on the message left on his answering machine.

The voice was Becky's.

"Call me," she said. "Please, Doc. I need your help."

Walter dialed her number. His pulse quickened.

"Doc," she answered with terror in her voice.

"What's the matter?" he asked.

"Wes beat me up. Jacob's gone after him in my truck."

"Oh Christ," Walter said. "You all right? How bad did he hurt you?"

"I'm just roughed up. My lip's cut. Come now. Jacob's going to do something crazy."

"Call the sheriff. I'll be right there."

"I ain't calling the sheriff until we get Jacob."

"Why not?"

"They'll arrest him. He's got a gun."

"Oh my God. I'm on my way."

With his heart pounding, Walter sped in his jeep toward Becky's trailer on Bear Wallow Road. The rain had started, a steady downpour that greased the asphalt. Walter turned on the windshield wipers. The rubber blades beat with a vengeance. Trees streaked by in the growing darkness. Gusts of a northerly wind thrashed the Jeep's canvas top and caused the vehicle to sway. Walter gripped the steering wheel tightly. He remembered Jacob picking at his thumbnail and saying how he was going to kill Wes if he hurt his mom. Walter's pulse sped. The rain beat down harder. Walter turned off Bear Wallow onto a gravel lane and Becky's double-wide rose in the jeep's headlights. On the stoop, Becky stood in the downpour and waved frantically. When Walter stopped in the driveway, she ran to the jeep and climbed in. Walter looked at her face in the dim grainy light from the dashboard. Strands of wet hair clung to her forehead. There was swelling and a dark bruise over the left side of her jaw. Her right eye was swollen shut, her lower lip split.

"God damn," Walter said. "That goddamned animal." Vengeance swelled in Walter's chest. He wanted to hurt that son of a bitch Wes.

"Drive," Becky said. "Go. Go."

"Where to?"

"Wes's brother's place. That's where Jacob thinks he'll be. I'll tell you where it is."

Walter dropped the transmission into low. The jeep's tires kicked up wet gravel as it bucked up onto Bear Wallow.

"When we get Jacob," Walter said, "we'll go the sheriff's office and file a report. Then we'll go my cabin until they lock Wes up. You and Jacob can spend the night in the loft."

"I pray to God it's not too late," Becky said.

Walter was driving fast, seventy miles an hour on a curvy county road with no center line. The jeep's tires sucked the wet pavement. In the beam of his headlights, he searched for deer, hoping one wouldn't dash in front of the jeep. It was like Nam. He had never imagined he would be involved in a war or something like this. In the seat beside him, Becky began to weep.

"It's my fault," she said. "My life's a wreck. I just go from one mess to another. Jacob hasn't had a chance."

"Don't blame yourself." Walter reached over and took her hand. He gave it a squeeze and held it for a moment. "It's never too late to change your life."

At the turnoff to Wes's brother's house, Becky told him to pull over. Walter steered the jeep onto the berm and stopped, but kept the engine running.

"I'll go get Jacob," he said. "Pull down the road out of sight and wait. If I'm not back in fifteen minutes, go get the sheriff."

"I'm going with you," Becky said.

"You stay right here. I mean it. Stay."

Becky slumped back in her seat. "Okay. Okay. I'll stay."

Walter opened the door and stepped out into damp knee-high weeds. He tugged the brim of his hat down. He looked straight ahead and hurried up the gravel lane lined with tall sentinel trees. His heart pounded against his chest. The rain had softened. Just ahead through a cold mist, Walter saw a small stone house with dark windows. In the yard a wagon wheel propped against a pole with a cow's skull on top of it. The door to a fenced-in chicken coop stood open. The air smelled wet and of poultry. Walter scanned the buildings and saw no sign of life. Then his gaze found Becky's red truck partially concealed in an opening in the trees by the road. As he approached the pickup, he saw a dark shape behind the steering wheel. Walter bent over and looked in the driver's side window. Jacob was dressed in a dark hooded sweatshirt and green camouflage pants. On his military web belt was a hunting knife in a leather scabbard. In his lap was a double barreled shotgun.

"What do you want, man?" Jacob said.

"I want you to hand me the gun and get out of the truck," Walter said, slow and evenly.

"Go on," Jacob said. "Get out of here."

There was such cruelty in Jacob's voice that Walter couldn't think of him feeding a hummingbird.

"Get out and give me the goddamn gun. Your mother's up the road in my car waiting for you."

"You seen what Wes done to her?" Jacob asked. "He's going to pay for it. Leave me alone to do my job."

"I understand you wanting to do this," Walter said. "And I don't blame you for it. But this isn't the right way. It won't settle anything."

"I'm different than you," Jacob said. "I've got a different way of handling things."

"But not a sensible, better way," Walter said. "Now hand me that goddamn shotgun."

Walter opened the door to the truck. Jacob raised the gun and pointed it at his chest.

"Go on," Jacob said. "Get out of here."

"Go ahead and shoot me," Walter said. "'Cause if you don't, I'm going to take that gun away from you. I'm not going to let you ruin your life and your mother's too."

Walter reached in and grabbed the gun by its barrels. He looked into Jacob's eyes, and Jacob looked back at him with eyes that were cold and hard. Then Jacob's grip on the gun went slack, and Walter took it. He broke open the double barrels. From the chambers, he extracted two shells and pocketed them.

"Slide over, son," Walter said. "I'll drive. We're leaving this godforsaken place."

As he pulled the truck out of the woods, Jacob began to cry. Walter reached over and patted his shoulder.

"It's all right," he said. "It's all right to cry."

On their way to the cabin, Walter stopped at the sheriff's office, and Becky filed a complaint against Wes. The deputy behind the desk told her not to worry. Where Wes was going he couldn't cause her any more trouble.

When they arrived at Walter's, the sky had cleared and turned deep and black; a harvest moon cast a sulfurous haze over the land. Becky and Jacob followed Walter into the dark cabin. The air was damp and chilly, and smelled of cold ashes. Walter turned on the light. In his wood burning stove, he laid seasoned hickory logs on a bed of kindling and lit a fire that ticked and spit. Then he cleared a bowl of apples and the salt and pepper shakers from the kitchen table. He asked Becky to lie down . Wearing rubber gloves, Walter opened a sterile suture pack that he had taken from his office when he retired. He drew up six cc's of 1 percent Xylocaine in a syringe. He dabbed at Becky's lower lip with a Betadine-soaked sponge.

"A little pinch," he said, injecting the local aesthetic.

Before he began to sew, he looked down at Becky. In the lamp's white light, she looked pale and fragile, damaged and afraid. Walter's heart went out to her.

"This won't hurt," he said. "You won't feel a thing."

"I ain't afraid of pain," she said. "It's other things I'm afraid of.

"Don't worry, darlin'," Walter said. "You're safe here."

He bent over her and began to sew. To minimize scarring, he sutured with tiny, interrupted stitches. *Frog hair* he called the fine monofilament thread. Cursing his old man's tremor, he steadied his working right hand with his left. But he was pleased to see he still threw a slick instrument tie with the needle holder.

While he worked, Walter pictured Wes, defiant and defeated, behind bars. He wondered what made the man so cruel and destructive. Was it fear of being seen as weak and insignificant? Was it fear of losing control in a world he didn't trust? Was it seeking revenge for the beating life had given him? Or had God just made him mean?

After he clipped the last suture, he studied his handiwork. He was satisfied with the way he had approximated the vermilion border of her lip. He smeared the cut with triple antibiotic ointment.

"Lips have good blood supply and heal fast," he said. "Your smile is going to be as pretty as ever."

Tears came to Becky's eyes. "You're always thinking of ways to make the world better for people," she said.

"Okay," Walter said. "We've had enough blubbering for one day. I've got some blue gill filets in the fridge. How about you fixing a fish chowder for me and Jacob while we finish up that stone wall?"

"It's dark," Jacob said.

"Ever hear of electricity?" Walter asked.

Walter uncorked his best bottle of Merlot, a 2003 Beringer, to let it breathe. From the refrigerator, he took a Ziploc bag filled with the filets he had caught with his fly rod in the pond.

He laid the fish on the counter with corn, potatoes, celery, and onions from his garden. "The way I make chowder—"

"Go on," Becky said. "Get outta here. I don't know much, but I know how to cook."

Walter stepped onto the porch. He switched on the flood lamps that were bolted to the eaves of the roof. Their light bathed the wall and the clearing below in a cold incandescence. Walter sensed that the stones were somehow alive and waiting for him. With Jacob trailing behind, he descended the hill to the pile of rocks. Walter had held back the largest rocks to use as "capstones" on the final top-course; their extra weight would stabilize the wall.

"These are big mothers," Walter said.

"Not to worry," Jacob said.

"Okay," Walter said. "Time to rock and roll."

Together, they muscled the big stones up the hill, flopping them end over end through the wet grass. At the wall, Walter counted to three, and they hefted each stone into place. Being careful not to smash his fingers, Walter tugged and turned the stones to make them fit. He was never satisfied until each one was properly placed in accordance with the laws of physics and masonry. He thought of the stones, not as inanimate objects, but rather as living things.

For a while they worked in silence. Walter hummed a hymn and sang the words to himself.

> We are building Jacob's wall,
> We are building Jacob's wall,
> Sisters, brothers, all.
> Every stone goes higher, higher.
> Every stone goes higher, higher,
> Sisters, brothers, all.

"I like laying stone," Jacob finally said. "Maybe that's what I'll do after I graduate."

"Masonry is a mighty fine profession," Walter said. "A lasting one. Man's been laying stone for ten thousand years or more. It goes back to the Egyptians and even farther."

Jacob brought him another rock.

"Just be sure of one thing," Walter said. "Whatever you do, do something you're not ashamed of."

The last stone was a monster, four feet long and at least ten inches thick. Walter was afraid that the two of them couldn't lift it. But between them the rock rose from the earth and onto the wall with what seemed to be a power of its own.

With the stone in place, Walter stepped back and surveyed their work. The flood lamps and moon cast a sanctifying light on the wall, causing the stones to glow a ghostly and shadowed gray. Walter took the plumb bob from his pocket and let it dangle on its string, testing the wall for pitch. He was pleased to see that its vertical face leaned into the hill about a half an inch for each course of stone. The wall was strong and would stand long after he was gone, even long after Becky and Jacob were gone if no man tore it down.

"It's a damned fine wall," Walter said, "if you don't mind me saying so."

"What you going to build now?" Jacob said.

"Haven't thought about it. These rocks are getting heavy. Maybe this is it for me."

"We could build a stone bridge over that ravine by

the pond," Jacob said. He pointed down the hill toward dark water where the harvest moon's reflection shimmered.

"You'd have to use mortar," Walter said. "And that's a whole different ball game."

"We could do it," Jacob said. "I bet we could."

Walter handed Jacob the plumb bob. "Keep it," he said.

"Really?" Jacob said.

"You earned it, son."

Jacob looked at the plumb bob and smiled. "Thanks," he said. "Thanks a lot."

Putting a hand on Jacob's shoulder, Walter turned from the wall and headed up the hill toward the cabin. Hickory-scented smoke rose from the chimney and wafted into the night. A full moon appeared from behind a cloud. Through the windows, he saw Becky's backlit silhouette moving around in the kitchen from the stove to the sink. A tranquil sense of family washed over Walter. He and Jacob entered the cabin where a bottle of good wine and Becky's supper awaited them.

BLOOD

IN THE CLAMOR and glare of a hospital trauma room, Stan Ward, a surgeon dressed in blue scrubs, bends over a critically injured boy on a gurney. Although the boy is a fair-skinned Black, he is pale from the loss of blood. With a gauze square, Stan dabs at a deep gash on the boy's forehead where it hit wet pavement when he went over the handlebars of his Kawasaki NINJA 500 motorcycle. The surgeon eyes the digital printout of the patient's vital signs; they flash in red across a monitor's screen. Stan shakes his head. The kid is headed for the grave if he doesn't get some blood in him. He turns to Hoa, a petite Vietnamese nurse with a gold tooth, sleek black hair and an accent that reminds him of his days as a battalion surgeon in the Mekong Delta. It seems as if he has always been in a war zone of one sort or another.

"Set up six units of blood stat," he says. "Type-specific. No time for a crossmatch."

"You got it, Bacsi," she says, using the Vietnamese word for doctor as she rings up the blood bank on the phone.

Stan is tall but stooped, with close-cut silver hair and narrow elegant wrists. Nodules of arthritis deform the knuckles of his long, once-clever fingers. He has been in practice for thirty years, and he is tired—tired of night call, tired of not getting paid for cases like this, tired of fools like the boy on the cart who ride their crotch rockets without helmets, tired of the discomfort he has been feeling in his chest the last few days. He is tired of feeling tired. The boy moans, thrashing his arms and legs.

"Lie still, son," Stan says. "That's it. Be quiet so I can take care of you."

With a pair of bandage scissors, he slashes open the camouflage poncho the boy is wearing. Then he asks him what his name is and flashes a penlight into his frightened eyes. Stan is relieved when the pupils constrict and the boy groans *Troy*, demonstrating that it is unlikely his brain has been seriously injured. Stan places his stethoscope on the patient's flat corrugated abdomen that he, with a middle-aged paunch, envies. When he presses the listening bell down, Troy moans and tries to push his hand away. Thinking, diagnosing damage, Stan knows by the way the boy tightens the muscle of his abdomen that he has bled into his belly, confirming what a just-completed CAT scan has shown: his spleen is ruptured. Struggling up from the cart, Troy leans on his elbows. A rivulet of blood runs down his temple from the jagged red star on his forehead. There is terror in his eyes.

"I don't want to die," he cries out. "Don't let me die."

"I'm not going let you die, son," Stan says. With a hand on his shoulder, he eases the boy back down on the stretcher. "You need an operation, but everything's going to be all right."

Stan's voice is calm and soothing. He checks the monitor and sees that the motorcyclist's pulse has risen to 120 and the systolic blood pressure has fallen to eighty millimeters of mercury. The deterioration of vital signs causes adrenaline to seep into Stan's circulation. He is aware of his own heart racing and a tightness in his chest. After all of these years in the trenches, a tough trauma case still excites him. He turns the IV wide open. Saline solution streams from a plastic bag through a tube into a vein in the boy's left arm.

"Busted spleen," Stan says to Hoa. "Time to cut."

He is thinking of an old adage from his surgical residency years ago: "A chance to cut is a chance to cure." Stan welcomes the opportunity to act, to be heroic. A savior. It seems to him that since his wife left him, surgery and his thirty-year-old daughter, Betsy, are the only thing left in his life that give it meaning.

"Patient seventeen," Hoa says. "Underage. Permission needed."

"Not if no one's here to give it," Stan says.

He moves quickly to the telephone on the wall and dials the number of the operating room. While he waits for someone to answer, he looks at the monitor and sees the boy's pressure is up to ninety. Stan breathes a sigh of relief, thinking the kid is young and resilient with a great cardiovascular system that will help him get through this if he can just get some damned blood in his veins. Stan shifts his gaze out the window. The landscape is dripping, gray and blurred as if seen through cataracts. Rain splatters on the street, and the pavement glistens black, dangerous. Stan wonders why someone would ride a motorcycle on a nasty day like this, wonders what Betsy is doing. He hopes she is safe and taking care of her diabetes. Alice, the nurse-supervisor of the OR, answers in her high, annoying voice. Stan tells her to get a room ready for a laparotomy and splenectomy stat.

"A little birdie told me about the case," she says. "Room one is set to go."

"Aren't you something?" Stan says. "Make sure my vascular instruments are on the table."

"They'll be there. Anything else you need?"

"A little luck and some blood."

Stan likes being in charge, likes the way the nurses follow his orders and take care of him in a way his ex-wife never did. Even in the days before his divorce, the hospital was the nearest thing to a home for him. Medicine was his marriage. As he hangs up the receiver, the door to the trauma cubicle springs open, and a heavy but solidly built woman bursts into the room. She wears a beige smock over a blouse and skirt in a printed, bright-colored fabric. Around her neck a pair of glasses hangs by a gold chain. Although he doesn't know her name, Stan recognizes her as someone who works at the hospital's information desk. He has always been impressed by her regal appearance and the way she answers people's questions.

"Troy," she cries, rushing to the boy's side and grabbing his hand. "Your head is cut. Oh, God, what happened? What's going on here?"

"He's your son?" Stan asks.

"Yes, I'm Ethel Wilson. What's the matter with Troy?"

"He's been in a motorcycle accident," Stan says. "He has a ruptured spleen. He's in shock from loss of blood. We're taking him to the operating room immediately."

"He's going to be all right, isn't he?" She caresses the boy's cheek, getting smudges of blood on her fingers. "Please tell me he's going to be all right."

"He's young and strong. He should do fine if we get some blood in him and get him to surgery."

The woman turns and looks at Stan. Her face is dark and gleaming. From her expression, he knows his authority is about to be challenged, and he doesn't like it. Not here in his domain.

"He can't have blood transfusions," she says.

"What? Why not?"

"We're Jehovah's Witnesses. It's not allowed."

Stan knows that Jehovah's Witnesses believe blood is sacred and not to be used for human consumption, and that they consider a transfusion the same as ingesting blood. Although he was raised Catholic, he considers religion to be a kind of infectious disease that produces far more evil than good. The absurdity of refusing lifesaving blood makes his own blood boil. He glances up at the monitor. The boy's pressure is down to seventy-five.

"Mrs. Wilson, your son's in shock. He'll die without blood."

"I said no blood transfusions."

On the gurney, the boy's eyes flash with fear, darting back and forth from Stan's face to his mother's.

"Please, Mom," he pleads. "I don't want to die. I want the blood."

Ethel bends over her son, her wide frame blocking him from Stan's view.

"If you receive blood, Troy," she says, "your chance for eternal life will be lost."

"No. I want the blood."

She presses her cheek to his.

"Trust in God," she says. "He'll get you through the operation without blood. You're in His hands now."

Stan moves to the gurney and picks up the boy's wrist. Troy's pulse is faint, a rapid tap against the tip of his fingers. The boy's cool, sticky skin tells Stan his blood volume is so low his heart isn't pumping well. Time is running out. He asks Mrs. Wilson to step away from the gurney with him.

In the corner of the room, Stan says in a forceful whisper, "Didn't you hear him? Your son's will is to receive blood. He wants to live, for Chrissakes." Stan fights to control the anger in his voice. Tightness returns to his chest. "It's his life, not yours."

"I'm his mother. He's a minor. It is God's will, not yours or his, that's to be obeyed. You're a doctor, not God."

Stan thinks of Betsy, his estranged daughter whom he hasn't seen since he left her mother six months ago to be with a woman he is no longer with. He imagines Betsy on the gurney. Although he disdains religion, he believes in God, believes he has been anointed by Him to be his daughter's guardian, to take care of her no matter what. For a parent to condemn her own child to death seems subhuman, senseless, like a mother grizzly who devours her cub to save it from a predator. For Troy's mother to with-hold blood from her son is the same as him not allowing Betsy to receive insulin if she was in diabetic coma.

"We don't have time for this," he says. "Your son's going to die. Why don't you just look the other way and let me do what has to be done to save him?"

The mother glares up at him. Her eyes are glistening with tears but also dark with anger.

"If you give him blood, I'll sue you. You'll be fighting the entire Watch Tower Society. I'll press charges. It's assault and battery to transfuse someone against their will."

"This is unbelievable," Stan said. "How can you let your child die? Don't you love him?"

"I love him more than anything in the world. If he dies, I'll want to die, too. But I can't condemn him to eternal damnation. If you had faith, you'd be able to understand that."

Stan looks at the boy, then at Hoa. He tightens his lips and shakes his head in disgust and disbelief. Hoa closes her eyes and shakes her head, too.

"Let's go then," he says. "Let's get him to the OR, Hoa."

Stan starts toward the door. Before he opens it, he turns toward the mother.

"Please," he says. "Let me give your son blood."

"No," she says, tears streaming down her cheeks.

On his way to the surgical suite, Stan hurries along beside the gurney through a sloping windowless tunnel with walls that are unnaturally white. Ahead are the operating rooms, cold and indifferent as caves of ice. He looks down at Troy, pale, shivering with shock and fear. Stan reaches down and rests his hand on the boy's shoulder. He remembers Troy's mother saying if he died, she would want to die, too. He thinks of Betsy. If she died, he would want to die too. He presses his hand against his chest, trying to compress the pain that is there.

ON A SATURDAY MORNING IN NOVEMBER, two weeks before the boy in the motorcycle wreck was brought to the emergency room, Stan had driven his mud-splattered Range Rover to the nearby Indiana town where Betsy lived. It had rained the night before. The landscape was damp and drab as if all the color had been drained from the day. Stan wore jeans and a heavy Irish wool sweater Betsy had given him for his birthday a few years ago. He didn't particularly like the sweater, but he wanted Betsy to see him in it and remember a time when they were a family and she cared about him.

Beside him on the seat were two framed needlepoint wall hangings. On one in blue capital letters was the word FORGIVE, AND on the other LOVE. Years ago, his deceased mother had embroidered them and hung them in her living room. As he drove, Stan thought about forgiveness: how discarding a burden of blame and anger can lighten life's load and how love was a continuum of little forgivenesses. Betsy had adored her namesake, "Mamma Betty." He planned to give his daughter the wall hangings as a peace offering, a plea for her forgiveness. How could Betsy not heed her dear grandmother's admonition to forgive? To be able to hold her father in her mind without anger was a gift Betsy could give herself and him, too.

Stan parked the Range Rover in front of Betsy's yellow clapboard bungalow where she lived alone with her black Lab, Ralph. He sat with hands on the steering wheel, trying to decide how he should present himself to her. Should he kiss her? Just embrace her? What should he say? He imagined her smiling, hugging him, putting the past behind her. But what if she wouldn't let him in? What then? In a moment of panic, he wished he hadn't come. He took a deep breath and picked up the wall-hangings. Stepping from his car, he trudged up the steps to her front door. He pushed a lighted button that rang a door chime. He was aware of his heart galloping. He could hear Ralph yapping, but Betsy didn't come to the door. Stan knocked and waited, staring down at the wall-hangings in his hand. Please, he thought, just let me in. I'll give these to you and everything will be all right. Still, the only sound that he heard was Ralph's bark. Was Betsy refusing to see him, or was she gone?

Stan knocked again and waited. Still there was no answer. He felt as if he were alone, stranded on the shore of a great body of water from which the tide had ebbed. Disheartened, Stan hung FORGIVE and LOVE on the door knob. He turned and started down the steps. The deep ache that had been plaguing him in recent weeks returned to his chest, nearly bringing him to his knees. He paused for a second and put his hand on the fence to steady himself. After a few seconds, the pain eased. He continued on to his car, wishing he had been a better father, a better husband, a better person in Betsy's eyes.

STAN STANDS at the scrub sink in the corridor outside operating room one. The tiled walls and floors, the porcelain fixtures gleam white and hard as bone. The air is redolent with an antiseptic, medicinal scent. Through the door he can see Troy asleep and strapped to the long narrow table, his arms extended on boards as if in crucifixion. The boy's eyes are covered with gauze patches to protect his corneas. Pale and waxen, he glows with an iridescence in the brilliant beams of two overhead lights. Lou, the surgical assistant, is rapidly draping his belly with blue towels. Ted, a young, nervous anesthesiologist just out of residency, slides a tube into Troy's trachea. The boy's breath fogs the clear plastic.

Everyone is masked and moving quickly. Stan feels as if he is watching a video on fast forward.

The squeezing ache that had plagued him at Betsy's house returns beneath his rib cage, nearly bringing him to his knees. He leans against the scrub sink and pushes his hand against his sternum to compress the pain. He draws in a deep breath that makes it worse. Sweat covers his forehead. Please. Go away and let me finish this case, and then you can do with me as you want. When the pain eases, Stan exhales a sigh of relief. There isn't time to scrub properly so he squirts his hands with an antiseptic foam while planning the incision he will make. He tells himself to get ample exposure and not to worry about the length of the cut. Wounds heal side to side, not end to end. But what about the blood? Will he transfuse the boy and face the consequences? Or will he let him die and live with that? He can hear an echo of the boy's mother's voice saying she will sue him if he transfuses her son, that he will be fighting the entire Watch Tower Society, whatever the hell that is. Stan feels the weight of the choices bearing down on him, testing his soul.

With his hands held up away from his body, he hurries into the room. A tall slim nurse with sleepy blue eyes and perfectly plucked brows holds out a gown of green cotton for him. Her name is Elizabeth, and for an instant, Stan thinks of Betsy, his own Elizabeth whom he hasn't heard from since he left the wall-hangings on her door. He wishes she could be here to see him operate, see him in this moment of heroism. Maybe then she would forgive him. He pushes her out of his mind and thrusts his arms into the gown's sleeves. He bellies up to the table and looks over the ether screen where Ted is adjusting the flow of oxygen into the respirator that breathes for Troy.

"How's he doing?" Stan asks.

"For shit," Ted says. "All he has in his veins is salt water. He needs some goddamned hemoglobin for Chrissakes. Friggin' Jehovah's Witnesses. Can't we just transfuse him, Stan?"

Stan glances at a cooler that contains the blood he had ordered. It sits on the floor like contraband.

"Time to get this show on the road," Stan says. He holds out his gloved hand to Lou. "Scalpel. Come on. Let's get this goddamn spleen in a pan."

Lou slaps the scalpel into his palm. In spite of the pain that grips his chest, Stan smiles under his mask, thinking that the good thing about having nothing to lose is that it allows you to do things you should do, but otherwise wouldn't. With a bold stroke of the knife, he makes his incision, reminding himself to do no harm. But then who is to say what is harm and what is not?

BOBOLINKS

ON A SUMMER MORNING when fog layered over the land and the coronavirus was raging around the world, Wayne Wilson started up a trail that led to a mountain pond in Vermont. Tall, fit, and straight as the white pines that lined the path, the retired orthopedic surgeon was a nearly handsome man for his age in spite of a scar on his left cheek where a basal cell had been removed. On a ball cap he had purchased in the Galapagos Islands was a blue-footed booby. Hot, dense breath filled his cloth face mask. Flies swarmed around a heap of horse manure left by someone's early morning trail ride. In his hand was the hickory walking stick he had carved himself, and in his chest, he could feel the weight of his heart. An unrelenting heaviness.

The last time he had made this hike was a few months before with Laura, his lover for the last three years. It was on that climb up the mountain when she told him that the reason she'd never had a baby was that she was afraid she would treat it like her mother had treated her, but now she wished they'd met years ago and that he had fathered her child.

"I want to marry as soon as we can," she said. "Will you promise never to leave me?"

"I promise," Wayne had said, hugging her.

Shortly after that, out of the blue, she had texted him and told him she was changing her life and wouldn't be seeing him again. In disbelief, Wayne had called her. In a cold and distant voice, she said the man she was with now was a jealous type and that if Wayne contacted her again, he would cause trouble. Her words put a knife in Wayne's gut, and ever since he had been immensely sad and humiliated. Unable to concentrate when he tried to read a novel or write one of his short stores, he was going through a couple of bottles of Scotch every week. He had let his coarse gray hair grow long and curl over his collar, and he seldom shaved. Weeds had taken over his vegetable garden. The deer were devouring his prize hostas. He no longer went to the gym or to grand rounds at the hospital. His bird feeders, empty of seeds, hung on their poles.

The trail grew steeper, and Wayne's legs began to tire. To catch his breath, he paused beside a hollow, black stone. Filled with water, the big rock served as a horse trough. Sucking in air, he leaned on his walking stick. His damp shirt clung to his chest. The rapid beat of his heart worried him. Was it atrial fibrillation or just a sinus tachycardia? Could he have contracted that goddamn coronavirus? He felt his forehead for fever and found none. While he waited for his pulse to slow and his oxygen level to rise, his mind sorted through all of the trials he and Laura had gone through together—the end of his career in medicine, the death of Laura's abusive mother, Wayne's wife in the nursing home descending deeper into dementia, Laura's breast cancer scare, the time she had left him briefly for the TV weatherman. Although he didn't believe in a god who intervened in the lives of individuals, he said a silent prayer that Laura would come back to him, just as she had done after her fling with the meteorologist. He ended his prayer by asking the Lord to watch over his wife.

Laughing and listening to their phones with earbuds, four girls in denim shorts and sorority T-shirts came toward him on the path. When he saw they were maskless, Wayne stepped off the trail into a bed of ferns. Before he'd gone to college, he joined the Marine Corps and spent a year as a medic with a reconnaissance battalion in Vietnam. He thought if he could make that sacrifice, these spoiled brats could wear a mask. He watched them waltz on down the trail.

"You're nothing but selfish," he mumbled into his mask. "I'm an old man who could die if I got this frigging virus. Show some respect. Consider someone other than yourselves."

Wayne turned and continued on up the mountain. He was Sisyphus, his rock a heavy heart and the world's indifference.

When he came to the pond, the trail leveled off, and Wayne's breathing became less labored. On the shore, he found the same split-log bench where he and Laura had sat together not so long ago. Engraved on the seat in capital letters was the old adage TOUGH WATER PETRIFIES WOOD. He thought the words were a message. Was life in a pandemic—coupled with the loss of Laura—supposed to toughen him up, or did the adage mean that what he had been through, and was still going through—his loneliness, his grief and guilt—had fossilized him, hardened him, leaving him nothing but a stone?

He took off his backpack and sat down on the bench. He watched a silver trout slither in the shallows and devour an insect. He retrieved a granola bar from his pocket and unwrapped it. He took a bite and washed it down with a swig of water. The taste of honey and almonds revived the memory of he and Laura sharing the same flavors and a kiss on this very bench. The longing he felt for her was fierce. He shook his head and wished he had brought a flask of brandy, something to deaden the pain.

Wayne wondered where Laura was and what she

was doing at this very moment. Had Covid-19 infected her? What were she and her new man doing now? Making love? He wanted to know, but at the same time he was afraid to know. He remembered her immune system had been altered by a chronic thyroid condition and that she would be at high risk if she became ill with the virus. He had always doctored her ailments—her headaches, sinus infections, torn rotator cuff, sore thumb, and the breast lump that turned out to be benign. He thought if she was sick with the virus, he should be the one who cared for her.

From his backpack, he retrieved his smartphone to Google her Facebook page. In her photograph, she was wearing intentionally torn jeans and a white turtleneck. Her straight, wheat-blond hair was parted in the middle. Her face was tanned, yet beginning to show creases around her eyes. He thought her beautiful in a natural, unadorned way. She was smiling, bending forward nearly nose to nose with her beloved Foxy, a rescue dog with a frizzy coat of red fur and a long, pointed muzzle. The sight of Laura caused Wayne's heart to seize.

"Man, oh man," he said, shaking his head.

She was a drug he couldn't live without.

With the phone in his hand, he was tempted to call her, but he remembered the threat from the man she was with. Wayne took in a deep breath and blew it out. It was hard for him to believe that she, a peaceful Christian soul who loved all of nature and would stop in traffic to carry a turtle across the road, could be with someone who threatened to do harm to one of God's creatures—specifically him.

When he scrolled through her Facebook photos, he stopped at a picture of Laura and her new lover eating at a restaurant where she and Wayne once had their own table and called the waitress by her first name. The man was pudgy, with a napkin over his potbelly and old man breasts showing beneath a lavender polo shirt. His hair was white and perfectly coiffed like that of an evangelical minister. All Wayne knew about him was that he was Canadian and had money. Laura was a sports nut and physically fit—a paddle boarder, former college tennis player, and shortstop on the school's softball team.

Wayne, in his day, had been a fine athlete and a track star. He couldn't believe she was attracted to someone so soft and unmanly. Canadian bacon, he thought with disdain and a slight smile. Surely, she would tire of him as she had of the weatherman and others in her past. He looked again at Laura's foxlike dog, and it occurred to him that no one had said he couldn't contact the pet. Even though he knew it would be a rather childish subterfuge, he began to compose a message to Foxy. He hadn't mastered thumb-typing, so he laboriously punched out the letters with his index finger.

Dear Foxy,

I'll bet you are surprised to hear from me. I was looking at a picture of you and your mother. It made me wonder how the both of you are. I was told not to contact your mother, but no one said that I couldn't contact you, and I know you won't bite me.

So tell me Foxy, do you still chase rabbits? Do you still cower when it thunders? Are you still as jealous as you were when I would sit on the couch beside your mother with my arm around her? Did you eat all of those many cans of dog food we bought you at PetSmart? Did you like that piece of filet mignon I brought you from the steakhouse where we celebrated her birthday? I don't need to ask how she looks in the beige sweater from Nordstrom's I gave her that day. I know she looks terrific. I don't have to tell you she is a woman of great beauty and that she adores you as I adore her and believe she once did me.

It may seem strange to you that a man would continually think of a dog he hadn't seen in a while. But I miss you. I miss you bounding on the bed to wake us up with face-licks. I miss those morning walks with you and your mother through streets lined with hibiscus and bougainvillea by the golf course with its sugar-sand traps and pristine green fairways, a stroll through paradise that seemed like it would never end. I miss your tail-wags when you greeted us at the door after an evening out. I miss you like hell. Will I ever see you again? I believe I will the way I hope there is a life hereafter. Until then, take care of yourself and watch over her. I worry about her in this time of corona. Make sure she sanitizes her hands, avoids crowds, and wears a mask. Keep her well and happy.

All the best,
    Your buddy, Wayne

When Wayne read what he had written, he felt foolish and wondered if he wasn't beginning to lose it.

Laura had made him feel young, alive, and loved. He wondered if, at his age, he could ever find another woman to replace what had been lost. With glistening eyes, he raised his finger to hit send, but something restrained him. Was it fear of further rejection more than of retribution? As he once had done in the operating room, he decided to weigh the risks against the rewards before he acted. He reminded himself to follow the dictum of Hippocrates and to do no harm.

Wayne returned the phone to his backpack. He took a deep breath and a drink of water. He covered his mouth and nose with his mask. He shouldered his pack and picked up his walking stick. With his head down, he headed off on the trail around the lake. His emotions were a tangle of sorrow and hurt, guilt and humiliation. He felt emasculated, unlovable. Why had this happened to him? What had he done wrong to deserve this? He had always treated her well, taken care of her needs, comforted her when she was down on herself. He had been careful not to criticize her, always complimenting her, telling her, in spite of what her mother had told her, that she was a good person. He knew he should be angry at Laura, but for reasons he didn't understand, he felt no malice, only longing. He thought how love, true love, was impossible to shed. He wondered if he was doomed to feel like this the rest of life. For an instant, he wished he would become infected with the coronavirus, a suffering that would end his suffering.

At the south shore of the pond, Wayne took the Red Pine trail that led into a forest of tall coniferous trees. Fallen needles carpeted the earth, and the air smelled piney and sweet. When he rounded a bend, he came across a park ranger standing by a sign that pointed to the mountain's summit. Nearly as tall as he was, she had graying hair in a frizzy, funky style and large, long-lashed hazel eyes above a cloth face mask. The pants of her baggy brown uniform were tucked into thick-soled boots. Wayne noticed that her only jewelry was a leather bracelet on her wrist. He thought her attractive in a fresh, woodsy, natural way. He estimated her age to be about sixty, the same as Laura's.

"Good morning," he said, keeping his distance.

"Good morning," she said. "Fine day for a hike. You been here before?"

"Many times," he said.

For a while, they stood on opposite sides of the path, introduced themselves, and chatted about the mountain and the history of the park. He told her he was a retired orthopedist who had moved his summer home to Vermont to be near his grandchildren, but that they had soon relocated to California. When he asked her where she was from, Olivia said Iowa and that she had taught psychology in a junior college there before she became a park ranger. The subject turned to the coronavirus.

"Covid-19 has turned this park into a ghost mountain," she said. "I seldom see anyone on the trails these days."

"Kind of apocalyptic." Wayne shooed away tiny insects that danced before his eyes. "Like the world is suspended in midair, and no one knows what's going happen."

"Yeah. This mountain is Vesuvius, and no one knows when or if it's going to erupt," she said. "Pandemic uncertainties seem as bad as the infection itself."

"Spoken like a psychologist," he said. "But the infection can be bad if you're not young and healthy."

"Spoken like a doctor," she said.

Wayne went on to talk about the absurdity of the anti-mask movement and how it angered him when he saw the girls coming down the mountain without their faces covered.

"I guess you would say masks are ambiguous." Wayne pinched the metal strip on his mask to fit it to his nose. "They disguise the wearer's identity and at the same time reveal who's under the mask."

"Right," she said, "the mask becomes their true face. It identifies the wearer as someone who cares about his fellow man and wants to protect them."

"Amen," he said. "I want the old world back when we cared for each other. A time before this damn bug."

Although he referenced the virus, he was thinking what he really wanted back were his halcyon days with Laura before she left him.

"Worrying about what happened or should happen or what might happen only leaves me frustrated," Olivia said. "I try to focus on positive things like the flora and fauna of this place." She pointed at the blue-footed booby on his cap. "You must like birds."

"I sure do," he said. "I'm an avid birder."

"Well, then let me show something." Olivia pointed up the trail. "It's not far."

While Wayne followed her, thoughts of Laura floated through his mind. He remembered how she had been avian-obsessed ever since college, when she'd worked in a raptor rehab center in Ohio. Ever since, she'd kept a list of the species she had seen and those she hoped to see. He remembered her joy when they saw an eagle flying over the Ottauquechee River and when they heard finches chittering in the willows at Dewey's Pond. He remembered their elation when, last winter, they spotted a roseate spoonbill above the mangroves on Sanibel Island. Now he realized that the disappearance from sight of the stunning pink bird was a foreshadowing, a representation of something brief, brilliant, and beautiful, but doomed to end.

Before long, the path brought Wayne and Olivia to a mountain meadow with a dense carpet of grasses brightly enameled with yellow butterflies and flowers. Bees buzzed around the blossoms of thistles and clover. The fog had lifted, and tufted white clouds paraded across a cerulean sky. Olivia paused, pointing with a stick she had picked up.

"This field is filled with the nests of bobolinks," she said in her Midwestern twang. "Early in the morning the fledglings emerge from the grass and fly about. It's really something to see. It's a gosh-darn bird circus."

"I've never seen a bobolink." Wayne wondered if Laura had. He wished he had known about this place when he'd brought her to the mountain. "Isn't their call distinctive?"

"It's what gives them their name. It's a metallic, bubbly, rambling song."

She stepped back and lowered her mask. Then, with sharp high notes and buzzy low pitches, she began to imitate the bobolink's call. Her performance made him chuckle, and she blushed. She went on to describe how, after breeding, the male's plumage molts from the bright black-and-white of a tuxedo to a drab brown camouflage, more like a park ranger's uniform.

"Post-breeding drab." Wayne looked down at his quick-dry khaki shorts and gray T-shirt. "I can relate to that."

"Drab is as drab does. You don't seem drab to me."

"Well, thanks," he said, smiling beneath his mask.

Wayne tried to think of something humorous to say that might impress her, something that would illustrate his love of nature. After an awkward silence he said, "When I was hiking here last summer, I took pictures of lichen with my phone, and then wrote haiku poems that the images brought to mind."

"I wish I could see them," Olivia said.

"If you have a smart phone, I'll send you a couple."

Olivia pulled an iPhone from the pocket of her shirt and held up it for Wayne to see. He retrieved his phone from his pack and emailed the letter to Foxy to himself. In PHOTOS, he found pictures of the lichen. Some looked like seashells, some like sconces, and some like snails on a log. They reminded him of Laura on the trail with him that day, her utter joy, the way she ran ahead of him, then stopped and teased him for being old and unable to keep up, but then she had come back to him, wrapped her arms around him, and kissed him hard on the lips.

"What's your number?" he asked Olivia, thinking that it would be nice to have it in his contacts.

Olivia recited it, and he texted her three photos. When they appeared on her screen, she said, "Amazing. These are quite lovely. Lichen, like much of nature, are under appreciated for their beauty."

"In all things of nature, there is something of the marvelous," Wayne replied, quoting Aristotle while still thinking of Laura.

"So true," Olivia said. "It's wonderful how old Mother Nature can free us from our despair and disappointments. After all, isn't that what a mother is for?"

"I published these photos and poems in a little monograph," Wayne said.

"You're a writer then."

"I am. Among other things."

A small brown bird flashed up from the grass. Olivia called to it, "Too-Wee. Too-Wee."

"You sound like you need oil." Wayne chuckled beneath his mask. "Is it a bobolink?"

"A sparrow."

"I was just testing you," Wayne said.

"Ha." Her eyes were smiling. "I'll bet you write fiction."

"Short stories mainly."

"I've always wanted to write a novel," Olivia said. "There's a story I want to tell."

He started to ask her what that story was about,

thinking it might reveal something intriguing, perhaps about her love life and the despair and disappointment she just referenced. But he thought better of it. The walkie-talkie on her belt began to buzz. She answered it and said she would be right there.

"Gotta go." She holstered the walkie-talkie. "No rest for the wicked."

"Thanks for the bird lecture," Wayne said. "And the serenade. Especially the serenade."

"I got carried away." Her cheeks above her mask reddened again.

"I liked the spontaneity," he said. "You be here tomorrow?"

"And the day after," Olivia said. "God and Covid-19 willing."

Wayne raised his elbow as if offering a bump. Olivia raised her elbow, too, but kept her distance.

"Like they say here in Vermont, stay a cow apart," she said. "You have a good day."

"Be safe," he said.

Olivia smiled with her hazel eyes. Then she turned and headed up the trail toward the summit. He watched her disappear among the trees, and he was reminded of the spoonbill he and Laura had seen disappear among the mangroves that day on Sanibel Island.

∿

ON HIS WAY down the mountain, Wayne chose a steep, but less trodden and leaf-covered, path that serpentined downhill in a series of switchbacks. Sunshine streamed through the branches of birch trees and suffused the land with ultraviolet rays that he knew killed viruses. A cool breeze stirred the ferns and purified the air, dispersing the gnats that had plagued him on his ascent. He could hear birds trilling. He stopped to watch a doe and her fawn browse on twigs. A yellow-and-black swallowtail landed on top of his walking stick.

"Well, hello there, pretty lady," he said. The butterfly quickly fluttered away. "Hurry back," Wayne called.

He resumed his hike, thinking how lucky he was, in spite of what was going on in the world and his life, to be in such a pristine place, away from the threat of pestilence and close to nature. He wondered if he should get up early the next morning and return to the meadow to see the fledgling bobolinks. As he walked, he twirled his hiking stick and planned what he would put in his backpack if he did come back—binoculars, bug spray, hand sanitizer, a thermos of coffee and two plastic cups, a couple of blueberry muffins he would pick up at King Arthur's Bakery, and a signed copy of his book of lichen and haiku. He would give Olivia the lichen book and wear something that wasn't so drab. Maybe he would tie a red bandana around his face to serve as a mask. For a moment, he considered how he could share his coffee with Olivia. He decided he could put on surgical gloves. Then he would fill her cup with coffee and place it and a muffin on a flat rock so that she could serve herself while staying a cow apart. From somewhere in the distance came the bay of a dog. Wayne continued on down the shadow-and-light-dappled path with Foxy's bark echoing in his mind.

PART III

IMMORTALITY

Unable are the loved to die, for love is immortality.

— EMILY DICKENSON

At the end of my suffering there was a door.

— LOUISE GLUCK

RESUSCITATION

DR. SLATER KNOTTS walked through the emergency room of the hospital where he was head of the pulmonary disease department. He was wrestling with what was best for Amoto Bertini, his Covid-19 patient who was critically ill in the ICU. Everywhere Slater looked, he saw people sick with the coronavirus struggling to breathe, being placed on ventilators, or getting CPR. He shook his head in disbelief. It was a war zone. Never in his fifteen years of practice had he seen anything close to the suffering this pandemic was causing, not even the AIDS epidemic when he was in training.

At Slater's side was Megan O'Neill, a tall first-year internal-medicine resident who was taking her rotation on Slater's service. She had gone to Notre Dame and had even spent a year in England as a Rhodes Scholar.

Slater considered her to be one of the brightest residents he had ever trained, but he thought her headstrong and somewhat arrogant. Dressed in personal protective equipment—N95 masks, face shields, gowns, and boots made of PVC—the two of them looked like astronauts in a space capsule. From the ER, they went to ICU where they stepped aside to let an orderly wheeling a gurney pass by. On it lay a body covered with a sheet.

In a cubicle near the nurses' station, Slater peered down at Mr. Bertini. He removed the semi-comatose man's mask to get a good look at him. A gray stubble of beard sprouted on his chin. His dark hair was oily and matted, his eyes closed. When he sucked in a breath, his lips pursed, and his skin bore the blue-gray hue of oxygen deprivation. Slater pressed his stethoscope to Mr. Bertini's chest. Each breath he heard was a bubbly heave, a heavy load lifted and dropped. Slater turned to Megan.

"Does he have family?" he asked.

"A son they can't locate," Megan said.

Slater tried to imagine what it must be like to be alone and drowning in your own bodily fluids—the terror, the utter loneliness.

"What are you going to do?" Megan asked.

For a moment, Slater pondered his patient's dilemma. Does his life have meaning? Should we let nature takes its course? Or should we save him and commit him to what might be a life of suffering?

Mr. Bertini gasped for air and moaned.

"Easy now," Slater said. "We're going to take care of you." He turned to Megan. "He's miserable. We need to make him comfortable. Morphine or a respirator? Those are the choices."

"There's a 'Do Not Resuscitate' order in his chart," Megan said. "You know he has cancer of the prostate with bony metastasis."

"Prostate cancer won't kill him anytime soon. The corona infection is benign," Slater said. "We're his caretakers. It's our obligation to do all we can."

Megan scowled.

Slater could feel himself growing impatient. "Didn't they teach you the Vatican Declaration on Euthanasia at Notre Dame?"

"No. Why?"

"It says those in the medical profession must not end a life either by a willful act or by withholding care."

"I don't agree with everything the Church says."

"Your concerns are legitimate, Megan. But trust me, the right thing to do is to put Mr. Bertini on a ventilator."

"The hospital is about to run out of them," Megan argued. "What if a young person needs one and none are available?"

"There's an ethics committee to answer that question," Slater said.

"The God Committee," she said.

"The Life or Death Committee." Slater looked directly at her. "Our job is to take care of Mr. Bertini."

Megan shook her head.

Slater stepped out of the cubicle and hurried to the nurses' station. Marlene, the charge nurse, was at the desk.

"What do you need, Dr. K?" she asked.

"A ventilator, Marly. Call respiratory therapy and help us get ready to intubate Mr. Bertini."

"You sure?"

"That's my decision."

Marlene picked up the phone.

"Make it stat," he said. "Mr. Bertini is in trouble."

Slater knew the intubation would spray the patient's respiratory droplets on him and even with his protective gear, put him at risk. For a moment, he thought of his own family: Owen, age seven; Mattie, age five; and his wife, Julie, an asthmatic. The last thing he wanted was to bring Covid home to them. He worried that his mask would leak or that his gloves wouldn't protect him. But he put those concerns aside and went back to Mr. Bertini. Soon a lanky inhalation therapist wheeled a ventilator into the cubicle. On a towel-covered tray sat a laryngoscope and a plastic endotracheal tube. Marlene appeared behind him. Slater turned to Megan and pointed toward the scope.

"You do the intubation," he said.

"I'd rather not," she said coldly.

"I'll guide you through it."

"I prefer you do it."

Slater frowned and stepped to the head of the bed. He inserted the blade of the laryngoscope into Mr. Bertini's mouth. Slowly, with practiced ease, he exposed the vocal cords and, beyond, the dark, hollow trachea. He held out his gloved hand, and the therapist placed the breathing tube into it. Slater quickly slid it through the vocal cords and into the trachea. Mr. Bertini's cough made Slater grimace. He blew up the balloon that held the tube in place. The therapist connected it to the ventilator and switched on the machine. Its bellows swished and sighed. With his stethoscope, Slater listened to Mr. Bertini's chest.

"Both lungs are aerated," he said.

Slater stripped off his rubber gloves and dropped them in a waste container. For a moment, he looked down at Mr. Bertini's chest. It rose and fell like a pendulum swinging in perfect rhythm. Slater turned to Megan.

"As a physician," he said, "there's a fundamental of medicine you need to remember."

"What's that?"

"Death is the enemy. Life is sacred."

Beneath her face shield, her cheeks reddened.

"The right of patients to choose for themselves is the most sacred thing in medicine," she said.

"I don't believe that's always the case," he said. "When you've been in practice a while, you will come to understand that."

Megan shrugged, then turned and walked away.

ON HIS WAY HOME, Slater drove through the rain. The silent, empty streets and unlit shops conveyed an aura of apocalypse. The drops that splattered his windshield reminded him of contaminated droplets spewing from Mr. Bertini's lungs. The car's wipers slapped side to side. Slater had read Camus' *The Plague,* and he felt like Dr. Rieux traveling through his plague-stricken city, finding it hard to believe that pestilence had crashed down on its people. He came to Shoofly, a chic bar and restaurant. Through a water-speckled window, he saw young people laughing and drinking, crowded together without masks. Their gaiety and disregard for the virus angered Slater. Didn't they care about others? He blamed them for him not being able to hug his children or sleep with his wife. He blamed them for Mr. Bertini's illness. He wished they could see his patient and understand what fighting for your life was like.

Slater pulled into the driveway of his house and

parked in front of the garage. He clicked an automatic opener. The door rattled up, revealing his isolation quarters. An old oriental rug covered the cement floor. There was an inflatable bed and a beanbag chair. Julie had covered a small table with a red-and-white checkered cloth. A bottle of Pinot Grigio was chilling in an ice bucket. Slater entered the garage and lowered the door. He stripped off his clothes and, with a towel around his waist, went into the house.

"I'm home!" he announced.

"I'm giving baths," Julie called from upstairs. "I'll bring the kids down after you shower."

In the laundry room, Slater deposited his clothes in the washing machine and started the cycle. Being careful not to touch anything, he went to the downstairs bathroom where he stepped into a shower with water as hot as he could stand. He soaped himself from head to toe. For a while, he stood in the steam and let hot water needle his skin. He felt contaminated and drained of energy. Mr. Bertini and his other critically ill patients haunted him. He wanted to put the hospital out of his mind, eat, and go to sleep.

Back in the garage he dressed in a warm-up suit and a paper mask. Soon Julie, in jeans and a sweater, appeared at the door with Mattie on one side and Owen on the other. Mattie wore pajamas decorated with pink unicorns. Owen was dressed in red soccer shorts and a pinstriped Yankees shirt. His kids were adorable. He wanted to hug them.

"Hi guys," he said.

"Can we play a game of ping-pong?" Owen asked. "Please, Daddy?"

"You know I can't."

"Can you read us a story in bed?" Mattie said.

"Honey, I can't. I'm sorry. I don't want to risk making you sick."

"I hate coronavirus," Owen said.

"I do, too," Slater said.

Mattie began to cry.

"You're both tired." Julie bent over and gathered the little girl up. "Say goodnight to your father."

Owen mumbled goodnight while Mattie wailed.

"I love you," Slater said.

Julie put Mattie down and herded them away. Through the open door, Slater watched his children climb the stairs. A swell of emotion overtook him. He filled the glass on the table with wine and drank it. Soon Julie returned with a plate of chicken Alfredo, a green salad, and a glass of Chardonnay for herself.

"They really miss you," she said.

"I miss them, too." Slater drew in a big breath and sighed it out. "This is the hardest thing I've ever done."

Julie passed him the plate and pulled a chair to the doorway. Sitting, she raised her glass to Slater.

"Here's to a true hero," she said.

"You're the hero," Slater said. "The kids must be driving you bats."

"They're sick of this damn virus just like I am."

After Slater finished his salad, he told Julie about Mr. Bertini and his disagreement with Megan, the resident.

"Maybe she was right," he said. "Maybe I should have let nature take its course."

"You did what you thought was best for your patient."

"Doctors of her generation are different."

"How so?" Julie asked, taking a sip.

"They place too much emphasis on risk avoidance and not enough on the patient." Slater washed down a bite of chicken with wine. "I always try to take the patient's side of things."

"I know you do," Julie said.

They were quiet while Slater finished his meal. Finally, Julie said. "Slater, how long are you going to keep this up?"

"As long as there are sick people." Slater folded his napkin. "It's why I went into medicine."

"The kids need you," Julie said. "I need you."

"Don't make it harder than it is," Slater said. "Listen, I'm dead tired. I need to go to bed."

"Okay, then. I'll leave you alone."

"I'm sorry, Julie. Things will get better."

"I hope so." Julie rose from her chair. She lowered

her mask and blew him a kiss. "Sweet dreams."

Feeling sad and totally alone, Slater went to the inflatable bed where he lay in the dark. What he craved was the love of his family. A cricket trapped in the garage chirped continuously. Slater thought of the unfairness of the world.

"Goddamn virus," he said.

TWO WEEKS later it was dark when Slater walked from his car to the hospital. Megan had moved on to an oncology rotation at the cancer hospital. Slater was glad to have her gone, but at the same time he felt he had somehow failed to mentor her properly. Mr. Bertini was still on the ventilator, and Slater was thinking that if the man wasn't able to come off the machine, he would have to do a tracheotomy. He knew a trach was a super-spreading procedure that aerosolized the virus and sprayed droplets on the doctor performing it. He prayed he wouldn't have to trach Mr. Bertini.

On a stool at the ICU nurses' station, he reviewed Mr. Bertini's medical record. When he saw that the patient no longer required high levels of oxygen and tolerated long periods of time off the ventilator, Slater managed a smile. For a moment, he sat thinking. Then he stood up and walked to the bedside.

"Mr. Bertini," he said, "if you can hear me, raise your hand."

Mr. Bertini's hand rose from the bed. With the endotracheal tube protruding from his mouth, he opened his eyes.

"Well, hello there." Slater placed his hand on Mr. Bertini's shoulder. "I'm going to let you breathe on your own."

Mr. Bertini nodded his head.

"Just relax and breathe." Slater disconnected the tube from the ventilator and switched off the machine. "That's all you have to do. Breathing is your sole purpose in life right now."

For a long while, he watched Mr. Bertini, noting the movement of his chest and the color his skin. He studied the vital signs that scrolled across the screen of the monitor above the bed.

"In and out. Deep breaths. You're doing great, man. I'm going to get that tube out of your throat."

Mr. Bertini made a thumb's up gesture. Slater called Marlene to the cubicle's door and told her he was going to extubate Mr. Bertini.

"Praise the Lord," she said.

She handed Slater a plastic syringe that he used to suck the air from the cuff that held the tube in place. Carefully, he slid it from Mr. Bertini's throat. The man sputtered and coughed. Slater stepped back from the bed to try and avoid contamination.

"Who . . . ?" Mr. Bertini growled. His voice was husky. He cleared his throat. "Who are you?"

"Your doctor," Slater said.

"Did you put me on that goddamn machine?"

Slater nodded his head.

"Yeah, I did."

Mr. Bertini cleared his throat again.

"You put me through hell!"

"I'm very sorry for what you've been through."

"Don't be sorry." A slight smile came to Mr. Bertini's face. "Thank you, Doc."

Slater's throat tightened and beneath his face shield his eyes glistened. He wished Megan were here. There was much to be learned at the bedside.

Whenever a corona patient came off a ventilator, a song was broadcast on the hospital's loudspeaker system. When Slater heard "Every Breath You Take," he smiled at Mr. Bertini and said, "They're playing your song."

But then the music was interrupted by the wail of a siren, and the red light of an ambulance flashed through the cubicle's window. Soon Slater's pager beeped. He took in a big breath and braced for whatever might come next.

ONE DAY IN THE LIFE OF DR. IVAN JONES

IT WAS morning at Mirror Woods, the nursing home where Dr. Ivan Jones lay on a narrow bed in the memory care unit. At 7 a.m. an attendant entered his room. Her name was Bobby. She was big-boned, with blond close-cropped hair and penetrating blue eyes.

Her clap sounded like a whip and startled him from sleep.

"Rise and shine, Doc." She raised the blinds. "Another big day ahead."

The room's only window looked out on an asphalt parking lot and a single tree, an anemic dogwood with dry yellow leaves that periodically fluttered to the ground. Watery light filled the room with its chest of drawers, a loveseat covered in orange corduroy, and a floor model television set that wasn't hooked up.

Unable to walk to the bathroom, the old neurosurgeon had wet himself. The paper diaper he wore was soaked and felt cold and clammy against his skin. He shivered. He turned his head on the pillow and looked out through cataract-clouded lenses at a gray sky. He blinked and rubbed his eyes, thinking he was seeing smoke—there must be a fire burning nearby. Immediately the thought fled from his mind. He wondered where he was and where he had left his car.

"Come on, sleepyhead," Bobby said. "Chow time. Get up."

Rather roughly, she tugged Ivan up by his shoulders, turning him so that he was sitting on the edge of the bed. He felt a click in his right hip. Two months ago, fleeing from a nightmare in which his body was enormous and his brain minute, he had tried to get up in the dark and had fallen, fracturing the neck of his femur. Because of his congestive heart failure and advanced age, the orthopedic surgeon at the hospital had elected not to pin the bone, even though it meant the rest of Ivan's life would be in a chair. A searing pain shot down from his groin into his thigh and made Ivan grimace, but he didn't cry out. In front of him on the wall, he saw an oil portrait of his wife Helen, who had died of metastatic colon cancer. Ivan was a self-taught artist. He had painted her from a photograph thirty-five years ago and given it to her as a gift on her fiftieth birthday. In the picture, framed in walnut, she was wearing a blue, belted dress with a gold broach. Her luxuriant hair, just beginning to turn gray, was immaculately coifed. He looked at her smiling, dark-eyed image and thought the woman in the painting was beautiful. He wondered who she was. Bobby rolled a wheelchair beside the bed. Ivan smiled up at her, revealing teeth that were stained yellow with a chip in an incisor.

"I don't believe we've been introduced," he said.

"Come on, Ivan. I'm Bobby. You know who I am."

"I'm very pleased to make your acquaintance," he said.

"My. Such a gentleman," she mocked.

"You bet," Ivan said. "Where's my money?"

"Under the pillow."

"May I have it, please?" he asked. "I want to pay."

Bobby reached under the pillow on his bed and retrieved a thin, worn leather wallet. She handed it to Ivan. He unfolded it and saw a faded snapshot of he and Helen standing in front of a pagoda. The picture had been taken on a trip to Japan years ago. His arm was around her waist. He was smiling as if he had never been happier in his life. For a moment, he looked at the two of them together. A pretty couple, he thought, wondering who they were. He pulled a ten-dollar bill from the money compartment and gave it to Bobby.

"Here," he said. "This should cover everything."

Bobby reached down her shirt and tucked the bill into her bra.

"You're all paid up," she said. "Don't tell anyone,

though." She tickled him under the chin. "These trans-actions are just between us."

"You bet."

With her hands in his armpits, she hoisted him onto the seat of the wheelchair. "Ouch," he said.

"Pee-yoo," she said. "You stink."

"Where's my car?"

"What are you driving?"

Ivan looked bewildered. "Damned if I know."

"I'll bet you drove a Cadillac," Bobby said. "You were a big shot. A rich brain surgeon. I can tell you were rich by the way your son acts."

Ivan smiled at her and nodded as if in agreement, trying to remember his son's name. As the years passed, his son Eric kept retreating, moving further and further back in time. The mention of his son brought him forward into Ivan's fleeting consciousness. He had been such a good boy. Ivan loved him deeply. Ivan felt the same way he'd felt when his son was a doctor with the infantry in Vietnam, and Ivan feared that he wouldn't come home. What torture that had been. Now he longed to see him.

"Eric," he said. "Where's Eric?"

"I don't know," she said. "Let's take a shower. Get ready for Bingo and therapy. But first some breakfast." Her voice was singsongy. Falsely cheerful. "You hungry?"

"I just ate," Ivan said.

"What did they serve?"

Ivan thought for a moment. "Rice," he said.

Bobby shook her head and chuckled.

"We haven't served rice in a coon's age."

As if he were a broken machine, she stood him up in the shower and stripped the wet diaper from him. Naked, a shiver passed through him and goose bumps dotted the gray skin that hung on his bent frame. To ease his shortness of breath, he pursed his blue lips when he exhaled.

"Jesus, Ivan," she said, looking down at his flaccid, uncircumcised penis. "For a little guy, you've got a big one. I'll bet the ladies liked you."

She turned on the water and tested the temperature with the back of her hand. Standing behind him, she wrapped her arms around his waist. He could feel her breasts. He pressed back against her. She eased him down onto a plastic chair. Ivan liked the warm spray on his face and chest. In a moment of reverie, it was a summer day, and he was a boy playing in the rain. His mother was standing on the porch in her apron, telling him to come in and have cookies and lemonade.

"Be there in a minute, Mom," he blurted.

Bobby looked at him quizzically as she lathered up a washcloth with a bar of soap. She began washing his testicles, shrunken to the size of acorns from the hormone shots he received for his prostate cancer.

Next, she wrapped the cloth around his penis and slid it up and down. Ivan smiled at her.

"You like that, don't you? You naughty boy."

"Helen," he said.

"It's not Helen, lover boy. It's Bobby."

When she was drying him off, a heavy nurse in tight slacks and a golf shirt appeared in the doorway. She came to Ivan and pinched his cheek.

"Hi, sweetie," she said. She turned to Bobby. "The funeral home is here for Mrs. Ringer. We need you for a minute to help lift the body."

Bobby threw a towel over Ivan's lap and left him sitting in his wheelchair.

"Be back in a jiffy," she said. "Don't do anything I wouldn't do."

Ivan's hair was wet, his skin still damp. He shook all over. He wanted his sweater. He fingered the cardiac pacemaker that was implanted beneath the skin below his right collarbone, wondering what he was feeling. Through watery, red-rimmed eyes, he watched the morticians wheel a body covered with a sheet out of the room across the hall. Ivan heard the gurney rattle as they turned a corner. He wondered where his car was.

Bobby came back into the room. She removed the towel from Ivan's lap and teased him with it, holding it out like a matador's cape, calling him *el toro*. He pretended to try and pinch her.

"I don't believe I've made your acquaintance," Ivan said.

"It's me," Bobby said. "The Queen of Sheba."

She finished drying him. As she slid a diaper under him, Ivan raised his hips from the chair. A stab of pain in his leg startled him. From a rod in the closet where his meager selection of shirts and pants hung, Bobby selected a brown long-sleeved knit shirt and a pair of gray cotton slacks with the belt already in the loops. She smelled the pants and wrinkled her nose. She knelt down and inserted his feet into the legs and jerked them up. They gathered around his shrunken waist when she cinched the belt tight.

"Where's my car?" Ivan said.

"In the shop getting new tires."

"They won't let me drive anymore."

"Thank God," Bobby said.

When he was dressed and Bobby had tied his shoes, she ran her hand over his cheek.

"A shave can wait till tomorrow," she said. "A little stubble is sexy."

She wet a brush and parted his hair. With a scissors used to clip his toenails, she chopped away stray hair that hung over his ears. She picked up an Indianapolis Colts cap with a horseshoe logo from the dresser and set it on his head.

"Where's my sweater?" Ivan asked.

"Jesus, Ivan, it's hotter than blazes in here. You don't need a damned sweater."

As she rolled him out of the door, Ivan turned, still looking for his cardigan, but all he saw was the picture on the wall. He felt a pang that quickly passed. The corridor had been decorated to look like a village street: imitation lampposts, a pedestal bank clock with Roman numerals, and brick-like floor tiles. Ivan thought he was on his way to operate on a patient. Bobby steered him around a galvanized bucket with a mop sticking out. The smell of Lysol mingled with the odor of urine. In doorways old men and women slumped in their wheelchairs, catheter bags dangling. Blankets covered their laps. Some snored. Some just stared at the floor as if waiting for their hearts to stop.

A man with one leg shouted: "Hey, you. Hey!"

Ivan didn't know who these people were or why they were here, but he felt a vague camaraderie with them. A heaviness pressed down on him. He wanted to do something to make them happy.

"I'm paying," Ivan called out. "It's on me."

They passed the swinging door to the kitchen. The scent of frying bacon wafted to Ivan's nostrils, and he realized he was hungry. Because of his high cholesterol, Helen had only allowed him to have two strips of bacon and one egg once a week on Fridays. He breathed in the aroma from the griddle. It was the smell of happiness.

Friday, he thought. Bacon day. His face lit up, and the pain in his bones and joints was forgotten.

It was monthly theme day at Mirror Woods, and the dining room was decorated like a circus tent with helium-filled balloons and crepe paper streamers. A sign above a counter with pitchers of juice and a coffee urn advertised THE GREATEST SHOW ON EARTH. Bobby rolled Ivan's chair to a table covered with a white linen cloth under a protective glass cover. An elderly lady was already seated there, drinking a glass of orange juice. She was wearing a blue pantsuit and furry house slippers. She was a regal woman with a large aquiline nose and an abundance of white hair. Her tremulous hands were covered with brown spots. Around her neck hung a lei of yellow paper flowers left over from last month's luau.

"Here's Madge," Bobby said. "Your favorite girl."

Ivan looked at her with his rheumy eyes and smiled. He noticed the scent of her perfume. There was something familiar about it. Also, the blue color of her clothes reminded him of something that he couldn't place. The vacuum in his mind brought a twinge of pain to his forehead, and he pressed his hand above his eyes.

"I don't believe I've made your acquaintance," he said.

"Here we go again," Bobby said. "It's Madge, Ivan. You know. You played checkers with her yesterday. Madge. M-A-D-G-E."

Madge looked at him as if he were an animal of a strange breed. Then she turned away and stared off into the distance without speaking. Gloomily, Ivan looked down at his silverware, trying to remember where he'd left his car. Ava, a registered nurse, sashayed up to the table. She wore a polka dot clown suit and a black top hat. Her face had been painted white with giant red lips.

"Welcome to the big top." She tied a bib around Ivan's neck. She took off his ball cap and ran her fingers through his hair. "No hats in the dining room, dear."

She gave Ivan a hug and pranced away, swinging her hips. Overhead, an inflatable giraffe and zebra bobbed on strings suspended from a chandelier. Ivan saw them and he was frightened. He tried to stand up and flee, but he was tied into the chair. For a moment he struggled against the strap then gave up. Ava reappeared and placed a plastic cup filled with Ivan's morning medicine in front him: a diuretic pill, two blood pressure capsules, a vitamin, something to make him breathe better, something to keep his urine flowing, something to calm his nerves, something to strengthen the beat of his heart, something to enhance his memory. She handed him a baby aspirin and a glass of apple juice. A smile creased Ivan's face. He was thinking it was wine.

"I'm paying for dinner," he announced.

"You're already covered," she said. "Come on. Bottoms up, handsome boy."

Ivan choked down the pills with gulps of juice.

When he was finished, he held his glass up triumphantly. Ava took it, and Ivan turned to Madge.

"I'm very pleased to have made your acquaintance," he said.

Madge didn't speak, but she returned his smile. Ivan reached under the table and put his hand on her thigh, letting it rest there. The thinness of her leg surprised him. When she didn't object, Ivan lifted his hand and slid it up to her breast. It was large and soft—like a pillow that he wanted to put his head on. She smiled at him and made a noise in her throat. He gave her breast a little squeeze.

"Ivan, what are you doing?" Bobby scolded. "Stop that right now!"

She moved quickly to Ivan and jerked his hand away from Madge. Ivan felt a stab of pain in his shoulder. He let out a groan and dropped back in his chair. Ava hurried up to the table.

"What's going on here?" she said.

"He had his hand on her breast," Bobby said. "He was pawing her."

"Ivan," Ava said. "Shame on you. We don't do things like that." She bent down and put her arm around Madge. "Are you okay, dear? Did he hurt you?"

Madge looked at the nurse, bewildered.

"Everything is all right," Ava said. "We'll take care this. It won't happen again." She turned to Bobby. "Take him to his room. I'll notify the Director."

Everyone in the dining room stopped eating and stared as Bobby hustled Ivan out the door. Ivan felt confused. His heart pounded like a hammer. In his own room she parked him by the bed.

"How would you like to be pawed?" Bobby asked. "How would you like for me to grab you by the balls?"

Ivan looked up at the tall woman. Her eyes were cold, blue, and angry.

"Now, I'll have to write a goddamn incident report," she said and hurried out of the room.

Ivan sat blinking. He felt like he had to pee. So, he let it go. He hugged himself and tears came to his eyes. Soon Ava, still in her clown suit, and Mary Beth, the Mirror Woods Director, came into the room. Mary Beth, short and serious, wore high heels and a white lab coat over her dress. She carried a manila file in her hand.

"Dr. Jones," she said. "Do you realize what you did?"

"I don't believe I've made your acquaintance," Ivan said.

He felt very tense and afraid.

"Look at him," Ava said as if he were a statue in a wax museum. "He's totally clueless. What do we do now?"

Ivan looked out the window for his car. It seemed to him that everything he ever had was lost. That he no longer possessed anything at all.

"I'll have to report the incident to the state," Mary

Beth said. "I'll notify Madge's family. Hopefully, they won't raise a ruckus. We'll start a surveillance of Dr. Jones to cover ourselves."

"I'll call his son," Ava said. "Maybe there's a medication that would help, something to knock his libido down."

"I can't imagine he still has a libido," Mary Beth said. "In the meantime, keep him away from the female residents."

She moved to Ivan and bent over him. He twitched away from her, trembling.

"We can't have you doing this," she said. "Don't let it happen again. Do you hear?" Her lips closed in an uncompromising line. A shiver passed through Ivan.

"I want my sweater," he said.

DUSK CAME EARLY. It was Ivan's least favorite time of day. The air was blue and heavy and hard for him to breathe. The dim light always made it more difficult for him to see and contributed to his state of emptiness and confusion: his loneliness. Because of the incident with Madge, he had been confined to his room where he'd spent the day, not even leaving for physical therapy. As if he were an inmate on death row, every thirty minutes someone from the nursing staff came by to check on him and make a note on a chart. Ivan sat in his wheelchair facing the wall. The day of immobility had caused his hip and back to stiffen. He ached all the way up to his shoulders. In front of him on a metal cart was the dinner that had been brought to him: Swiss steak, macaroni and cheese, and fruit cocktail. His appetite was poor, and he had eaten little. He tried to think, but his mind was scattered. He didn't know where he was or why he had come there. He felt cold and he wanted his sweater. In the doorway, a tall, middle-aged man with a receding hairline appeared. He was wearing khakis, a blue blazer, and a club tie. With a wary look, Ivan watched him enter. In the dim light the man's face looked blurry but familiar.

"Hi, Dad," the man said. He bent down and gave Ivan an awkward hug.

Ivan's face broke out in a smile. "Hi, old friend."

"Don't you know who I am?"

"My number one son," Ivan said.

"That's right. And your only son. Name's Eric."

"Eric," Ivan said. "It's good to see you, old friend."

Eric carried Ivan's dinner tray to the hall and set it on the floor.

"How have you been, Dad?" he asked when he returned.

"Getting along pretty good."

"What did you do today?"

Ivan thought for a moment.

"Damned if I know," he said. "Took it easy, I guess. What's next?"

"Continue to take it easy," Eric said. "I brought your favorite dessert."

In front of Ivan on the metal cart, Eric placed a piece of strawberry cheesecake wrapped in cellophane.

"It's from Shapiros," Eric said. "You know, the deli where you and Mom took me when I was in medical school."

"Ooo-wee," Ivan said in falsetto.

Eric settled onto the orange loveseat. For a few moments, they sat without speaking. Ivan's head bobbed continually in a palsied nod. He took off his hat and held it close to his eyes, straining to see the horse-shoe logo embroidered above the bill.

"Cubs," he finally said.

"Colts," Eric said.

Ivan rubbed his eyes. "What do I do?"

"Just take it easy," Eric said. "Let's talk about what happened today. The nurse tells me you touched a lady on the breast. They're making a big fuss about it. What's the story?"

"Where are we going to have dinner?" Ivan said. "I'm treating."

"Let's talk about this deal with the lady's breast. What exactly did you do?"

"Where's your car?" Ivan asked.

"In the lot right outside the window."

"I don't drive anymore."

"Tell me about it. I almost had to knock you over the head to get the keys away from you."

"It's good to see you, old friend," Ivan said.

"About the lady, Dad. You can't do that. I know it's hard with all the girls after you." Eric cleared his throat. "But it's against the rules, even if she wanted you to. You can't put your hands on people, particularly women. You've always been a perfect gentleman. You don't want to ruin your reputation at this late date. They aren't going to put up with it."

"It's sure good to see you," Ivan said.

Eric shook his head and unwrapped the cheesecake's cellophane. It was a gorgeous dessert, four inches high of creamy cake topped with big red strawberries in a thick glaze. Ivan picked up a fork and cut off a piece. He wanted something to drink with his dessert. He looked around for Helen. He didn't like that she wasn't there to get him a glass of something to drink. He wanted her to sit down and keep him company while he ate. He put the bite of cake in his mouth. He smiled at how sweet and good it tasted.

"Who do I owe for this?" he said.

"Don't talk with your mouth full," Eric said.

"Where's your car?" Ivan asked after he'd swallowed.

"In the parking lot. I haven't moved it since you last asked." Eric let out a sigh and leaned back in the loveseat, watching his father, wondering how it had come to this.

Ivan ate the cake slowly, savoring each bite, thinking of nothing but the taste in his mouth.

"That cheesecake, it must be good," Eric said. "I'm glad something gives you pleasure."

"Damned if I know," Ivan said. When he was finished, he placed his fork on the table and looked up at Eric. "Where are we going for dinner?"

"Dinner's said and done," Eric wiped strawberry glaze from the corners of Ivan's mouth with a Kleenex.

"Who do I owe?" Ivan asked.

"Nobody. Your owing days are over."

Carrying a flashlight and a chart fastened to a clipboard, the night nurse appeared in the doorway. She was heavyset and wore a plastic back brace outside of her clothes. Ivan noticed her large bosom.

"How's it going in here?" she asked.

"He hasn't attacked anyone," Eric said, "if that's what you mean."

"I'm sure he hasn't," she said. She moved to Ivan and ruffled his hair with her hand.

"I don't believe I've made your acquaintance," he said.

"I'm Lois," she said. "The nurse." She looked at Eric. "We just have to keep an eye on him. It's part of the routine."

"Look at him," Eric said. "He's just an old man who

doesn't know where he is. He can't walk. He's weak as a cat. He's not a threat to anyone. This is a massive overreaction to what happened."

"It's the rules. If we don't follow them, we lose our license. I'm just following orders."

"He's my number one son," Ivan said, smiling.

"I know," she said. She made a note on the chart then looked at her watch. "It's time for bed, Mr. Jones. I'll take you to the bathroom."

"That's okay," Eric said. "I'll do it tonight. If the rules allow it, that is. And by the way, he's Dr. Jones."

"You can take him if that's what you want," she said.

Eric rolled Ivan into the bathroom and helped him onto the stool. He pulled off Ivan's pants and wrestled him out of his diaper. While Eric waited outside, he read a profile of Ivan that was displayed on the wall under a clear plastic cover:

I prefer to be called Ivan. My home state is Indiana. I was a neurosurgeon at Ball Hospital. I have one child named Eric. My wife's name was Helen, and she is deceased. Special people in my life are my family. My areas of interest are checkers and exercise group. I used to golf at Delaware Country Club. My favorite words of wisdom or advice are "Be Kind."

Eric shook his head. He was near tears.

"I'm finished," Ivan called. "Come get me."

Eric put a new diaper on Ivan and dressed him in the striped pajamas he had given him for Christmas. He transferred his father back to the wheelchair. He squirted paste on a toothbrush and handed it to his father.

While he cleaned his teeth, Ivan puzzled over his reflection in the mirror. He thought he was looking at a picture on the wall. He wondered who the old man with a funny haircut and red-rimmed eyes was. He dropped his toothbrush in the sink. Eric wet a comb and parted his hair.

"Worst haircut, I've ever seen," Eric said. "What did they use, pinking shears?"

"Where's my car?" Ivan asked.

"I think I'm talking to a parrot," Eric said.

He wheeled Ivan to his bed and helped him in.

"Where's my car?"

"Oh Dad, Jesus," Eric said. "Stop it. I can't take it anymore. Just don't say anything."

At the angry sound of the voice, Ivan cowered, covering his face with his arms.

"Don't hurt me," he said.

"I'm sorry, Dad. I'm not going to hurt you. I know you can't help it." For a while, Eric sat on the corduroy-covered couch with his head down. "Your mind is a mystery to everyone but you, isn't it?"

Ivan nodded and smiled.

"Damned if I know," he said. "It's cold in here. I want my sweater."

Eric found an old cardigan golf sweater on a hanger in the closet. He held it as Ivan worked his arms into the sleeves.

"You wore this when we played golf with Mom," Eric said. "We had a lot of fun, didn't we? I wish we could play again." His eyes glistened. "Just the three of us."

"You bet," Ivan said.

Eric reached down and buttoned his father's sweater. Ivan fell back on his pillow. Eric pointed at the portrait of Helen hanging on the wall.

"Do you know who that is?" he asked.

Ivan thought for a moment, and then he nodded his head. "You bet."

"Is it Mom?" Eric urged.

"Yes," Ivan said. "It's Mom."

"That's right," Eric said. "That's who you thought the woman in the dining room was. You thought she was Mom. It's okay that you touched her." He pulled the blanket up to Ivan's chin. "You're a good man, Dad. If they don't want us here, we'll go somewhere else. Go to sleep now." He switched off the bedside lamp. "Sweet dreams."

Eric moved to the doorway. He stood silently backlit by the nightlight in the corridor. For a while he gazed at his father. With the back of his hand, he blotted his wet eyes. Then he turned and disappeared down the hallway.

For Ivan, the day was over and forgotten. He felt exhausted as if he had been on a long forced march to a place he didn't know. He heard the crescendo of Eric's car engine as his son drove out of the parking lot into a world that was inconsequential to Ivan. Thin lines of light leaked through the blinds from the streetlamp outside the window and striped the portrait of Helen. Ivan looked at the painting he had labored over years ago. His mind didn't know who the woman was, but something in his heart did. He moved his gaze back to the ceiling. He felt under his pillow and was relieved to find his wallet. The cardigan sweater he wore over his pajamas warmed him. He closed his eyes, feeling as if he were about to be set free. And soon he was asleep.

OLD DOGS

KREBS HAD PRACTICED general and vascular surgery in Southern Indiana for thirty-five years. He was the first surgeon between Louisville and Indianapolis who was board certified. A surgeon was who he was. It was as if he had been born to operate. Since Elsie, his wife of forty years, died five years ago, Krebs felt there was nothing else left for him but medicine. The hospital and the operating room had become his home, the nurses and his patients his family. It was well past midnight when a ring awakened him from a dreamless sleep. Krebs groped in the dark for the phone. His hand found the receiver, and he pressed its cold plastic to his ear.

"Dr. Krebs?" the voice said.

"Yeah. Who's this?"

"It's Vandergraff. I'm in the ER. I've got a guy with a leaking aneurysm."

Fuck, Krebs thought.

"You sure of the diagnosis?" he said.

"The CAT scan confirms it. There's no doubt."

"What kind of shape is he in?"

"Bad. Can't keep his pressure up. I doubt he'll survive."

"Get his ass to the OR," Krebs said. "I'm on my way."

"We'll be waiting for you."

Krebs heard the receiver click. He hung up and, with stinging eyes, waited for the fog of sleep to clear. He pictured the man on an operating table. A pool of blood in his belly. For an instant, he wished the patient dead so he could escape back into the warmth and sweetness of sleep. But then he pried himself from the bed and made his way to the bathroom. His knees were stiff, and the joints of his fingers ached. He splashed cold water on his face and ran a brush through a nest of gray hair. He pulled on a fresh set of scrubs that he kept at home for occasions like this.

In a yellow slicker and hunting boots, Krebs hurried through the dark to his car. Through ghost-ridden streets, he drove his Mercedes diesel with 100,000 miles on the odometer toward the hospital. It was cold in the car. Without a moon or stars, the sky was black. A light rain fell. He could see the drops slanting through the beams of his headlights. The streets downtown were empty, the windows of the storefronts dark.

Krebs felt as if he were the only person on earth. The life of a surgeon seemed unbearably hard, a young man's game. He wondered if he should still be playing it. But what else was there?

Krebs saw the hospital looming before him, and with it, stacks spewing smoke into the night. Adrenaline seeped into his circulation, and his pulse sped. He thought of the last aortic aneurysm he'd operated on. It was two months ago. Vandergraff, the resident on his service, had assisted him with the surgery. The bulge in the aorta was small and hadn't ruptured. In his prime, Krebs, a former basketball player, would have called the surgery a slam dunk. But the operation had gone badly. The suture line where he sewed the graft to the aorta had bled in the recovery room. Krebs rushed the patient back to the OR, but it was too late. The man's blood wouldn't clot in spite of transfusions of fresh frozen-plasma and platelets, and he died on the table. After the surgery, Krebs was in the bathroom of the surgeons' locker room, grieving for the patient and himself. He overhead Vandergraff talking to a first-year resident about the case.

"He's over the hill," Vandergraff had said.

Krebs was ashamed of what had happened. His very essence was in doubt. He felt as if he were merely an impersonation of the surgeon he once had been. Every time he thought of the case, he felt miserable. Now, remembering the man's death brought a cold hollowness to his chest. Was he up to what lay ahead?

KREBS STEPPED into the operating room. White light. White tile walls. A gleaming terrazzo floor. Everything was clean and cold, white and hard as bleached bone. In green gowns and latex gloves, his surgical team was preparing the patient for him. Sue, the circulating RN, lathered the man's belly with an amber solution of Betadine soap. Vandergraff stood by a lighted view box on the wall; it displayed a CT scan of the patient's abdomen. Over his gloved hands a sterile towel was draped. The young resident was lean with doubting metallic-blues eyes above his mask. Even before he overheard Vandergraff's "over the hill" accusation, Krebs didn't care for him. He thought the rookie was cocky, and he didn't like the way he treated the nurses in the operating room. Vandergraff was smart, but Krebs believed that becoming a good surgeon involved more than mastering operating techniques and the science of medicine. It required a sensitivity and compassion that he didn't see in Vandergraff. Gerta, a sturdy scrub nurse who came from down near Paoli, a small village in southern Indiana, arranged instruments in tidy rows on a Mayo stand—brushed steel hemostats, German-made needle drivers, forceps, towel clips, and thousand-dollar Metzenbaum scissors. To Krebs, the expensive hardware had become as commonplace as tools to a builder.

"Howdy, Dr. K," Gerta said in her Hoosier twang.

"Howdy, Gerta," Krebs said.

He was grateful Gerta was on the case. The former farm girl was hardworking, smart, and plain-spoken. She had scrubbed for Krebs for years and knew his routine nearly as well as he did. She anticipated what he needed and stayed a step ahead. His operations went smoother when she was passing the instruments.

At the head of the operating table, Bill Riley, the anesthesiologist, stood pumping blood into the patient's IV line with a rubber-gloved hand. He was a likable Irishman with a ruddy face, big belly, and orange eyebrows. Pasted to his gas machine was a sticker with VIGILANCE in red letters. On the stool behind him sat a copy of *The Wall Street Journal*. He saluted Krebs.

"At ease, Private Riley," Krebs said.

Krebs was a hunter of quail and pheasants before their habitat was plowed under and the birds disappeared from the state. In the operating room, all his senses were sharpened as they once were with his beloved English Pointer and a 20-gauge Browning Citori in a cornfield. He saw everything. He saw the monofilament sutures on the Mayo stand. He saw the aortic grafts made of corrugated Dacron. He could smell the hot, dry odor of instruments fresh out of the autoclave.

He could hear the green bleeps of the cardiac monitor. In the blaze of the operating light, he saw the anesthetized patient on the table. Just as Krebs had pictured him over the phone, the patient was fat and grizzled, with a scruffy beard and white hair that curled over his ears. His eyebrows were thick and wild, his toenails yellow and gnarled. A catheter in his long, flaccid penis drained dark urine into a plastic bag. Krebs wondered who the man was, what family he had, what he would say if asked to prove he still had a meaningful life.

Krebs moved to Vandergraff's side. The young resident towered over the short and stoop-shouldered Krebs.

"So, Doctor," Krebs said, keeping his eyes on the view box. "Tell me about the patient?"

"He worked at the grain elevator in Seymour," Vandergraff said. "He's sixty going on a hundred. He's a diabetic with emphysema and prostate cancer. He's on Digoxin, Lasix, Lipitor, Lupron, and GlucaGon."

"Piss poor protoplasm," Krebs said. "He'd be high risk for a haircut."

Krebs studied the grainy CAT-scan images of the swollen aorta. He noted the interruption in the ring of calcium in the wall of the aneurysm and the puddle of white contrast material that had leaked through the blockage. He estimated the diameter of the aneurysm to be a large 12 to 14 centimeters. He was relieved to see that the dilatation started below the renal arteries.

"So, Dr. Vandergraff," Krebs said, "based on your vast experience with abdominal aortic aneurysms, what do you think of the case?"

"We've got a tiger by the tail," Vandergraff said.

As an undergraduate at Wabash College, Krebs had been an English major as well as a premed. He still loved literature, particularly modernism with small details of sensory input and psychic life. Recently he had been rereading Faulkner and Hemingway. He thought of Hemingway's "The Short Happy Life of Francis Macomber" and the Somali proverb that said a brave man is always frightened three times by a lion: when he sees his track; when he hears him roar; and when he first confronts him.

"No, son," Krebs said. "Not a tiger. It's a lion. A big one."

Krebs swung his gaze from the view box back to the patient on the operating table. As if he were wearing a pair of tie-dyed pants, the man on the table was blue and mottled from the umbilicus down. It was an ominous sign that meant the circulation to the lower half of his body was inadequate. The mountain of the old man's belly caused a voice inside Krebs to groan. Everything about the surgery was going to be a bitch. There was a time not too long ago when Krebs believed he could rip an aorta in two with his hands and repair it before the patient bled to death. He wondered if he still possessed the technical skills to do the job. A sense of dread crowded in on him. He looked up at the cardiac monitor above Riley's head. A hieroglyph of blips scrolled across the screen.

"How's the guy doing?" he asked.

"He ain't no rose," Riley said from his seat behind the ether screen. "But he's got a pressure. At least for the time being."

"How much blood you got?" Krebs asked.

"Four units typed and crossed," Riley said. "We're working on more."

Sue finished her prep and tossed a sponge into a metal bucket. Gerta stepped up to the operating table and, one at a time, handed Vandergraff folded blue towels. The resident began draping the belly.

"No. No," Krebs said sharply. "Don't fence me in. Go wide with those drapes. He's a big boy. We're going to need all the room we can get." He turned and started toward the door. "I'm going to wash my paddies, then we'll get this show on the road."

Krebs stood at the sink in the corridor and scrubbed his hands with a stiff brush and cold water. He rehearsed the techniques and pitfalls of aneurysm repair, and warned himself to stay away from the ureters. Would he need to open the chest to get control of the aorta? Would he be able to use a straight graft instead of a Y-graft? Krebs reminded himself to release the aortic clamp slowly to avoid a drop in blood pressure. He didn't want the guy to suffer a myocardial infarction or stroke while he was on the table.

When Krebs finished his scrub, he held out his hands. He turned them slowly and studied them. His fingers vibrated with a tremor. This surgery required more fine-motor control than most. He hoped he could still do the job.

With water dripping from his elbows, Krebs backed through the door into the operating room. Gerta handed him a towel, and he dried from fingertips to elbows. The scrub nurse held out a green cloth gown, and Krebs plunged his arms into its sleeves. While Sue tied him up, Gerta gloved him. He could smell Sue's perfume, the scent of sandalwood.

"Sue City Sue," Krebs said. "Sweetest girl I ever knew."

Sue patted his butt. Krebs smiled under his mask, thinking he didn't have much of an ass anymore.

"Oh, Jesus," Riley grumbled with a twinkle in his eyes. "It's a love-in."

Krebs bellied up to the table beside Greta and across from Vandergraff. He rested his hands on the patient's big abdomen. The pulsations of the aneurysm banged like an angry fist on a door. He held out his open hand, and Gerta slapped the handle of a scalpel into it. For a moment, Krebs peered over the ether screen at the man's pale face. Riley was patching his eyes with gauze to protect them from corneal abrasions. With each puff of the ventilator, the plastic tube in the old man's trachea frosted like breath on a cool window. Saliva gurgled in his mouth.

God help you, fellow, Krebs prayed silently. God help me.

He swung his gaze away from the man's face to his belly. With a single swipe of the knife, Krebs cut him from sternum to pubis. A fatty red gash appeared. Vandergraff jabbed at oozing capillaries under the skin with the cautery. A blue spark sizzled at the tip of his instrument, and smoke wafted from the wound. Krebs frowned beneath his mask. He didn't like the young resident's surgical technique, his herky-jerky moves. An operation should have rhythm and grace, like a waltz.

"Easy there," he said gruffly. "You're a bull in a china shop."

"Then you do it," Vandergraff said, offering him the cautery.

"You do it. But do it right. Be gentle. Be smooth."

Using a pair of Mayo scissors and taking care not to nick the underlying structures, Krebs opened the membranous lining of the abdomen. The filmy curtain of the peritoneum parted, and he looked down into the abdominal cavity. Although he had entered this canyon of anatomy thousands of times, he still found it a place of mystery. The organs it contained were strangely beautiful. A "sweet work of nature", he thought—a line from Shakespeare. The man's liver, cobbled from alcohol, crouched beneath the dome of the diaphragm. His omental fat was an apron of glistening, gold globules. Like a nest of snakes, the small intestines gleamed and writhed in the light. Krebs dove his hand deep into their midst and felt warmth and wetness through his glove. His fingers found the big aneurysm, tense and beating as if it were an extra heart. Krebs took a deep breath and began packing away the intestines in a plastic bag that he covered with laparotomy sponges.

Chitlins, Gerta called them.

Krebs handed Vandergraff two silver retractors to hold for exposure; he wanted to tie up the resident's hands and keep them out of the way. Then he changed his mind and asked Gerta for a self-retaining retractor so Vandergraff's hands would be free when he needed them. Now, Krebs had a clear view of the aneurysm, throbbing and tawny. He thought again of the lion-hunting proverb's three times of fright. The size of his prey gave Krebs a cool, electric sensation.

"Caramba," he muttered.

His eyes found a blue hematoma in the tissues that surrounded the aorta; blood had leaked from the crack in the aneurysm's weakened wall. A clot had formed that tamponaded the hemorrhage and saved the old man's life. Krebs wanted to get control of the aorta quickly before the clot had time to let go.

"Right angle," he barked.

"Which one?" Gerta asked.

"Give him the Mixter clamp," Vandergraff said.

"Christ, no," Krebs said. "Something blunter."

Gerta passed him the instrument he wanted, and he began to dissect around the neck of the aneurysm. With the tip of the clamp, Krebs cautiously probed and spread dense tissues. Even though he had lost some of his dexterity, his instincts were still intact. The going was tough, and he worked slowly through the inflammation. Frequently he changed the direction of his dissection to try and find the path of least resistance around the aorta. The renal vein was stretched precariously over the aorta. To damage it could be fatal.

"Don't tear, you son of a bitch," Krebs said silently as he nudged the big vein aside with his clamp.

Sweat beaded his forehead and soaked his cap. During the past couple of year, Krebs had lost the fortitude to accept complications. At times he was overly cautious, playing not to lose in the operating room. *First, do no harm* had always been his credo. But he knew that by trying to do no harm, he could, in fact, do harm. Now he told himself to be bold.

Krebs returned the right-angle clamp to Gerta and began dissecting behind the aorta with the index finger of his right hand. Blindly, painstakingly, he pushed and probed, wiggling the tip of his finger. The aortic pulse was savage. After a while, his hand began to cramp. But he kept working. Finally, he found his thumb and index finger encircling the aorta. He let out a long, sighing breath.

"Give me the Riley clamp," he said to Gerta. "The big ugly one?" Krebs was trying to relax everyone, including himself, with a little humor.

"Oh great," Riley said. "It's *Saturday Night Live*."

Gerta slapped an aortic clamp into Krebs's hand. The instrument was a DeBakey, named for the great Texas cardiovascular surgeon who was one of Krebs's heroes. Most all of his heroes were doctors like William Carlos Williams, Jonas Salk, and Chekhov. The DeBakey was a beautiful instrument, long and light with its handle gracefully curved like the neck of a heron. Krebs loved the clamp the way he had loved his favorite shotgun. When he ratcheted its jaws down on the artery, he felt a crunch as it crushed the calcium in the wall of the vessel. He cringed, hoping he hadn't loosened atheromatous debris that would embolize to the legs. But what was done had to be done. It was an example of risking harm to do no harm. He sighed. Sewing in the calcified artery would be difficult, and he prayed that his sutures would hold.

Krebs took a scalpel from Greta and opened the aneurysm with a longitudinal incision in the big bulge. The artery was filled with clot and a soft ripe material that looked like Limburger cheese. Krebs could almost smell it. How could something this rotten exist inside a living human being? For an instant, Krebs resented the man's bad habits, his smoking and the dietary indiscretions that had created this surgical ordeal. Gerta handed him a serving spoon that he used to scoop the cheesy material from inside the aneurysm. Vandergraff held out an emesis basin, and Krebs dropped the spoon's contents into it.

"Good old Hoosier gunk," Gerta said.

Since his wife's death, Krebs' own diet was unhealthy, deep fried and full of unsaturated fats. It occurred to him that he ate no better than the man he was operating on. He wondered what his own aorta looked like, but at his age, he didn't much care. When he analyzed the patient's distal aorta, he was relieved to see that a straight graft could be used rather than a Y-graft. That would cut down the operating time, and he could get the old boy off the table sooner.

Krebs took the tube of Dacron and soaked it in pool of blood to pre-clot it and cut down on blood loss.

"Why aren't you using Gortex?" Vandergraff asked.

"Because he likes Dacron," Gerta said.

Krebs smiled at her loyalty. Blood was pooling around the aorta.

"Suck the goddamn puddle," he said. "Come on, son. Keep it dry."

Krebs began to sew—graft to host, Dacron to tunica. From across the table, Vandergraff grasped the suture.

"Keep the son-of-a-bitch tight," Krebs said.

"I am," Vandergraff said.

"Then keep it tighter," Krebs said.

With each stitch, calcium plaque dulled the needle. He tipped his head so that his bifocals focused better. The armpits of his scrub suit were soaked. His back ached. He steadied the needle holder with his left hand and took big bites in hopes the stitches wouldn't tear out. He worked without talking except for essential commands to Vandergraff like "Sponge," or "Come on, Doctor, suck."

Krebs came to a difficult corner of the anastomosis. His angle was bad, and he couldn't position his hand properly to take the stitch.

"I have a straight shot," Vandergraff said.

He reached for the needle driver. Krebs pushed his hand away. He flipped the needle over in the jaws of the instrument and took the stitch backhanded.

"Nice, Doc," Gerta said in her country voice.

"Old dog. New trick," Krebs said.

He glanced up at Vandergraff. For an instant, their gazes locked, then Vandergraff looked away.

"Old dog can still hunt," Gerta said.

"Old dog's bark is worse than his bite," Riley quipped. On his stool, he was drinking Coke through a straw that ran under his mask.

Krebs was fighting to keep his concentration. He was aware of the quick, deep stabs of the ventilator's breaths. The green sound of the monitor's bleeps.

"Enough chatter," he said, and he kept suturing.

When the anastomoses were complete, Krebs took a deep breath. He turned from the operating table to let Sue wipe sweat from his brow with a towel. He looked up at the clock on the wall. Two hours had passed.

"How's he doing?" he asked Riley.

"Hanging in," Riley said.

"When you think he's ready," Krebs said to Riley, "I'm going to release the clamp."

"Let me fill up his tank," Riley said.

He turned a valve on the IV line, and a stream of saline poured into the patient's vein. With his hands resting on the drapes, Krebs waited. I'm nothing but a high-priced plumber, he thought. But that's okay. Plumbing was an honorable way to make a living.

When the systolic pressure rose to eighty, Riley told him to try opening the aortic clamp. Krebs slowly released the DeBakey while Riley counted out the systolic pressure.

"Seventy. Down to sixty," Riley said.

Krebs clicked the clamp closed. He wondered if the old guy's heart had given up.

After a couple of minutes, Riley said, "Up to ninety. Try it again."

Krebs opened the clamp very slowly, and this time the pressure held. He was relieved to see that there was minimal leakage from his suture line. He stood for a few seconds, watching the tubular conduit of Dacron pulsate, bringing blood and life to the man's legs. In the bright overhead light, the graft shone with the white radiance of a star. Krebs was aware of the beat of his own heart. He thought of the man's age, how far his legs had taken him, how tired they must be. His own legs felt heavy.

Krebs took his time tidying up the belly. Cauterizing bleeders. Pleating the wall of the aneurysm over the graft with 3-0 Vicryl. Irrigating the wound copiously with saline. When he was certain there was no bleeding and there was nothing else do, he said he was ready to close. Gerta and Sue counted the blood-soaked sponges, and Sue announced that the count was correct.

"You must be pooped," Vandergraff said. "Want me to close?"

"Who's tired? Not me."

Then, Krebs told himself to be patient with the resident. Performing surgery wasn't like learning to ride a bike—you didn't get it all at once. But then once you did, you never lost it, so in that it was the same.

"Okay," Krebs said. "You can close." He stepped back from the table. "Use retention sutures. I don't want this guy coming apart."

"I know the drill," Vandergraff said.

Krebs stripped off his gown. He balled it up and tossed it toward a hamper as if the gown were a basketball. It went in like the two-handed set shot he'd made in the regional tournament against Muncie Central back in 1958. How great it would be to have his youth back, to play the game and win.

Krebs went to the foot of the table and raised the drapes. The man's legs were still cold and blue, but Krebs could feel a weak pulse in the arteries of his ankles. Satisfied that his patient had circulation to his feet, Krebs moved to the head of the table. Riley patted his shoulder and handed him the chart.

"Good work, Old Dog," he said.

"He going to make it?" Krebs asked.

"I don't know. He's rocky, but he's got a chance. I'm going to keep him on a ventilator."

Krebs nodded. Even though he had reached an age when the possibility of death had lost most of its impact, he didn't want the patient to die on his watch. Gerta was placing dirty instruments in a stainless-steel dishpan. Krebs picked up his DeBakey clamp. After he retired, it would make a nice memento of his years in the operating room.

With his head down, he started toward the recovery room. At the door he stopped and looked back at the old man on the table. Riley had removed the patches from his eyes, and the patient appeared to be human again. His face was pale and gray. His chest rose rhythmically with the beat of the ventilator. Krebs felt one with him. If the man survived, would his life be meaningful? But then, when it came right down to it, the value of the man's existence was not Krebs' to judge.

He was trained to be a keeper of life, not a terminator, not a critique of its value. Life itself was a terminal illness. All that he had ever done in the operating room was mere palliation.

"Thank you all," he said, turning to his team. "You did great. You, too, Vandergraff."

Krebs raised the DeBakey clamp in a salute. Then he turned and walked from the operating room into the corridor.

MORNING SUNLIGHT BLOOMED in the windows to the east of the hospital. A nurse and an orderly wheeled a gurney that carried the first case of the day. Their green gowns rippled like sails gathering wind. The patient was a frightened child with a fractured femur. Krebs smiled down at him in a reassuring way.

In the recovery room's dictating booth, Krebs sprawled onto a chair. For a moment, he thought of all the years he had practiced surgery and how many abdominal aortic aneurysms he had repaired. He did the math in his head and decided it was close to three hundred. That's a hell of a lot, Krebs thought. Man, time went by fast. A pigeon perched on a windowsill, and it occurred to Krebs that the bird would likely outlive him.

Rosemary, a veteran RN with dyed ginger hair,

brought Krebs a cup of hot coffee and two homemade deviled eggs. She called Krebs "Special K." Rosemary had worked around the OR as long as Krebs had. Like Gerta, she'd been through the wars with him. Krebs thanked her and told her she still looked damned good for an old dog.

"Best in show?" she said, posing with her hands on her hips.

"You bet," he said.

Krebs ate the eggs slowly, savoring their mustardy flavor. He sipped the coffee and started to write the post-operative orders: Morphine for pain, vital signs q 15 minutes until stable, and then every hour. He couldn't remember the dose of the new cephalosporin antibiotic everyone was using. He'd better let Vandergraff write the orders.

Krebs closed the chart and picked up the aortic clamp. For a while he sat, clicking its jaws open and closed. He liked the way the instrument felt in his hand. He tipped his chair back, closed his eyes, and waited for his patient.

PALLIATION

ON A WINTER NIGHT, the ring of a telephone awakens David Fuller from a brooding, sepia-toned dream where he is standing at an operating table paralyzed with indecision and unable to act. The surgeon knows the call will be about his patient, Joe Turner. A year ago, David removed a colon cancer that was blocking the legendary Presbyterian minister's large intestine. David believed he had cured Joe, but at the man's six-month follow up, a CAT scan revealed grape-sized metastases to his liver. The tumor resisted 5FU chemotherapy and spread to other organs until his belly was solid with tumor. Joe is dying slowly. David can't look at him, gray and gaunt, consumed by malignancy, without feeling that he has failed him.

With burning eyes, David glances at a digital clock on the bedside stand. It is twenty-two minutes past midnight. He gropes in the dark for the receiver. Finally, his hand finds the phone. He presses it to his ear, hoping a voice will announce that death has put an end to Joe's suffering.

"Dr. Fuller," David says.

"It's Ruth," Joe's wife of fifty-two years says in an unsteady voice. "We need you. Joe's miserable." She sounds as if she has been crying. "He moans continually. Sometimes he's out of his head. The pain medicine isn't holding. I can't stand seeing him like this. Please come over."

"I'll be right there," David says.

For a moment, David doesn't move, remembering his conversation with Joe when he made a house call a week ago. In his book-walled study, Joe, exhausted and short of breath, was sprawled on a leather recliner. Because his liver was failing, he was deeply jaundiced, his skin the color of summer squash. His eyes, sunken in their sockets, were glazed. Once defined by his wit and intelligence, now he was defined by his pain and suffering. For David to watch him die was like seeing a tall building implode and crumble into dust. On a small table next to the recliner sat a cardboard box filled with yellowed manuscripts. One by one, Joe was reading them and then pitching them into another box.

"What's up, old friend?" David said. "Cleaning house?"

"In a manner of speaking," Joe said. "These are old sermons and my poems. I'm getting rid of them."

"Jesus, Joe," David said. "You can't do that. They're valuable. They're great literature full of wisdom and history."

"Yeah, yeah," Joe said. "What they are is ancient history. Nothing but detritus. Just as I am." He tossed another sermon into the box. "My life on earth is complete."

"Don't be so sure," David said. "There's a new experimental protocol for stage IV colon cancer. It's a combination of chemotherapeutic drugs. I could see if you're eligible for the study."

"Surely you jest," Joe said. "Look at me, Doctor."

He unbuttoned the shirt of his pajamas to display a washboard chest. Hairless and emaciated, he looked like a patient in the Buchenwald typhus ward.

"There's nothing left of me. Why would you even think of more chemotherapy? If Pontius Pilate had access to chemotherapy, he would have prescribed it for Jesus before he sent him to the cross."

David agreed that some chemotherapy was as barbaric as some religions. He believed that years from now, the way hopeless cancers were treated would be viewed in the same way cranial trephination, cautery with a hot iron, and bloodletting by leeches were now viewed.

"If you feel that way, then it's time to bring hospice

in," David said. "They're experts at palliation. They can make you comfortable. Make your days as full as possible."

"I'm nothing but a burden to you and Ruth and everyone else," Joe said. "It's senseless to go on. Why prolong things?" Joe paused a minute to regain his breath. "Look, what I feel more than anything is gratitude. I've had a rich life. I've had the privilege of being a minister to people on this wonderful earth. I've been loved and I have loved. It's been a terrific ride, but now my earthly life is over."

David shifted in his chair.

"So what exactly do you want from me?"

"I've come to the shore of a wide river," Joe said, ever the poet. "I want you to help me across to the other side where there's green grass and shade." With his jaundiced eyes, he looked at David. "Give me medicine that will put to me to sleep."

David took a deep breath and thought for a moment.

"I can't do that, Joe," he said. "To withhold care's one thing. To do something active to end a life. Well, that's something else. I'm sorry. I just can't do it. Not even for you."

"Why not?" Joe cocked his head and looked at David. "It can't be because of your fear of God."

"Jesus, Joe," David said. "I'm a doctor. I'm a life extender, not an ender. I took an oath to do no harm."

"Maybe you ought to rethink 'harm.'" Joe rolled on

his side and let out a groan. "Let me ask you something. What do you think death is?"

David thought for a moment. "I don't have a good answer. Somehow it seems more what isn't than what is."

"Explain that," Joe said.

"Well, when death happens, the body becomes an empty vessel. There's no heartbeat. No brain activity. No thoughts. No emotions. It's nothingness. I would define it by what's gone from a person. So what do you think it is?"

"I see it differently," Joe said. "Death isn't the end of anything, even your body. The atoms and molecules that make you up don't die when you decay. They continue on as something else in other living forms. In grass and trees and the critters who eat them. Your atoms become other living things, just as they were part of something else before they were you. And that's just your body." Joe paused for a drink of water. "Then there is your soul. It lives on in those you love and those who love you. I will live on in Ruth and my parishioners. You will live on in Marie and your patients. And, of course, there's God's eternal love for us. That's what I believe immortality is. Life may seem to fade with time, but life is endless." He rummaged through the box of sermons. He pulled one out and held it up. "I preached about immortality in this sermon. I titled it 'God Loves You. Endlessly.' I consider it a summation of my theology."

"You make a great case for death's glory," David shook his head. "I'm sorry. I'd do almost anything for you, but I can't end your life here on earth. It would go against the oath I took to preserve life."

"Then I'll do it myself."

"What do you mean?"

"I'll stop eating and drinking."

"Come on, Joe. Let's give hospice a try."

"Gandhi did it," Joe said. "So can I."

He pitched his "God Loves You" sermon into the box. The effort left him winded.

IN THE DARK, David climbs out of bed. He stubs his toe on a bedside stand.

"Damn it," he says.

"What's the matter?" his wife Marie asks. She sits up and turns on a lamp. "Are you all right?"

"No. I'm not okay."

"What's the matter?"

"The call. It was Ruth about Joe. He's not doing well."

"That poor man," Marie says. "He's so dear. What are you going do?"

"I don't know. Go see him. Try to make him comfortable."

"Isn't it time for Joe to go?"

"Yes, but how? Do you think I should put him to rest and betray my oath?"

"When you see him," Marie says, "you'll do the right thing."

DAVID DRIVES slowly through the winter night, thinking, trying to decide how best to palliate Joe. The air is cold and glass-like. It seems as if the night might shatter. In the downtown, windows are dark, the streets deserted. A liquid moon casts the shadows of clouds on the sidewalks. He continues by the hospital where he is a member of the medical staff and Chief of Surgery. On the second floor, there are lights in the windows of the operating suite where he removed Joe's cancer. When he agreed to do Joe's surgery, he violated his own rule that he wouldn't operate on close friends or family because he knew he couldn't tolerate complications or failures in someone close to him. The emotional strain would be too much for him to handle, and he would lose his objectivity. Now that fear has come calling again, and he regrets agreeing to perform Joe's surgery.

David parks in a dark alley behind his office and unlocks the back door. He feels as if he is breaking and entering. He punches buttons to disarm the alarm system and turns on the lights. In his minor surgery suite, David fills a large doctor's bag with what he might need: a stethoscope, a liter bag of IV fluids, needles, an intracath, tubing and tape, vials of morphine and Valium, Compazine for nausea, everything he can think of to make Joe comfortable.

The windows of Joe's Cape Cod cottage glow with pale orange light. David pulls into the driveway lined with a white picket fence. Carrying his bag, he climbs out of the car and moves through brittle icy air on frosted grass. He feels as he does when entering an operating room for a difficult case, knowing everything depends on him. Before he can knock, Ruth opens the door. She wears a blue housecoat over a flannel nightgown. With dark circles around her eyes and no makeup, she looks old and frail, as if she too were critically ill. David steps into the house. The odor of urine and malignancy greets him as if his friend were in a nursing home.

"Thank you for coming, David," Ruth says, exhausted, desperate. "Thank you. Thank you. I can't stand to see him like this. I don't know what to do."

David puts his arm around her shoulder. "Let's take a look."

She leads him to the dining room with lace curtains and painted china in a glass-fronted cabinet. Joe lies on a hospital bed. Whiskers stubble his sunken cheeks and chin. His belly is swollen and tense from the malignant fluid that distends it. His lips are cracked, his nostrils caked with flecks of mucus. He smells like spoiled milk. Beside him on the floor is the box of sermons.

Jesus, David thinks. All the medical training in the world couldn't prepare a person for this. He moves to the bedside and places his hand on Joe's shoulder.

"Hey, old friend," he says.

Joe moans and plucks at a sheet.

"I'm sorry." He groans. "I'm sorry."

"Sorry? You don't have anything to be sorry about."

"I can't do it. I've failed."

Spittle sticks to his lips. His voice is a dry whisper.

"Can't do what?"

"The fast. I can't keep it up."

"Don't apologize. You haven't done anything wrong."

"Water. Please get me water."

David turns to Ruth and asks her to bring a glass of water and a damp cloth. She hurries to the kitchen. Hoping to ease Joe's breathing, David raises the head of the bed. Ruth returns with a wet washcloth and a glass with a straw. David lays the cloth on Joe's forehead and sticks the straw between his lips. Joe tries to suck the water down, but it dribbles from the corner of his mouth.

"I'm so sick," Joe gasps. "Help me."

Ruth looks at David, her eyes pleading and red-rimmed.

"This can't go on," she says. "Please do something."

For a minute, David stands looking down at Joe, gray and gaunt, consumed by malignancy. He feels he has failed him both as a doctor and a friend. He glances down at Joe's "God Loves You" sermon in the box, and he recalls what Joe believes about death and how love makes us eternal. He tells himself it is time to do no harm.

He looks at Ruth and says, "I have some things in my bag that will help."

"Morphine?"

"Yes."

"Enough to end his suffering?" Ruth says.

David hesitates a moment, then he says, "Yes, there's enough."

"Give it to me," Joe says. "All of it."

"Are you sure that's what you want?"

"We're sure," Ruth says.

"I'll start an IV."

"Give me a minute with him," Ruth says.

David steps out into the entryway. Through the dining room's door, he watches Ruth lean over Joe's bed. She runs her fingers over his face, tracing his nose and mouth and ears. David sees her kiss his cheek, and his heart constricts. It is as if he, Joe, and Ruth are the last people left on earth. Ruth straightens up and moves around the foot of the bed. As she passes David, their eyes meet.

Tears stream down her cheeks. "Thank you," she says.

On the bedside table, David lays out an eighteen-gauge intracath, an alcohol swab, a 20 cc. plastic syringe, and four vials of morphine sulfate. He fills the syringe with the morphine. For a moment, he rests his hand on Joe's chest. Joe reaches up and covers his hand with his cold, bony hand. The house is deathly quiet. David ties a rubber tourniquet around Joe's biceps. He wipes the back of his friend's hand with an alcohol swab and slaps the skin to make a vein stand up. David's own hands are trembling, but he easily threads the intracath into Joe's vein. Dark blood backfills the plastic tube. David plugs the syringe into the IV line. He releases the tourniquet. With watery gray eyes, Joe slowly turns his head and looks at David.

"Everything's fine," David whispers. "Everything is wonderful. Think of something beautiful, Joe. The other side of that river."

"I'm not afraid," Joe says. "God loves me." Joe closes his eyes. "And don't you be afraid. He loves you, too."

David checks his watch. The time is two o'clock. Slowly, he pushes the plunger of the syringe until all of the drug flushes into Joe's vein. With his eyes on Joe's face, he waits for the morphine to travel from Joe's arm to his brain. Joe's eyelids flutter. On his lips a slight smile appears as if he were seeing something glorious.

David stands beside the bed listening to the rasp of Joe's breath, watching the rise and fall of his chest. A column of moonlight angles through a window and covers Joe in a blanket of soft light. Joe's respirations gradually slow until the movement of his chest is no longer perceptible. His body seems to relax. His eyelids quiver and then become still. David places his fingers on Joe's carotid artery. He feels no pulse. He removes the intracath from his hand and covers the puncture site with a strip of tape. He returns the syringe and empty morphine vials to the bag. He waits for a while, then he checks Joe's carotid pulse again. He finds none. David pulls a stethoscope from his hip-pocket and listens to the silence of Joe's heart.

"Ruth," he calls. "You can come in now."

She returns quickly to the bedside, looks down at her husband and then up at David with glistening eyes.

"Thank you," she says.

David squeezes her arm. Then he bends over and takes Joe's "God Loves You" sermon from the box. He folds it and slips it in his pocket. He leaves Ruth with Joe and walks to the front door where he steps outside into the night. The air is cold and has a crystalline clarity that amazes him. The entire universe seems near. He hears the sound of a car shifting gears. The quiet, easy drone of the engine fades into the distance. Then everything is silent as if the moment has been emptied, but the presence of Joe is there. David can feel it all around him. In wonderment, he gazes at the sky. It is black, but harbors no dread, only the moon and a sprinkling of stars.

CORKS IN THE OCEAN

HANK AND JANET SHEPHERD sat anxiously in the living room of their beachfront home on the Gulf Coast of Florida. They were waiting for the doctor to call with a report on Janet's chest X-ray, taken that morning. It was a near perfect day. The clouds in a blue sky were suffused with golden light that was almost savage in its brilliance. Along a shore, lined with tiny shells and yellow foam, sea gulls dove for silver sardines. Janet had a history of breast cancer. Although it was fifteen years since her surgery, the dread of a recurrence was always lurking in the shadows of her life. The physician in Hank told him the news wouldn't be good. He was a retired dermatologist and Mohs skin cancer surgeon. Tall and reed thin with pale, sun-protected skin and a handsome high-domed forehead, he was a sociable, but also impatient, man. Both divorced, he and Janet had been married ten years. They were childless, but a couple whose compatibility others envied. He considered the time he had spent with her the best of his life. She had given him a self-confidence, a feeling of worth, a happiness that he had never known before. He liked to say that Janet was the icing on his cake.

Janet began to cough, a dry, hacking cough. She covered her mouth with her left hand. The two-carat diamond on her finger sparkled in late afternoon light that came through a picture window with a view of the Gulf. Her chest heaved violently. Nothing came up.

Janet had majored in French at Wellesley. She had gone to class in wool Bermuda shorts, knee-length argyles, and a raccoon coat that had belonged to her grandfather. Her boyfriend had played pulling guard for Army. After she graduated, she taught in a school in Alsace. She read Balzac and Flaubert in their native language. She could quote Baudelaire and Prévert with a good accent. She wore Stubbs and Wooten shoes, linen slacks, and silk blouses. On her chest where her right breast had once been, dots of blue ink were tattooed to mark the field that had been radiated years ago at Sloan Kettering.

When her cough finally subsided, she closed her eyes and shook her head.

"I'm sorry," she said.

"Christ," Hank said. "Don't be sorry. You're sick. It's not your fault." He glanced at his watch. The nurse had said the doctor would call at four. It was ten after five. "What the hell is he doing?"

"He's busy," Janet said. "Doctors are always busy. You were always busy."

"Not busy enough to keep someone waiting when this much was at stake. A doctor's job is to alleviate suffering. Dr. Johnson's prolonging yours."

Hank thought the young family practitioner should have asked them to come to his office to get the report. What if the X-ray revealed metastases? Wouldn't he want to tell Janet in person? Hank would have done it that way if the diagnosis in question was melanoma. He believed there was much to be learned about the patient —like body language and facial expression—that went beyond words. Nothing could replace eye-to-eye contact or the laying on of a hand. Hank considered it a privilege to care for the sick and suffering. The cavalier manner medicine was practiced today disappointed him. The older he got, the more the indifference of the world angered him.

Hank gazed around the room at mementos the two of them had accumulated in their travels. An oriental rug from a bazaar in Istanbul. The Chéret poster from a gallery on the Left Bank. A Hopi bowl purchased in a shop on Canyon Road in Santa Fe. Would there be another cruise? Another fine meal in a starred restaurant? Another room with a view in a boutique hotel? More treasures to bring home? He rose from his chair and paced to the window. He looked out at sluggish water the color of tarnished metal. A line of white pelicans skimmed low over the surface of the Gulf. Small waves lapped listlessly on the shore. High, ragged clouds were moving in from the west.

Years ago on warm nights the two of them often swam naked together. They would spread a beach towel on the sand then shed their clothes. Holding hands, they would walk into the ocean. Now, Hank remembers the two of them clinging to each other, the dark water wrapping around them like a garment of black silk. It seemed all the pleasures of life were suddenly relegated to the past. All joys were on hold.

"Would you like a drink?" he said.

"Not now," Janet said. She smiled at him. It was a fearful smile. "But thank you. Damn, I wish he would call."

Hank returned to his chair. From the cushion beside her, Janet picked up a belt she was needlepointing for Hank. The design was of a flying eagle, the logo of his golf club. She began to embroider, her fingers working robotically. Something told Hank he would never wear the belt. The ring of a telephone caused Hank's heart to thud. He and Janet looked at each other. Hank nodded toward the receiver on the rattan coffee table.

"You need to answer it," he said.

Janet put down the needlework and picked up the phone. She pressed the talk button.

"Shepherds'," she said. "Oh yes, Doctor. Thanks for calling. I'm feeling all right. Just anxious about the X-ray."

For what seemed like a very long time, she didn't say anything, just listened. Her face turned gray. Her eyes became lifeless. Her expression made Hank feel sick to his stomach.

"Talk to Hank," she said.

She handed him the receiver and closed her eyes.

"So, what's the diagnosis?" Hank asked.

"There's a new density in the left lung field," Johnson said in his North Carolinian accent. "It's in the upper lobe."

Hank pictured the film hanging from a view box, backlit by a soft white light. The gray, grainy lung-fields and boot-shaped heart that he'd first learned about in medical school so many years ago. The amorphous and ominous shadow Johnson described caused a cold shiver to run up the back of Hank's neck. The differential diagnosis of lung lesions flashed through his mind. Pneumonia. Pulmonary embolism. Tuberculosis. Fungal infection. Tumor. Please don't let it be a tumor, he thought.

"Is it a malignancy?" Hank asked.

There was a long silent pause on the other end.

"Are you there?" Hank said.

"Yes, I'm here," Johnson said. "It does appear malignant."

"Oh God, no," Hank exhaled into the phone. "Metastatic breast?"

"Most likely." Johnson cleared his throat. "It could be a new primary. I can't remember. Was she a smoker?"

"Years ago." Hank was dazed. It was as if he had just seen the angel of death.

"We'll need a CAT scan to confirm the diagnosis." Johnson said. "The nurse will schedule the scan for the morning. She'll call you with the time."

The doctor said something else that didn't register with Hank. He couldn't think. His mind was spinning too fast.

"Okay, then," he said.

Hank pushed the off-button on the phone, feeling as if his and Janet's future had been vaporized. His hand shook so violently he nearly dropped the receiver onto the table.

"It's bad," Janet said. "Isn't it?"

"Doesn't sound good," he said.

"It's cancer," she said. "I knew it would be. I've always been afraid it would come back."

Hank felt as if the two them had been flying in an airplane that fell from a clear blue sky. He rose and walked around the table. He sat down beside Janet and took her in his arms. She felt quite small and fragile, the bones of her shoulder blades, the vertebrae in her neck.

"I can't fucking believe it," he said.

After a few seconds, Janet said, "I'll have that drink now."

"Vodka or wine?"

"How about vodka and wine?" Janet said. She shook her head in regret. "Vodka will do."

In a state of shock, Hank walked to the bar in the kitchen. He thought of what lay ahead—chemotherapy, radiation, hospice—the exact things he was trying to exclude from his mind. He heard Janet begin to cough so hard he thought she might fracture a rib.

EVENING CAME WITHOUT A TRUE SUNSET. The gray haze on the horizon smothered the last light of day. Neither Janet nor Hank had an appetite. For supper they shared some crackers and cheese Hank found in the fridge, a bowl of dry-roasted peanuts with a couple drinks. They tried watching an old Peter Seller's movie on television, but neither of them was able to concentrate. Fatigued by worry and grief, they went to bed early. Through a partially open bathroom door, Hank watched Janet's reflection in the mirror over the sink. On the counter were tins, tubes, and jars of her cosmetics and lotions. She stepped out of her slacks, hanging her bra and panties on a hook. On her chest where her right breast had once been were the dots of blue ink.

A dark bruise on her thigh troubled him. Was that a sign that the tumor had already altered her clotting mechanism? She dressed in a flowered, silk nightgown with spaghetti straps. The gown came only to her knees. With her slim figure and good legs, Hank still found her alluring. She removed her makeup with a washcloth and brushed her teeth. She pulled open a drawer. From it she took an old blond wig styled in a pixie cut. She had worn it when chemotherapy stole her hair. She looked at it for what seemed like a long time and then put it away. Hank gazed at her, and another vision of what awaited them came to him. Wasting and pain for her. Loneliness and grief for him. He decided he wouldn't let her suffer at the hands of an aggressive oncologist whose therapy would give her an extra month or two of scalded skin, mouth sores, puking, and indignity.

From the medicine cabinet, Janet selected a plastic container of Ambien and a bottle of Robitussin with codeine. She swallowed two sleeping pills and drank the cough medicine straight from the bottle. As she made her way to the bed, she appeared a little unsteady. Lying prone beside him, she coughed convulsively. Hank turned onto his back. He stared at the ceiling of white pebbled plaster, trying to shut out the sound of her bark. Above him was a black circular shadow cast by the light of a digital clock shining up through a lampshade. He thought the shadow was a foreshadowing of the dark entry to the infinite and unknown where Janet was soon to pass. How empty and insignificant his life would be without her. She was the lucky one. She wouldn't have to face being alone.

Hank slowly turned his head and looked at Janet. In dim light, she was lying on her side toward him. Her face was pale, her lips parted. For an instant his heart seized, thinking she might be dead. Hank took her hand in his. He was struck by how cold her skin felt. He knew certain lung cancers produced a hormone that constricted blood vessels and diminished circulation. He covered her hand with his other hand to warm it. It seemed as if her body had been taken over by alien forces that were stealing her away from him. You know too much, he thought.

"How do you feel?" he asked.

"Punch drunk."

"So do I," he said.

"*Aujourd'hui, maman est morte. Ou peut-être hier, je ne sais pas,*" she said. Wine and sleeping pills caused her to slur her words.

It annoyed Hank when she spoke in French, made him feel unenlightened.

"What does that mean?" he asked.

"Mother died today. Or maybe yesterday. I can't be sure," she said. "It's Camus. *The Stranger.*"

"For God's sake, why did you think of that?"

"It just came to me. I don't why. I can't get it out of my mind." Her voice was thick. "I guess it's because the future seems so hopeless."

Hank felt hopeless, too. He could find no meaning in any of this. He pulled up the comforter to cover her shoulders.

They were quiet for a while, and then Janet said, "I am so scared."

"Don't be frightened," he said. "I'll take care of you."

"I know you will."

She kissed his cheek.

Hank spent the night in a state of restless wakefulness. Through the window he heard the rush of waves. He felt as if his life were an ocean, governed by forces beyond human control or understanding.

For a while, he listened to Janet's breathing. He stared at the dark circle on the ceiling. The night seemed interminable. The surf pounded. To live without her was unthinkable. He decided when the time came, he would set up a hospital bed in the living room so Janet could see the ocean. He turned his back to her and buried his face in his pillow.

∾

MORNING FINALLY CAME. Strange, solid white clouds domed the coast. On the way to the CAT-scan appointment, Hank's mind vacillated from anxiety to anger. All of his ideas about fairness and fate, faithfulness and good fortune seemed false. From the island's bridge, Hank looked out at the Gulf. Streaks of blues and greens variegated the water like a tapestry of raw silk. The surface of the sea was deceptively calm with occasional swells that seemed to come from nowhere.

The waiting room was crowded with snowbirds, old frail folks from the Midwest with their walkers and canes and Ace bandages. From his chair in the corner, Hank looked at their wrinkled faces, blank with resignation. It occurred to him that most of the people were about his age. His own demise suddenly seemed imminent, and he really didn't care. When the receptionist called for Janet, Hank asked to speak to the radiologist. A short dark-skinned man in a white lab coat appeared. His name tag read DANIEL GHOSH MD. Hank introduced himself as a fellow physician. He warned Ghosh that Janet was claustrophobic and would panic in scanner's narrow tube.

"I suggest a little a Valium IV," Hank said. "And send her through feet first."

"Oh, Hank," Janet said. "Don't worry. I'll be all right."

"We'll use some sedation." Dr. Ghosh's smile was

sympathetic. "And a sleeping mask." He turned to Janet. "Don't worry, dear. We'll take good care of you."

"I'm not worried," Janet said. "It's my friend here who is."

She gave Hank a shoulder pat. Hank thanked the doctor and returned to his chair in the waiting room. He thought about where they should spend Janet's last days. He decided it should be somewhere in a wilderness close to the earth. Where he could keep her comfortable while nature took its course.

IT WAS early afternoon the following day. Hank and Janet sat on metal chairs in Johnson's examining room. The doctor hadn't returned from lunch, but he would be along shortly, a nurse had assured them. On the wall in a gilded frame was a copy of Winslow Homer's *Hurricane, Bahamas*. In the painting, the sky was bruised with dark unruly clouds, the sea roiled by wind. Hank looked at Janet. She was nervously leafing through an old edition of *Bon Appétit*. He thought she appeared worn out. As a young girl, she had been a sun-tanner. He examined her skin with his dermatologist's eye. The pleats above her upper lip. The furrows around her eyes. The actinic keratoses waiting to become basal cell carcinomas. The blemishes of aging. Solar damage. Pre-malignancies. But things like that no longer mattered. It was time for him to completely rethink the future.

Janet looked up from her magazine. She smiled at him tentatively. He thought her beautiful. He wondered what kind of god would want to end the life of someone as lovely as her. He smiled back at her.

"I was just remembering the first time we met," Janet said.

"At the party," Hank said. "I'll never forget how you looked. I knew right away."

Janet was quiet for a few seconds. Then she said, "You know I've always believed my breast cancer would come back."

"Don't jump to conclusions," Hank said. "Let's just wait and see what the scan shows."

Janet began to cough.

Hank's stomach churned. He felt vaguely ill himself. The door opened and banged against a scales in the corner. Hank's pulse leapt.

Johnson breezed into the room. Heavyset, he wore a rumpled white lab coat and tinted, dark-rimmed glasses. His cheeks bore the scars of acne. He perched on a stool and greeted Janet with a nod. His open-collared shirt and the absence of a necktie annoyed Hank. Reaching over, Hank took Janet's hand. Her fingers still felt cold. Hank's heart pounded.

"Well," Johnson said. "I have some good news."

"What?" Janet said. "No. Tell me."

"It's not a malignancy," Johnson said.

"Oh my God." An enormous wave of relief washed over Hank. He let out a long exhale of gratitude.

"What is it, then?" Janet said.

"A pulmonary embolism," Johnson said.

"A pulmonary embolism?" Janet said.

"A blood clot to the lung," Hank said.

"Isn't that serious?" Janet asked. "Am I going to be all right?"

"You'll be fine," Johnson said.

He went on to explain she needed to be on an anti-coagulant to prevent further clotting while the existing clot was allowed to dissolve. He would order an ultra-sound of her legs to see where the clot came from. Hank tried to listen, but his head was swimming. Johnson spun on his stool. He typed something into the computer on the desk behind him. Then, with a ball-point pen, he wrote on a prescription pad.

Hank looked at Janet. He closed his eyes and shook his head in disbelief.

Johnson handed Janet the prescription. "Coumadin," he said. "Five milligrams a day." Then he stood. "All's well that ends well."

He turned and hurried out of the room. Hank watched him. Great communicator, Hank thought.

"Oh my," Janet said. There were tears in her eyes. "I just feel so—I don't know. I just feel so lucky."

"What a relief," Hank said. "I can't believe it."

"How serious is a pulmonary embolism?" Janet asked, dabbing at her eyes with a Kleenex.

"It's serious," Hank said. "But it isn't a malignancy." Why had Johnson put them through this? Where was his empathy? "Goddamn that man. He could have been truthful but kept a door open. I want to talk to him." Hank started toward the door. "I'm going to call him back in here."

"No, Hank," Janet said, reaching for his hand. "Don't do it. It will do nothing but reactivate our agony."

"He needs to learn a lesson," Hank said.

"Let's go home," Janet said. "Let's go home and restart our life."

She dropped her Kleenex in a wastebasket, gathered up her purse, and headed toward the door. Hank followed. His hands were trembling.

THAT EVENING, Hank and Janet took a bottle of white wine and two plastic glasses to the beach. The clouds had disappeared. Stars sprinkled a clear and darkening sky. The tide was on the ebb. The sand cooled and dampened their bare feet. Janet wore a loose-fitting Hawaiian dress covered with a pattern of hibiscus blossoms. Hank, in Nantucket-red shorts and a ball cap, spread a striped beach towel on the sand for

Janet. He sat down beside her with his legs crossed. He breathed in the salty, lustrous night air. With a corkscrew, Hank popped the cork from the bottle of French Chablis. He poured a glass of wine and handed it to Janet. Then he filled one for himself. Like schools of tiny, silver fish, phosphorescent waves rolled to shore and then retreated. He listened to the water whispering a secret to the night.

"I feel like Lazarus," Janet said. She sat with her knees drawn up to her chest. Hank raised his glass in a shaky toast.

"Here's to the resurrection," he said.

"A bullet dodged," Janet said. She coughed into her hand.

"Damn that Johnson," Hank said. "Why did he tell us it was a malignancy before the CAT scan? I'd like to wring his neck."

"*Aimer la verité, mais l'erreru de pardon,*" she said in her flawless French.

"Translation please," Hank said. "I wish you would speak in English."

"Love truth, but pardon error," she said. "It's Voltaire." She coughed a little. "This was a learning experience. A chance for us to know more."

"What did you learn?"

"How much I want to live," she said.

"And I learned how much I want you to live," Hank said. "How precious you are."

Janet leaned over and kissed his cheek. Hank grew quiet, thinking. He watched the lights of a shrimp boat bob and sway in the distance. He tried to imagine what it was like to be so far from shore in the dark. He had a strange urge to wade into the water and swim out to the lonely boat. The vastness of the sea overwhelmed him. A gull called in the dark.

"Has this changed the way you think about God?" Hank asked, sipping his wine.

"No. He didn't get me into this, nor do I think He got me out of it. It just happened for no good reason. It's pretty much the way I've always believed things happen."

"The randomness of the universe," Hank said. He threw the wine cork into the water and watched it bob. "We're just a couple corks floating in an ocean."

"At least we're still afloat," Janet said. She coughed again into her hand. "Let's take a swim. We haven't skinny-dipped in years."

"Maybe we should wait until your lung's had time to heal," Hank said.

"We shouldn't put things off," Janet said. "That's the other lesson I learned."

She rose from the towel and slipped out of her dress. She let the flowered garment drop onto the sand. She wore no underwear. Trembling, Hank pulled off his T-shirt and stepped out of his shorts. He looked at Janet, slender and naked under the gaze of a full moon.

He thought her still a goddess. She covered her mastectomy scar with her hand. The skin of her abdomen
appeared pale and wrinkled. His own hairy body felt
lumpy and soft. It was hard to believe how age had
reshaped them, how old they had become. There was
no escaping it. He took her hand and led her to the
water's edge. Together they waded in. Janet let out a
little gasp. She patted the surface with her hands. A
swell lifted Hank onto his tiptoes. Cool water bathed
his bare skin. A liquid chill rose from his thighs and
spread through the rest of him. He looked out to sea
and saw that the lights of the shrimp boat were still
there, bobbing and flickering.

THE COVER ART

The scene on the cover of the book is a reproduction of *The Doctor*, a painting done by the British artist, Luke Fildes. In 1890, Sir Henry Tate commissioned the painting. The artist chose to represent a personal tragedy of his own. In 1877 his first son Philip had died at the age of one.

Fildes's other son and biographer wrote: "The character and bearing of the doctor throughout the time of their anxiety made a deep impression on my parents. Dr. Murray became a symbol of professional devotion which would one day inspire the painting of *The Doctor*." Fildes himself described the shaft of daylight that blanketed the child as signifying the imminent recovery of the doctor's patient.

He wrote: "At the cottage window the dawn begins to steal in—the dawn that is the critical time of all deadly illnesses—and with it the parents again take hope into their hearts, the mother hiding her face to escape giving vent to her emotion, the father laying his hand on the shoulder of his wife in encouragement of the first glimmerings of the joy which is to follow." The painting is now exhibited in the Tate Museum in London.

ACKNOWLEDGMENTS

I wish to thank my dear cousin, the writer Lou Ann Walker, for her sensitive editing and guidance in the creation of this book and many of the stories that appear in it. I am grateful to Elizabeth McKenzie, George Core, Patrick Perry, Nancy Baxter, Rust Hills, and Michael Curtis who have edited my stories and to Sterling Lord, my agent for many years. I have been fortunate to have been taught, edited, and published by two brilliant authors and master teachers, Sena Jeter Naslund and Barbra Shoup. Thanks go to Tom McGuane who has served as an inspiration and friend. I value the encouragement given to me by fellow writers Fred Bales, Lucinda Sullivan, Bill Pierce, Alice Gorman, Jane Geniesse, Nancy Kriplen, Candy Hooper, and Roger Howe. I appreciate the critiques of my stories by Roger Hanlon, Terry Darcey, and Linda Smiddy, participants in the Fiction Writer's Workshop I teach at Dartmouth College's Osher Lifelong Learning Institute. I am particularly indebted to Beverly Marshall for her devoted editing of the manuscript and her keen-eyed advice about how to make it better. Thanks to Eric Kelly and Bobbie Marquis for their counsel. I am grateful to Marylee MacDonald for bringing this book into the world. My love goes to Toni Wolcott and my sister, Sandra Kelly, for their support through the years.

And finally, much more than thanks goes to Betty Daly Walker, my mother, who taught me to read and write and embrace the written word. This book is dedicated to her memory.

ABOUT THE AUTHOR

Daly Walker is a retired surgeon. His fiction has appeared in numerous literary publications including *The Sewanee Review, The Louisville Review, The Southampton Review, Catamaran Literary Reader, The Saturday Evening Post,* and *The Atlantic Monthly.* His stories have been short-listed for Best American Short Stories and an O'Henry award, nominated for a Pushcart Prize, and been finalists for Best Magazine Writing. His collection of stories, *Surgeon Stories,* was first published by Fleur-de-Lis Press. A native of Indiana, he now divides his time between Boca Grande, Florida and Quechee, Vermont where he teaches a Fiction Writer's Workshop for Dartmouth College's Osher Lifelong Learning Institute. More information about the author and his work can be found on the website www.dalywalker.com.

Made in the USA
Columbia, SC
10 July 2021